TEMPTING BELLA

AN ACCIDENTAL PEERS NOVEL

Other books by Diana Quincy

SEDUCING CHARLOTTE
COMPROMISING WILLA

TEMPTING BELLA

AN ACCIDENTAL PEERS NOVEL

DIANA QUINCY

This book is a work of fiction. Names, characters, places, and incidents are the product of the author's imagination or are used fictitiously. Any resemblance to actual events, locales, or persons, living or dead, is coincidental.

Copyright © 2013 by Dora Mekouar. All rights reserved, including the right to reproduce, distribute, or transmit in any form or by any means. For information regarding subsidiary rights, please contact the Publisher.

Entangled Publishing, LLC
2614 South Timberline Road
Suite 109
Fort Collins, CO 80525
Visit our website at www.entangledpublishing.com.

Edited by Alethea Spiridon Hopson & Rima Jean
Cover design by Liz Pelletier

Ebook ISBN 978-1-62266-248-7

Print ISBN 978-1493703012

Manufactured in the United States of America

First Edition September 2013

To my mother

Prologue

OXFORDSHIRE, ENGLAND

Sebastian Stanhope's first glimpse of his future wife came minutes before they were bound for all eternity.

He'd rushed from university in a haze of disbelief after receiving the urgent summons from his father. His father now sat across from him during the long carriage journey to the bride's ancestral home, barely acknowledging his son's presence, his open disdain crowding the closed space.

Sebastian sucked air into his lungs, his unease growing as the coach-and-four closed the distance between him and the stranger with whom he would be forever intertwined. He should be grateful. Being joined to the daughter of a duke was a much better match than he, a mere mister, had a right to expect. And, more importantly, the alliance would save his family from certain financial ruin.

A mammoth baroque edifice rose into view, dwarfing

the surrounding landscape, its numerous chimneys, towers, and domes sprawling across a blue, cloudless sky. Sebastian's stomach loosened, a faint cramp deep in his belly.

The fortress hovered over them as the carriage jerked to a full stop on the circular drive. The heavy front doors gaped open. Sebastian alighted and strode into the clutches of a murky future, barely noticing the stone-faced butler who showed them in. Squaring his shoulders, he walked ahead of his father through the mirrored hall. His black Hessians clicked a protest against the marble floor, the sound echoing high into the endless ceilings before trembling away.

His hand went to his cravat, adjusting it even though it had been perfectly wrought that morning. He always took care with his grooming because his appearance was not extraordinary. He stood only average in height, lacking the towering elegance of his four brothers. He'd always been different from the rest of the family. His powerful build and dark features lacked the gilded radiance of his lithe brothers. And their father.

They were shown into a massive receiving room that smelled of beeswax and lemon. Wood surfaces shimmered, reflecting shards of sunlight from tall, arched windows at the far end of the chamber. Formal furniture in the French empire-style crowded the space, lions' faces carved into the mahogany side tables seemed to mock him. He surveyed the chamber, every muscle in his body taut, and caught sight of a girl sitting in a window seat by the arched windows. Swinging her hanging legs to and fro, she regarded them with an expression of mild curiosity.

He looked at the butler, acknowledging the portly man for the first time. "Will Lady Mirabella be joining us?"

The butler nodded in the direction of the girl. "This is Lady Mirabella. His Grace will join you presently." He bowed out of the chamber.

For a moment, his mind went blank. Feeling the blood drain from his face, he turned to his father and murmured, "You cannot be serious." The bride, apparently having already lost interest in them, turned her gaze to the bucolic scene outside her window.

Cyrus Stanhope, never a patient man, was always even less so with his third son. "It is done. You will make the best of it. One day you shall thank me."

Nausea swelled, threatening to topple his composure. "That *cannot* be she."

His father shot him an obdurate look. "You are nine-and-ten with no serious prospects. Duty requires you do as bid."

Sebastian turned back to the girl. She was plain and somewhat plump, with large, dark, almond-shaped eyes and a pudgy nose. His betrothed's full, heart-shaped mouth looked like it belonged on a doll. A fresh white dress matched her wintry skin. Anxiety stretched his chest. She didn't deserve this. The poor girl clearly had no understanding of what they all planned for her. A booming voice from the room's threshold startled his thoughts away from her.

"Ah, there you are! I see you have met your future bride." Aubrey Wentworth, Duke of Traherne, lumbered toward them. A tall man, he was almost slender except for a prominent belly, which seemed too much of a burden for his birdlike legs. Sebastian had never met Traherne, but the man had a reputation for whoring, drinking, and gaming. The latter was no doubt the reason Sebastian found himself in this predicament.

The duke's bleary gaze rolled over him, his loose jowls hanging like drapes beneath a florid face. "You are Sebastian." He bounced a bloodshot glance between father and son, seeming to enjoy the contrast between the two, between light and dark. "The boy must take his looks from his mother."

Cyrus's stiff lips contorted into a joyless smile. "Perhaps it is time for Sebastian to meet his betrothed. After all, there is no reason to delay."

Traherne's features grew more pointed. "No reason at all. It will be my pleasure to have Sebastian Stanhope as my son by marriage."

Cyrus flushed beneath his polite mask. Sebastian's gaze narrowed as he darted a look between the two older men. Their obvious mutual dislike arced through the air. The undercurrent of an unspoken conversation, one that only the two of them seemed to understand, raged between them.

Traherne held a beckoning hand out to his daughter. "Bella," he said, loose jowls flapping. "Come and make yourself known to Mister Sebastian."

The girl's almond-colored gaze edged in on them, as though she'd just parsed that the appearance of these strangers had something to do with her. Her eyes rested for a moment on Sebastian before she rose from the window seat and came toward them.

"There now," Traherne said to her. "This is Mr. Stanhope, and one day you shall be obliged to obey his commands." She hesitated.

His gut gnarled. This was wrong. Abominably so. Yet, minutes later, after a stilted exchange of pleasantries, he found himself back in the carriage with his father while his betrothed rode in the forward carriage with Traherne.

"How did this happen?"

His father stared ahead. "Your betrothal settles a gaming debt. It is an incredible coup for our family." Cyrus flicked an unseen spot of dirt from his sleeve. "I am still waiting to hear your thanks, but then again, you've always been an ungrateful boy."

He braced his jaw, well aware this marriage would save the family from destitution. His father should be thanking *him*. "I see." He gazed briefly out the window. "Traherne must owe you a great sum of blunt."

Even now, the man could not spare him a glance. "You have no idea. Do you realize what I have done for you?" Cyrus turned a frosty gaze on his third-born son. "He has no male heir. She is to inherit it all. A special act of Parliament assures that girl will be a duchess in her own right. You will wield the power of Traherne until your own son becomes the next duke."

Icy disbelief whooshed through him. "Why have you chosen me for this great honor? Why not Arthur or Edward?" *The sons you love* he wanted to say.

"Don't be absurd," his father said. "Your uncle has no male heirs, and that ancient wife of his is unlikely to give him one. God willing, Arthur will be the next Marquess of Camryn and Edward must be available as well."

Ah. The heir and the spare. As the third son, this grand alliance, and the burden of rescuing the family from destitution, fell to him. The enormity of it astounded. As consort to a future duchess, untold power and prestige awaited him. Although the Traherne finances must not be particularly healthy if the duke had to resort to this farce in order to satisfy a debt.

Confusion and incredulity clouded his ability to think. Something was amiss. He shot a suspicious glance at Cyrus. Why would the father who rarely showed him anything other than cool contempt arrange an exalted marriage for him when another of his younger brothers would do just as well?

The conveyance jerked to a stop in front of a white stone structure. The chapel. For a brief moment, madness loomed and he contemplated bolting. Of course, he could never act so dishonorably as to break the marriage contract his father signed on his behalf. He would never allow his brothers, mother, or his father for that matter, to fall into the misery of destitution.

Reality and acceptance settled over him. The entire family would benefit from the alliance. His younger brothers' place at university would be assured, long-time family servants could be properly pensioned, while he endured the consequences of a loveless marriage with no hope of escape. After all these years of suffering Sebastian's presence, Cyrus had finally found the perfect way to exact his revenge.

The duke clapped a weighty hand on his shoulder as they entered the chapel. "I want you to know I take my daughter's future seriously. When your father proposed this alliance between our two families, I stipulated that I would only accept you as my daughter's husband. All of your brothers are fine gentlemen, but I quite insisted upon you."

Understanding hit like a slap in the face. Of course, his father would never arrange this grand alliance for him. Cyrus had no real choice in the matter.

Traherne chuckled at the surprised look in his future son-in-law's face. "I am a betting man, but I am not an idiot. Despite your youth, you've developed a reputation for your clever mind and firmness of character. It is what I want for my Mirabella." He looked toward his daughter, who had taken a seat in the front pew, her narrow shoulders rigid. "You have the correct temperament to oversee the dukedom until my daughter's son can inherit it."

His head swimming, he cleared his throat. "Thank you for your confidence in me, Your Grace. I will endeavor to live up to your high opinion of me." He willed himself to ask the question that had troubled him from the first moment he set eyes on Mirabella Wentworth. "May I ask, Your Grace, how old your daughter is?"

Traherne gave the girl a fond look. "Bella is in her thirteenth year. Sadly, she is plain, but the girl will be a peeress in her own right. That should be recompense enough for you. And she is young enough to be biddable."

Practically a child. And she appeared even younger with her round face, pudgy form, and complete lack of customary female curves. Nausea bubbled into his chest. Gulping a wretched breath, he swallowed down the sensation, his face breaking into a cool sweat. He darted a look at the girl, who now stood to the side of the altar with her wide arms folded tight across her flat chest. Her full face pale, she focused on something on the floor, an unreadable expression on her face. He realized he hadn't heard her speak. Did she even comprehend what was happening? He could learn to live with a dowdy wife, but what if she was simple as well?

Wrongly guessing at the trail of his thoughts, Traherne bared his crowded teeth in a knowing smile. "You impudent pup." The smell of vodka blasted Sebastian's face. "I know young flesh has its appeal, but there is to be no wedding night until my daughter is ten-and-seven. Until then, you must slake your desires elsewhere. Has Stanhope not explained any of it to you?"

Rivulets of perspiration scurried down his back. "He has not, Your Grace."

Traherne's generous eyebrows rose. "Then allow me to. For all intents and purposes, you become my heir after today. You will return to Cambridge posthaste to continue your studies. Traherne assumes all costs of your education. Once you complete your university studies, a tutor will be employed to accompany you on a grand tour of the continent." He clapped Sebastian's shoulder again. "You will assume most of the ducal duties until my grandson, your son, comes of age. You will move at the highest levels of government. You must be educated in a way that does credit to your new station in life."

He mopped perspiration from his upper lip with the back of his hand. His own father was merely the second son of a marquess and he himself was untitled, but would now one day assume the reins of one of the largest dukedoms in the realm. The Traherne holdings were of enormous consequence, the political clout unparalleled. He should be pleased, honored even.

He discreetly tugged at his cravat, trying in vain to improve his airflow. Mirabella Wentworth was ushered to the altar. The duke's firm hand touched his shoulder, urging him toward his bride. Sebastian's fine lawn shirt clung to clammy skin underneath his waistcoat. Forcing his tense jaw to relax, he stiffened his spine and went to it.

Upon reaching his bride, it occurred to him that he should reassure her. He forced a smile, but it did not have the desired effect. She squinted back at him, suspicion edged her gaze in a way that made her appear older than her years. She might be young, but perhaps life with a father like Traherne had taught the girl to be wary. Disheartened by the thought, Sebastian turned to face the vicar, barely registering the murmur of words that made them man and wife. All he heard were shackles snapping shut around his future.

When it was over, the groom headed back to university while the bride returned to the nursery. After a while, as memories will do, the events of the day faded into a gossamer sort of thing. In the years that followed, Sebastian sometimes wondered whether the dreamlike afternoon wedding had ever happened at all.

Chapter One

LONDON, ENGLAND
SIX YEARS LATER

"It is time for you to take your wife."

Sebastian cocked a dark eyebrow. "Where would you like me to take her?"

The Duke of Traherne pushed to his feet, the red in his ruddy face deepening. Planting his hands wide on the enormous wooden desk in his study, he leaned over to peer into his son-in-law's face. "Damn your insolence, boy!" The shadows from the afternoon sun danced across his flapping jowls. "You take my meaning and do not pretend you don't."

Sebastian walked over to the sideboard to pour a glass of water. He forced a deep inhale, taking in the rich aroma of books and leather intermingled with stale cigar smoke. Glancing out the window, he watched a coach-and-four amble along the tidy Mayfair street and suppressed a mad impulse to run after it and jump aboard. It didn't matter where its unknown inhabitants were headed, as long as it provided a reprieve from Traherne's dark-paneled study. His gaze followed the conveyance, watching the tenuous chance of escape slip out of sight.

He turned toward his wife's father, ready to face the man's palpable sense of growing outrage. "I am not here to discuss Mirabella." He gestured toward the documents on the duke's desk. "I have personally invested in a number of properties, including two factories near Manchester and one in Stockport. They are sound investments. I propose we attach Traherne funds to the same interests. The papers have been prepared. All they require is your signature."

"To hell with estate matters." The older man's scarlet face emphasized the broken blood vessels in his bulbous nose. "Married six years and you've yet to get your hands on her apple dumplin' shop. What's wrong with you, boy?"

He swallowed down the disgust at Traherne's vulgar reference to his own daughter's anatomy. Leveling a direct gaze at the duke, he said, "Please refrain from referring to my wife in such a coarse manner."

Plopping back in his chair, he rested his elbows on the armrests. "What is it about you? Bella is already nine-and-ten. You were to consummate the marriage two years ago."

Sebastian took the seat across from Traherne's desk. "What my wife and I do, and when we do it, is none of your concern."

"Or if you do it at all. You have not even laid eyes on her

since your wedding day."

"Upon her seventeenth birthday, my wife wrote to me from her finishing school and requested to go abroad. I acquiesced."

"I should never have allowed it."

"It was not yours to allow or disallow," he said quietly. "She is my wife. I alone command her now." And he would give her as much freedom as was in his power. It was the least he could do after what they'd all done to her.

Traherne's eyes widened at Sebastian's impudence. "She's been abroad for two years! This is preposterous."

A burning sensation unfurled in his chest. "On that we agree. Preposterous is a word that could be rightly applied to this marriage you and my late father arranged."

Traherne shook his head with obvious incredulity. "Most youngbloods would be grateful to be consort to a duchess and to wield real power." He slammed the rosewood desk with his hand, unsettling the tangle of papers upon it. One broke free and sailed to the ground. "Any man of sound mind would be thrilled to know his son would one day be a duke."

Sebastian resisted the urge to tidy the disordered documents strewn about duke's enormous wooden desk. "I have done my part in this devil's bargain. When the time comes, I will do my duty. I already oversee Traherne's vast holdings. Pray sign the papers so I may go about my business."

His Grace's hands fisted under his chin, his elbows resting on the armrests. "I have no argument with your oversight of the duchy. It pleases me to know I didn't misjudge your character and abilities. You've proven yourself adept." His voice rose in exasperation. "Except for one. Will you bed your wife? That is your duty above all else. Or is it that you do not like women? All these years and I have never heard of you keeping a ladybird or visiting the bawd houses." He waved a dismissive hand. "Indulge whatever tastes you have. It is of no matter to me, but you must consummate the marriage. It is imperative you beget an heir."

"My tastes are none of your concern, but I assure you they are quite mundane."

"Then get your nose out of the estate books and your person out of the boxing and fencing clubs. Get on with the business of claiming what is yours."

"My attention to estate matters is precisely why the Traherne accounts are robust once again." Eager to be out of the duke's presence, he rose, impatient to unleash the growing pent-up energy inside of him. "Speaking of Gentleman Jack's, I do have an appointment. Please excuse me."

"I am warning you. Go to your wife and make her yours. She is headstrong, more so than you, if that is possible. You must bring her to heel."

He bowed, cheered now that freedom was close at hand. "I shall take your comments under advisement. About the investments?"

"God's teeth, but you are stubborn." Traherne glanced at the papers. "If you think it is sound, then it is." He scratched his signature across the agreements and threw sand on them to set the ink. The duke handed the papers over. "Bella needs a strong hand to cope with her rebellious and obstinate nature."

Taking the documents, Sebastian headed for the door,

welcoming the cool burst of relief at having brought today's business with the duke to a rapid conclusion. "I bid you good day."

He was surprised to hear Traherne chuckle behind him. "One thing is certain. Once the two of you come together, even the devil himself will be running for cover."

The duke's words echoed in Sebastian's head as he set off in the direction of Gentleman Jack's. There was no putting off the inevitable. For six long years, he'd born the guilt of what they'd done to Mirabella. He was a grown man who'd never truly been free to do as he pleased, the same as when he was a boy. Yet Traherne had the right of it. He must summon Mirabella home.

His friend, Lucius Penrose, fourth son of the Earl of Allston, was standing by the entrance when he arrived at the boxing club.

"How was your audience with His Grace?" he asked as they made their way inside for their boxing lesson. The two friends came three times a week and Sebastian never missed a workout. He reveled in the physical challenge and exertion.

They entered the changing room, where humidity and the pungent scent of male exertion hung in the air. "His usual pleasantness, I am afraid."

"What did he want?"

He pulled off his shirt and folded it with care. "He wants what he always wants."

Shaking his head, Pen chuckled. "When will he realize you do no one's bidding but your own?"

They headed out to the boxing floor. Gentleman John Jackson himself was on the crowded floor instructing a young buck. As always, the champion wore the vibrant colors he favored, which today included an orange-striped tailcoat.

A familiar surge of anticipation shot through Sebastian's veins, his muscles poised and anxious for the fight ahead. "I suppose Traherne still sees me as the young pup who married his daughter. Unfortunately, he is right in this. I cannot put off the inevitable any longer."

"So the mystery bride finally appears?" Taking a seat on the hanging scale, Pen regarded the measurement with evident satisfaction. "I haven't gained an ounce." He studied Sebastian's face. "She's just your wife, Stan. Get a babe on her and then get on with your life. The world is full of highfliers for the taking."

He wrapped a protective muffler around his fist. "It's not my way, Pen, as you well know."

"How could I forget?" Pen held out a fist for Sebastian to wrap. "It's unnatural to go without a woman for as long as you have. I hold out hope the saint will one day allow the true Sebastian to emerge."

He exhaled through his nostrils. "What utter nonsense you speak. Do favor me with a change of topic?"

"Very well. Are we attending the opera this evening? Adelaide says you promised her. After all, you do have the best box in the house, next to Prinny."

"You mean to say Traherne has the best box in the house. But yes, I've made arrangements for its use this evening." He slammed his wrapped fists together, testing his mufflers. "If Adelaide wants it, she shall have it. You know I cannot deny your sister anything."

Chapter Two

"Discover anything that'll send Sebastian to Newgate?" Popping his head through her sitting room door, Cary Orford eyed the papers and account books littering Mirabella's escritoire.

"Not as of yet." Sitting back in her chair, she released a frustrated breath, stirring a renegade spiral of auburn hair that had escaped the bun atop her head. "Traherne's accounts are quite complicated. Finding irregularities is no easy task."

"I did a bit of investigation on my own, as you requested." He shut the door, wandering into the powder-blue sitting room originally designed for the mistress of the house. But years ago, during finishing school breaks, Bella had taken the comfortable space as her own. There was no one to object; her mother, the duchess, was long dead and, although the property wasn't far from Town, the duke never ventured to Strawberry Hill.

She gave Orford her full attention. "What have you learned?"

"I haven't actually laid eyes on the man yet, but from what I can gather, Sebastian runs everything." Ambling over to the blue, felt-covered card table with a chess set perched atop it, he ran his fingers over the carved wooden pieces. "Your husband oversees all of the estate business."

"Please don't call him that," she said.

"Very well." He shot her a bemused look. "Even though that is exactly what he is."

"In name only."

"Yes, wedded but not bedded." He ran an appreciative gaze over her petite, curvy frame. "Which I cannot begin to understand."

"I comprehend perfectly," she said tartly. "There's no gold hidden on my person."

"The man's a fool not to see you for the treasure you are." He regarded her with startling blue eyes that left women all over the continent breathless and swooning. But not Bella. They'd been friends far too long for that. "Tell me what you've learned."

Walking over to the unlit marble hearth, he folded his lithe frame into a chair covered with a blue-and-bronze paisley fabric. "He controls the duchy, including all of the assets, and is quite wealthy as a result."

"Our marriage has certainly served him well."

"He didn't have a farthing to his name before your marriage. The family was on the verge of destitution."

"Dare I ask how flush in the pockets he is?"

"Stanhope's personal fortune rivals that of the duke himself."

She sucked in a sharp breath. "Good Lord."

"Surely you're not surprised he helps himself to a bit of extra fruit from the tree."

"It sounds as if he's made off with entire orchards. Where is His Grace in all of this?"

"Your father, the duke, retains official control. However, he doesn't appear to trouble himself with business concerns." Orford adjusted the cuffs of his snowy-white shirt. "He leaves that to Sebastian."

"And while my father empties bottle after bottle of his beloved Russian vodka, Sebastian makes off with chunks of the family fortune."

"Perhaps there's another way he came by the blunt."

"Not likely." She stacked the ledgers to keep her hands busy. "From what I can discern, he receives a fixed allowance from the duchy. It's a healthy portion, but nowhere near enough to account for that kind of wealth."

He gestured toward the account books and documents cluttering the desk. "What do you hope to accomplish with this?"

"I am my father's heir. It's time I began acting as such."

"Meaning?"

"I can't allow Sebastian to bankrupt the duchy. Everyone will expect a duchess in her own right to make a hash of things, but I vow Traherne will never fall to ruin under my watch."

"I know that look. It means nothing will deter you." He smiled as if enjoying a marvelous joke. "For the first time, I don't envy Stanhope his place as your husband."

"I cannot leave my children a debt-laden inheritance."

"Ah yes, *les enfants,* who will also be the fruit of

Sebastian's loins."

"I have no choice in that regard." Although she preferred to avoid thinking about the intimacy required to breed, she was fully prepared to do her duty when the time came. It would be worth the sacrifice. Her chest constricted at the thought of having a baby to love. The lively laughter of children would be most welcome after the solemn quietude of her childhood.

"Saving Traherne from Sebastian is a laudable goal. However, once the duke passes, your husband will control everything, even more so than he does at present."

"Stop calling him that."

"What do you plan to call him?" he said. "He *is* the man you married. It's only a matter of time now before you submit to him."

"I submit to no one." But Orford was right, of course. She *would* see Sebastian soon. Not that she'd recognize the man she'd been forced to marry. All she recalled from that long-ago afternoon was a dark, masculine presence with a grim countenance. Yet his eyes had been kind. She remembered that much about him.

Clearly, she'd been wrong. The scapegrace abandoned her the minute he got his hands on her fortune. He'd had even less use for her than her father. The sharp edge of sorrow comingled with fury razored through her. It was a familiar sensation, one thoughts of *him* always evoked. So she stored it away and harnessed it for the day they would meet again. Only this time she wouldn't be a helpless child. Sebastian Stanhope would learn how unwise he'd been to treat his wife with complete disregard.

The future Duchess of Traherne had plans for her

husband.

...

"Oh, look! There is Baron Beresford's daughter. They say she is this season's incomparable," exclaimed Adelaide Penrose, looking around from her excellent vantage point in the Duke of Traherne's box.

Sebastian gave her a slight smile. "I myself think you are the season's incomparable, Lady Adelaide. What do you think, Pen?"

Pen took his seat, already looking bored. "Hmm? Yes, of course Adelaide is the loveliest girl in the room."

Adelaide's bright blue eyes sparkled. "Thank you for bringing us, Sebastian."

He took his seat, hardly in the mood for the opera, but he resigned himself to it this evening due to his fondness for Adelaide. He'd known her since girlhood from the many times he'd visited on school breaks with her older brother. Anything to avoid going home to his own family. Now eighteen, Adelaide relished all of the firsts that came with her come-out Season. She had taken well so far, thanks to her sweet, sunny nature and petite, blond good looks.

He looked around absentmindedly while Adelaide continued chattering with her brother. His eyes moved over the tiered boxes. People in evening dress milled about waiting for the performance to begin. A movement in one of the boxes across the way caught his attention.

A woman in white muslin stood with her back to him, her gown cascaded down over soft curves in expensive simplicity, its short sleeves trimmed in lace. She wore long, white evening gloves and a snowy fur tippet sloped neatly over her shoulders. The woman's auburn curls were pulled up, but ringlets cascaded down the back of her smooth, pale bare neck. The hair on the back of his neck tingled. Intrigued in a distant way, he kept his gaze on the woman, waiting for her to turn around for a glimpse of her face.

When the woman turned to take her seat, his heart spasmed as though it parsed something of critical importance. She had a wide, elegant face punctuated by prominent, but gently sloping, cheek bones, and a straight aristocratic nose. He brought his opera glasses to his eyes for a clearer view. At the same time, her large, almond-shaped eyes turned in his direction and locked with his. Darkness swallowed her. Startled by a profound feeling of loss, he pulled the opera glasses away from his face only to realize the lights had dimmed because the performance was beginning.

"It's starting." Adelaide scooted up to the edge of her seat angling for a better view of the stage. Sebastian turned toward the stage but in his mind's eye could still only see the marvel in the box across the way. Who was she? He had never seen her at any other functions even though the season was well under way. Chagrined, he suddenly remembered something he never forgot. His wife.

He struggled to bring his thoughts under control. It did not matter who the beauty was, he harshly reminded himself, because she could never be anything to him. Still, as the sounds of the opera crashed around him, his wayward thoughts drifted back to that astounding face. The image of those large, dark eyes widening in surprise floated in his mind.

At intermission, Adelaide turned to him with glistening

eyes. "This is marvelous." Wonder filled her voice. "I cannot wait to see the rest of it."

He smiled, but barely saw or heard her. Pushing to his feet, he excused himself, only vaguely aware of Pen's faint look of surprise when he left the box. Forcing himself to breathe evenly, he walked at a swift gait, acknowledging the people who greeted him without stopping. Rounding a corner, he collided with a wall of soft curves and the subtle scent of jasmine. His hand shot out in a reflexive gesture to right the woman.

It was her.

Recognition flickered in her eyes, the color of toasted almonds, an intriguing soft brown dappled with flecks of gold. Up close, the unique details of her face, including the imperfections, made her even more mesmerizing. She had the faintest white line of a small scar high on her left cheek that he longed to softly trace with his finger.

"I do beg your pardon," he finally said, belatedly remembering to remove the hand he'd instinctively put on her shoulder to keep her from falling. She no longer wore the fur tippet and part of his gloved hand touched the bare skin where her neck and shoulder met. The feel of her supple warmth sizzled through the thin cloth of his glove.

"Do you?" she asked, drawing his attention to an impossibly sumptuous mouth, with a top lip as full and plump as her lower one.

"Yes. Well. Quite." He winced at the inane words. What the devil had come over him? He couldn't begin to remember the last time he'd lost his tongue over a woman.

Blinking, she smiled, and it completely transformed her, throwing him off balance again. That unapproachably beautiful face appeared open, expressive, and even more devastating in its loveliness.

Clearing his throat, he tried again. "I should have watched where I was going. Please excuse my clumsiness."

"Not at all." Those watchful almond eyes fixed on his. "I, too, was distracted."

He dared not ask what distracted her. Becoming aware that they were in the middle of the walkway, he moved aside and felt grateful when she mirrored the movement. A glance down at her hand provoked an irrational inward throb of jealousy. An apparent wedding ring encircled her gloved finger.

"Is your husband accompanying you?"

"No, I am alone…with friends of course." Her voice took on a hard edge. "But no, my husband is not with me."

Could she possibly have a neglectful husband? What a clod pole. If this extraordinary creature were his, he'd never let her out of his sight.

"My lady?" someone called out, causing her to turn around. "The performance is about to resume."

"Oh, Orford," she said easily to a man who stepped out from behind the curtain of a nearby box. Handsome, with a bored glint in his striking blue eyes, he stood tall, several inches above Sebastian, and moved with the lanky elegance bred among the highborn set. His inquiring look cooled when it found and clashed with Sebastian's, a sliver of something rivalrous touching his gaze.

The man offered a tight, dismissive smile before taking hold of the woman's arm in a familiar manner, which filled Sebastian with a senseless urge to pummel him.

"Yes, of course, I am coming." Flashing a quick glance at

him, she disappeared back into her box with the man.

...

She invaded his dreams that evening.

He awoke with a start, sweating and disconcerted, his body on edge. Sitting up, he pressed his palms against his eyes, frustrated by his lack of control over his dreams. These were the times when the unbidden reminder of how long he'd been without a woman intruded upon the careful order of his life. He stilled for a moment, allowing the feeling to wash over him, to accept how much he missed the touch of a woman.

Forcing the thoughts aside, he glanced toward the window where darkness still clawed the sky. He rose and sluiced cold water on his face from a basin his valet set out each evening without fail. Towelling off, he contemplated waking a groom to saddle his mount. He rode almost every day, long and arduous outings during which he exerted himself to extreme endurance. Perhaps he'd let the groom sleep and just slip out for a brisk walk.

He dressed swiftly, pulling on the shoes he'd had specially made for mornings like this. Slipping out of his spartanly decorated bachelor's apartments, he headed for the street at a brisk pace, his steps accelerating into a slow jog.

At least it was before dawn, when few were awake to witness what would be perceived as foolishness. But it calmed Sebastian, helping him keep tight control over certain elemental urges he wished to ignore. He relished the strong, steady movements of his powerful legs and the rhythmic sounds of his breathing, all the while looking forward to the rush of exhilaration he would soon feel from his exertions.

Thoughts churned in his mind, images of the beauty at the opera, remembrances of his long-ago nuptials, his father's austere gaze, Traherne chuckling. Blowing out a heavy, loud breath, he quickened his pace.

The time had come to reunite with his wife and finally reconcile himself to a union neither of them had wanted. They'd been apart for too long. It was the only explanation for his incomprehensible reaction to the woman from the opera. It shamed him to realize he wouldn't even recognize his own wife when he saw her. It was long past time to summon her home. Straining his memory, he tried to recall Mirabella's whereabouts. Last he'd heard she was in Spain. He would send a note through their mutual solicitor. The man who took care of his wife's financial needs would certainly know her whereabouts.

His mind made up, his breathing fell into a heavy pattern as he ran faster and faster, until he raced through streets of Belgrave Square in an all-out run.

Chapter Three

"Oh, you wound me, my dear," Orford protested when Bella sank the last ball into a far pocket of the billiards table.

She straightened with a saucy smile and perched her chin on the tip of the mace. "I win again. You owe me three pounds."

He moved to the mahogany sideboard to pour himself a drink. "You have a man's thirst for gaming. One would think you needed the funds."

"The last thing *m'petite* needs is more gold," said her friend, Josette Laroux, in her lilting French accent, from where she reclined on a green velvet chaise. "That husband of yours is most generous, no?"

The mention of *him* drained the thrill of victory out of Bella. Feeling cross, she threw her stick across the table.

"They are *my* funds, Josette." She stalked away from the table and plopped down onto a chair next to her friend. "Anyhow, I'm certain he is much more generous with himself."

Orford held up his glass, inspecting the amber liquid inside. "Still, by rights he can do as he chooses. You are fortunate it pleases him to be generous with you. For now."

Tabitha, their fellow traveling companion, sat by a large window working with her watercolors. "Exactly so. He could have withheld funds."

Trying to ignore the plaintive prick in her chest, Bella scowled. "Isn't it obvious? The lubber pays me off to keep me from bothering him so he can go about his life." She picked at the gold-corded trim that embellished her scarlet velvet chair. "He has his wife's blunt without having to bother with a wife. It is a perfect arrangement for him."

Josette stretched along the chaise, her delicate body arching into the movement. "Husbands are such a bore. You are fortunate to be free of such trouble. Look at all the amusement we enjoy without him here making a nuisance of himself."

Bella felt a rush of warmth for Josette, for all of her friends really. Without them, she would have been utterly alone.

"And he's given you leave to use this lovely house," said Tabby.

"Please." Bella rolled her eyes. "This is my father's house, my house, by rights, if there were any justice in the world for females. Sebastian isn't even aware that we've encamped here."

Indeed, she'd specifically chosen Strawberry Hill secure in the knowledge the staff would be discreet about her presence while she acquainted herself with ducal affairs. It wasn't just because the servants were well aware she would one day be duchess and they, in turn, hers to command. She'd spent much of her growing up years here and the staff was more like family than her own father. Or husband for that matter.

"When will you tell him you are in town?" asked Monty, an Englishman who'd joined them on their travels after a chance encounter in Spain.

"When I am ready. I need to learn everything I can about Sebastian's business dealing, and that is best done when no one knows who I am."

"It's a lucky thing neither your father nor your husband ever bothered to bring you to town before now," Tabby said.

"I didn't used to think so, but it certainly has its advantages at the moment." She'd been able to slip into town, mostly unnoticed, and Orford had taken to vaguely introducing her as his cousin, which she was, albeit a few times removed. Except for Lady Florinda, her old finishing-school friend who she planned to meet for a quiet luncheon, almost no one in town would recognize her. Except for her father, of course, and a few of his cronies, who she planned to steer clear of.

"I demand satisfaction." Orford's voice broke into her thoughts. Reclaiming his mace, he inclined his head toward Bella. "My dear?"

She shook her head, irate with herself for allowing talk of *him* to cause the twinge in her throat. "I am bored with billiards. Let Monty play with you."

Monty turned at the sound of his name from where he stood behind Tabby assessing her painting. He walked over and picked up a stick. "Very well. Your play first, Orford."

Folding her legs beneath her, she waited for the pain in

her chest to recede back to an ever-present dull ache. Chin in hand, she watched her friends. They had traveled together these last two years, this group of misfits who, for the most part, had no one else in the world who cared for them.

Bella's gaze flitted out the window, her mind returning to the masculine specimen from the opera who plagued her thoughts. With his inky curls and wide, impervious jaw, he wasn't terribly handsome like Orford, who possessed refined features and a lean elegance. The man had a dark complexion and was of average height, with a powerful physique and serious countenance. He'd been smartly attired in fine-cut clothing, the dark formal wear and snowy cravat providing a sumptuous contrast with his smooth caramel skin. But what drew her most were his eyes. Slightly hooded and fringed with dark velvet lashes, they were the purest green she'd ever seen—bright pools that shone against his bronze skin, radiating both strength and kindness. And when he'd focused that keen gaze on her, it was as if the sand had shifted beneath her feet, leaving her completely at the mercy of an approaching swell that promised danger, but also something sublime.

"My lady, you have a message."

Lost in her thoughts, she'd not heard Hastings, the butler, approach. She looked up to find him standing before her bearing a silver tray. Taking the note, she scrutinized the firm, sweeping curves that formed her name. Not recognizing the seal, she unfolded the foolscap and scanned its contents. When their meaning became clear, the words began to whirl on the page.

"What is it, *m'petite*?" Josette sat up on the chaise, her eyes alert. "You have lost all color in your face."

Orford and Monty paused from their game to look at her. Even Tabby stopped painting, her round, dark eyes fixed on Bella. Forcing a weak laugh, she waved the missive in the air. "It is from Sebastian. He has summoned me home. It seems my husband has found a use for me after all."

. . .

Sebastian reluctantly made an appearance at Lady Claymont's musicale a few days later. The occasion marked the inauguration of the society matron's newly renovated ballroom at her Curzon Street mansion, but he'd come for his brother, Will.

Lucius Penrose's distinguishing mop of fiery-red hair made him easy to spot, his coppery eyebrows rising in surprise when he caught sight of Sebastian. "This is hardly the kind of rout that entices you, Stan."

Skimming the crowd, Sebastian nodded every so often when he caught the eye of an acquaintance. "My brother just completed a commission for Lord Claymont. It's to be unveiled this evening."

"I suppose it is of Lord Claymont's favorite mount. Is the great artist in residence this evening?"

"He'd better be, as Will is the primary reason for my attendance."

"And I thought you came for Amelia Claymont's superior singing skills," Pen said with a wicked gleam in his eye. Claymont's plain eldest daughter was not known for her superior musical talents. Just then, a curvaceous widow with an impressive décolletage glided by, distracting Pen with her generous, sashaying hips.

Sebastian followed his friend's gaze. "Wander away at your leisure, Pen. I'll endeavor to run Will to ground."

"Good of you to be so gracious, old man. After all, we cannot all be saints," he said, disappearing into the throng. Sebastian moved about the public room searching of his younger brother, but Will was nowhere to be found. Giving up, Sebastian resolved to get a quick look at the painting and then be on his way.

Lady Claymont came bustling over once she spotted him. "Your brother sent a note saying he's been unavoidably detained. However, he did promise to make an appearance after dinner in time to hear Amelia sing."

Sebastian bowed with utmost courtesy. "I do look forward to it, Lady Claymont. What a treat, indeed."

The lady beamed. "In the meantime, should you like to see the painting, you will find it in my husband's study."

He made his way there and, upon finding the study empty, entered to examine the massive painting. Will had outdone himself. Standing at least eleven feet high, the composition magnificently captured the prancing thoroughbred's sense of movement and grace. Everything about the animal seemed to be in motion, from its wind-tousled mane to its swaying tail.

"The animal shows more personality than most people," said a woman's voice from behind him. "He would probably be better company, too."

He turned toward the source of the clear, confident voice and froze. The woman from the opera.

The lovely creature's eyes widened in recognition. "Oh, so it is you again," she said pertly, her sun-burnished brown eyes assessing him with amused interest.

His heart picked up speed. She looked as entrancing as the first time he'd seen her, perhaps even more so. This evening, she wore a gown of purple silk with golden embroidery along the generously cut neckline. He forced himself not to stare at the soft swell of her pale breasts. "So it is."

Seeming amused by his formality, she favored him with an arresting smile before gazing up at the portrait. "The artist is very clever."

"He is undoubtedly talented." He had to force his eyes away from her to concentrate on the painting, but couldn't resist casting a sidelong glance at that incomparable face. "But clever? How so?"

She tilted her head, assessing Will's work. "He was commissioned to paint Lord Claymont's mount. This could have been an indulgent, pedantic piece. Instead, it is a remarkable piece of work with such adroit composition and attention to detail." She turned to him with a dazzling smile that spoke of her satisfaction. "His vision is uncompromising. He made it his own and in doing so demonstrates an incredible mastery of his craft."

"A woman gifted with uncommon beauty and a keen mind. Are you a student of art?"

She laughed again, her golden-brown eyes sparkling. "Hardly. I appreciate beautiful things." Her eyes returned to the painting. "And am fortunate enough to be able to indulge myself on occasion."

"You're a collector."

She kept her gaze on the painting. "I have not collected any of Will Stanhope's works as of yet, but he truly is a forward thinking artist."

Will? Sebastian thought his brother's nickname rolled too easily off the woman's pillowed lips. "Have you made the artist's acquaintance?"

She perked a perfectly arched brow and seemed to consider the question. "I suppose you could say that. In a manner of speaking."

His brother knew this woman? His gut twisted a little. Just how well acquainted were they? She was obviously enamored of Will's work. Sebastian had witnessed firsthand the number of women who threw themselves at artistic types like his brother.

"There you are, Stan—" Pen popped his head into the study, stopping abruptly after catching sight of the woman. He cast an inquiring appreciative look in her direction. "Oh, do excuse my interruption. Dinner is being served," he announced without taking his frankly admiring eyes off the woman. "Adelaide says you promised to escort her to dinner."

The last thing Sebastian wanted to do was leave. What he really desired was to slam the study door in Pen's face, hopefully blackening at least one of those impudent eyes. Instead, he merely bowed in her direction. After all, he already had a wife and couldn't even offer to escort this woman to dinner since they'd not been formally introduced. Longing to thrash Will for being late, he resolved to waylay his brother as soon as he arrived to ensure the proper introductions were made.

"Pray do go on. I will make my way in a few minutes. My escort is to meet me here."

Her escort? Sebastian noticed she did not refer to her husband. The ignorant oaf apparently allowed this remarkable woman to flit about the metropolis escorted by other men.

Later, after supper, when Will still had not made an appearance, Sebastian decided to depart. Taking leave of his hostess, he turned into an empty hallway off the main public rooms.

"Why, Sebastian Stanhope," chirped a breathy female voice, "you are not trying to sneak away, are you?"

Masking his annoyance, he turned and executed a cordial bow before Jacintha Belfield's modest, but overexposed, bosom. "Lady Hawke," he uttered with cool civility. "How exceptional you look this evening."

The stunning blonde flicked her fan open in a practiced flirtation. "Exceptional enough to tempt a saint?"

"I trust Lord Hawke is well?"

"Well enough." Irritation sparked in her pale blue eyes at the mention of her current husband, an aging marquess forty years her senior. "But his lordship is most unsatisfactory in some areas, as you are aware."

He ignored the insinuation, and its unspoken invitation. "Do give him my regards."

She drew closer on a husky laugh. "You would do better to give them to me."

The once-familiar scent of her perfume reached him, recalling lust-soaked hours of mindless pleasure and startlingly inventive bed play. "As always, it is kind of you to offer, Jacintha, but I must decline."

Coming even nearer, she brushed her hand between his legs. To Sebastian's disgust, his body responded even as he stepped away. "I am married, Jacintha."

"As am I."

"All the more reason for restraint."

"One is hardly married if his wife stays abroad for years and never warms his bed." Her fingertips teased along his forearm. "She's a fool, that wife of yours, to leave you unattended. It wasn't so long ago that you allowed me to satisfy your needs."

"Our circumstances were different then. You were between marriages and I had yet to take a wife."

"You are a most entertaining lover," she said with a languid blink. "I will always welcome your attentions."

His body's natural inclinations hummed in response. Blood rushed to his nether regions, eager for a lusty bout of tupping, even as the thinking part of him dashed all hope of it. "You honor me." Forcing a stiff bow, he turned to go. "I regret I must depart."

"As I recall, you were well pleased by my skills." Her silky voice followed him down the hall as he rounded a corner. "A vigorous man like you cannot go without forever."

He quickened his pace, eager to be away from her.

"Are you running away?"

"What?" He caught sight of her—the mystery woman—in an alcove off the large hallway. He pulled aside the curtain that hid most of the cozy space. "Are you hiding?"

Her wicked smile singed his already sensitive loins. "Yes, I most assuredly am."

"Why?" he asked with sincere curiosity. "Are you in need of rescue?"

"But I asked you first. Why are you running from Lady Hawke?" She tilted her adorable chin downward as she assessed him. "I met her earlier this evening. I understand her charms are most sought after."

He savored the sight of her, allowing her vivacious energy to drift over him. "Not by me."

"A discriminating man. How refreshing." Her eyes sparkled. "Most will do anything for a beautiful woman."

She should know. He guessed most men would be willing to do anything for her. And she seemed well aware of her own staggering appeal. What a dangerous combination.

"Darling?" Jacintha's voice drifted from around the corner.

Without thinking, he stepped into the alcove and pulled the curtain closed behind him, casting her a sheepish look as they listened to Jacintha wander past the alcove. Once the danger had passed, the woman laughed. Not a practiced, quiet laugh of a lady, but a throaty, unabashed sound. He frowned momentarily and then saw himself through her eyes. The absurdity of a grown man hiding from a woman prompted him to smile. They both enjoyed the private joke for a moment.

Her delicate scent—this time of lavender instead of jasmine—reached him. Longing surged. He wanted her. Not just to bed her, but to talk and laugh with her, to know her thoughts and to feel her warmth as she slept next to him. Seeming to sense the change in him, the laughter left her eyes. The obvious magnetism between them surged, swelling the air. "Neither of us should be here." Her words were almost a whisper.

He took her hand, reveling in its petal-like softness, admiring the delicate lines and tapered fingers. He pressed a light kiss near the base of her thumb, his lips lingering a beat longer than they should, before letting her slip away. "You have the right of it, of course. Dishonor is not an option. For either of us."

He heard her sharp intake of breath at his tacit acknowledgment of the sensual lure between them. They quieted for a moment—gazes meshed—listening to the buzz of conversation from the nearby public rooms and the occasional spates of laughter, muted by distance. A languorous heat stretched between them. The color in her face grew more radiant. Her luxuriant lips parted slightly, her breathing became more apparent. Every part of his body pulsed.

"Darling?" Jacintha's voice again. "Come and have a drink with an old friend."

The moment splintered and he had the despairing sense he wouldn't know another like it.

Bold amusement crossed his mystery lady's face. "Tell me," she whispered, "do ladies often try to run you to ground?"

"Lady Hawke is most persistent."

"It seems you are the one in need of rescuing." Before he knew what she was about, she stepped through the curtain and pulled it closed behind her. "Lady Hawke, what a delightful surprise," he heard her say, her voice drifting away as they moved down the corridor. "I am quite lost. Could you direct me back to the parlor?"

Chapter Four

"I wonder if they employ a four-crop rotation," Bella mused, surveying the latest documents she'd requested from the estate steward at Traherne Abbey. The man hadn't questioned her interest, likely assuming Sebastian was aware she'd asked for the papers to be sent up.

Monty sipped his wine. "Most farmers do." They were out on the front lawn, lunching at a linen-covered table that had been set out for their meal. "They alternate wheat, barley, and a root crop like turnips."

"And the fourth field is planted with feed for the livestock?"

He nodded. "I see you've learned well from your study of French and Spanish farming methods during our travels."

"Yes, that explains why I'm so well acquainted with barley and turnips." She fixed a pointed look on him. "But where did the mysterious Monty gain his vast knowledge of agriculture?"

"It is no mystery," he said, putting his glass down on the table. "I've managed an estate book or two in my time."

"You've worked for a grand estate?" Tabby interjected from behind her easel.

"Something like that." Rising from the table, he wandered over to look at her painting of the house. "Lovely use of color. What shades did you use for the sky?"

Blushing with pleasure, Tabby explained her color choices. Bella noted how deftly Monty deflected attention from himself—and his past. Taking in his tall, trim frame and unassuming posture as he bent over Tabby's painting, she decided if Monty had secrets, they were his to keep because her every instinct suggested he was as honorable as he appeared. Returning her attention to the papers before her, she said, "Traherne Abbey appears profitable enough now, but it wasn't doing very well just a few years ago."

Josette groaned. "Must you always speak of such boring matters? It is a waste of time when one could be dancing or shopping."

"These boring matters, as you call them, are what keep us all comfortable and well fed," Bella said. "I should dearly like for that to continue."

"You are running out of the money?"

Reaching for a meat pastry, Orford answered for Bella. "She thinks Sebastian is helping himself to a bit too much of the pie, a sum far beyond his fixed allowance as her husband."

Silly as it was, Bella winced inwardly at his reference to Sebastian as her husband. For a moment, she allowed herself to imagine the dark stranger in his place. A pleasant sensation flowed through her at the memory of his quiet strength and the lingering scent of musk shaving soap and male skin. One look into those vivid emerald eyes was enough to make her want to forget all about honor and duty. She sighed. "I wonder how long it will be before I become accustomed to thinking of Sebastian as my husband."

Tabby cast her a sympathetic look. "But what can you do? A husband retains all power over his wife."

"Perhaps." She'd given that point a great deal of thought. "But at least I shall be duchess while he remains a mere mister. I must use the power of my rank to exert influence over ducal affairs."

"Such lofty goals." Josette yawned. "I tire just thinking of it."

Bella did have ambitious aspirations where Traherne was concerned. Gazing across the verdant lawn to the gracious, unfussy lines of the ivory-tinted Palladian villa, she experienced a sense of homecoming. Although it was a minor property in comparison to the ducal seat at Traherne Abbey, she felt far more at home within Strawberry Hill's cozier confines. She'd hated ambling around the abbey's vast emptiness, with little in the way of company save the assortment of nurses, governesses, and servants who'd been paid to keep her company in lieu of the family she'd never had.

A deep-rooted connection bound her to both properties and, indeed, to all of Traherne. The duchy was what grounded her and gave purpose to her life. As a child, she'd barely seen her father, but for as long as she could remember, she'd known she'd inherit the title when he died.

She felt the weight of that responsibility as keenly as any male heir, perhaps more so as a female who hadn't been properly groomed to assume the reins. Her father might not take his duties seriously, but she certainly did. And that meant doing everything in her power to keep Traherne safe from Sebastian's apparent poaching.

"It does seem like an awful lot of work," Tabby said, echoing Josette's sentiments. "I'm not sure why you bother."

Relaxing back in his chair, Orford closed his eyes and tilted his face toward the sun. "She doesn't want it said the duchy fell to pieces after being placed in the care of her feminine hands."

"Quite right." Determination surged within her. "I'll do whatever it takes to protect my birthright and I won't allow Sebastian Stanhope to stand in my way."

. . .

"*Poussée*! *Parade*!" The fencing instructor called out instructions from the sidelines. "Excellent! *Une telle grace*!"

Sebastian thrust forward with vigor, landing yet another hit on his embattled opponent.

"Such a magnificent combination of flexibility and power." Master Henri's black, bushy eyebrows rose in admiration as Sebastian launched a forceful final series of offensive moves with little apparent effort. "*Il est formidable*!"

"Yes, yes." Pen watched from the side, having already finished his turn. "He's superior in every way."

Sebastian's exhausted opponent seemed to agree, given his obvious relief when the practice match ended and two other men moved into position to take their turn. Sebastian stepped out of their way, his bared broad chest glistening with a fine sheen of sweat from his exertions.

Pen handed him a towel. "You're in rare form today. You practically ran poor Darley into the ground."

"Nonsense." He mopped his face, his attention on the start of the next match. "He acquitted himself well."

"There are already few enough men willing to take you on." Pen looked to where the weary man now sat, trying to regulate his labored breathing. "I doubt Darley will offer you a rematch anytime soon." He started toward the changing room but halted when Sebastian didn't follow. "Are you coming?"

Sebastian shook his head. "No, you go ahead. I think I'll await another match up."

Pen looked incredulous. "You are going to have another go at it? You've already been at it for hours."

Sebastian tracked the movements of the two fencers as they parried and thrust. "Just one more."

"I say you are even more vigorous than usual, Stan. And distracted, too. Wouldn't have anything to do with that woman from Claymont's library would it? Tasty piece that one. One could not help taking notice of that delightfully full bosom. Perhaps she will be the one to finally tempt the saint."

"At the moment, the only thing I'm tempted to do is run you through with my foil," he said, without taking his eyes from the bout. "Without the safety button on the tip, of course."

Chuckling, Pen backed away. "Have I hit a nerve?" He pondered aloud moving in the direction of the changing room. "Interesting."

Once he'd gone, Sebastian exhaled loudly through his

nostrils. Pen *had* hit a nerve.

He couldn't stop thinking about the saucy beauty. Any liaison was unthinkable, of course. It was completely against everything he believed in, totally at odds with the example his moralistic father had set, which he had always tried to emulate. Still, he imagined what it would be like to nourish his hunger with the sumptuous taste of her, to pull her into his arms and share the events of his day.

Blast and bugger his eyes. What had come over him? He knew the agonizing cost of infidelity better than anyone. He'd seen firsthand that children suffered the most. They grew up not quite bastards, but not exactly legitimate either. Fruit that had fallen a little too far from the tree, which, nonetheless, still had to be gathered along with the finest pickings.

He would prove himself worthy of his father's approval, and he had thus far lived up to his child self's long-ago vow to never do as his father had and risk having a bastard child.

Until now. With her.

It occurred to him that in the future he would dissect his life into two parts: before the knowing of her and the after. And in this after, he felt like a different man. He now comprehended that his resolve had never truly been tested and he feared failing as magnificently in this as he had always excelled in everything else.

"*Avancer, commençons!*" Master Henri's strident voice broke into Sebastian's thoughts. The master summoned his star student for another match. Grateful for the distraction, he picked up his foil and headed back to the floor, his worn muscles once again on edge.

Sebastian joined Pen and Adelaide at Vauxhall that evening, attending at the invitation of their mother, the Countess of Alston. She'd organized a small party in their box with a light supper before dancing and fireworks later in the evening. Lord and Lady Hervey were also in attendance, accompanied by their young daughter, Grace, a friend of Adelaide's.

As always, Adelaide glistened with excitement, reveling in her first visit to the pleasure gardens. "Sebastian," she asked breathlessly. "Are you going to ask me to dance this evening?"

The countess looked up with a frown from where she supervised the laying out of the refreshments. "Adelaide! You never ask a gentleman to dance."

"But it's just Sebastian. You don't mind, do you, Sebastian?"

He responded with a warm smile. "Not at all." He turned to her mother. "I assure you, it is always my pleasure to dance with Lady Adelaide."

"Nonetheless," the countess said, "this is your debut season. You are no longer in the nursery. You must act with appropriate decorum."

Adelaide looked down at her clasped hands in her lap. "Yes, Mother."

The countess flashed an apologetic glance at him. "And Mr. Stanhope is far too mannerly to refuse you."

"Basil, there you are." Penrose greeted the latest arrival to their box. The sudden appearance of Sebastian's younger brother spared Adelaide from any more of her mother's admonishments.

Basil stepped into the box with a bow. "I hope I haven't missed supper. I'm famished." The youngest of the Stanhope men was easily the most classically handsome. Not only did he possess the tall, lithe frame and golden mane that marked all of Sebastian's brothers, but nature had also arranged his patrician facial features in perfect symmetry.

One could practically hear Adelaide and Grace's combined intake of breath in the presence of Basil's vigorous masculine beauty. Even the dour Lady Hervey seemed affected by Basil's physical perfection, which the brothers had laughingly dubbed the "Basil Effect."

"I've never seen anyone with an appetite like yours," Pen remarked. "Where do you put it all?"

The Adonis greeted his brother with a winning smile. "We Stanhopes have hearty appetites. Even the saints among us, isn't that right, Seb?"

"I wouldn't know," he said a little testily, knowing his thoughts of late were far from saintly.

"Saints?" breathed Adelaide, still staring at Basil, her eyes wide with entranced admiration.

Sebastian felt a tug of amusement at how quickly the young girl had fallen under Basil's spell. "My brothers' misplaced, unfortunate, and untrue nickname for me," he said. "Trouble always seemed to find my brothers when we were growing up. Because I did not always follow their reckless path, they dubbed me the saint."

"Only he became even more saintly after we grew up," Basil said before popping a tartlet into his mouth.

"I'll say." Pen exchanged a knowing look with Basil, no

doubt referring to Sebastian's prolonged abstinence from carnal pleasures, something the two of them couldn't begin to comprehend.

The countess smiled at Sebastian. "There is no finer, more honorable gentleman." He felt a twinge of guilt at her words, given his recently acquired obsession with another man's wife.

A missive he'd received this afternoon from Mirabella compounded his short-tempered frustration. He'd been at the townhome he would soon share with her, overseeing preparations for her return. He rarely stayed at the lavish Park Street address, usually preferring the simple comfort of the bachelor's quarters he still kept. Just this afternoon, he'd had his things moved into the master's chambers, anticipating Mirabella's scheduled arrival the following day. He'd ordered fresh flowers laid out in the main rooms of the house, saving the largest bouquet for her bedchamber, the one that adjoined his through a shared sitting room. The usually solemn, empty house had been abuzz with activity as the staff prepared to finally have a master and mistress in residence. Servants had spent the past few days airing out the place, cleaning the large, empty rooms that now smelled heavily of lemon, soap, and beeswax.

He'd experienced a surge of optimism as he strode from room to room inspecting the activity, his Hessians clicking against the marble floors, the seductive aroma of flowers wafting through the rooms. He looked forward to reuniting with Mirabella and hoped they would soon be blessed with a child. Perhaps it would draw them together. Focusing on his wife and family would help him overcome his unfathomable infatuation with the beauty from the opera, which was beyond ridiculous. For devil's sake, he didn't even know her name.

It was while contemplating a hopeful future with his wife that his butler found him, bearing a note on a silver tray. In a brief, formal missive, Mirabella informed her husband that her return had been delayed, their reunion deferred for another sennight. She asked for his understanding. Sebastian scowled. His patience had already run out.

"I say," said Basil breaking into his thoughts. "Isn't that Cam's friend, David Selwyn?"

Sebastian caught sight of his eldest brother's longtime friend walking with a small group of people. "So it is."

"I hear he is finally betrothed," Basil said.

Selwyn's rank did not match that of their brother, the Marquess of Camryn, but he made up for it with an obvious intelligence and a good-natured temperament. Not a particularly handsome man, Selwyn had a pleasant demeanor and took a great deal of care with his appearance and manners.

"Isn't he betrothed to Bromley's daughter?" Penrose asked.

Basil whistled. "Bromley? David Selwyn and the daughter of an earl? It's a fine match."

"He is not a born gentleman," remarked Lady Hervey. "I understand the sister married a baron. Those commoners have done a fine job of marrying their betters."

"Mr. Selwyn is a fine gentleman." Sebastian did not care for Lady Hervey on account of her being both a snob and a gossip.

"It's a match made in heaven. Selwyn's flush in the pockets and Bromley's got pockets to let," said Pen.

Basil crossed his arms over his chest. "The perfect marriage. Bromley gets the blunt and Selwyn lands a lady above his station."

Spotting them, Selwyn waved his friends onward and stepped toward their box. "Gentlemen."

"Basil here tells us you're about to get leg shackled," Sebastian said after the introductions were made all around.

The other man nodded. "Yes, I'm fortunate Lady Florinda was gracious enough to accept my suit. And how are Camryn and his lovely marchioness?"

"They are well," answered Basil. "They'll be in town with the children soon enough. Charlotte isn't one to rusticate for long periods of time."

"Why, look," said Penrose, watching people strolling by, "isn't that the woman from Claymont's library?"

Sebastian's heart bucked. Following the direction of Pen's gaze, he caught sight of her chatting animatedly with her companion. She wore a full-length cornflower-blue pelisse trimmed with steel-blue cording. The two of them strolled down the main walkway between the supper boxes at a leisurely pace, seeming to enjoy the amusements, pointing at something that caught their fancy. Irritation shot through Sebastian when he recognized her companion as the same cur who'd been with her at the opera. Orford. What else did they share while her addle-pated husband obviously sated his needs elsewhere?

"She's lovely," remarked Basil to Pen. "Who is she?"

Selwyn followed their gaze. "That's Traherne's daughter."

"I beg your pardon?" gasped Pen.

"The Duke of Traherne's daughter," Selwyn said. "The one who inherits after her father's passing. She'll be the rarest of creatures, a duchess in her own right."

"That's Mirabella Wentworth?" Basil's mouth gaped like a fish on a hook. "How can you be certain?"

"I met her at luncheon this afternoon. She's a particular friend of my betrothed. They attended Miss Langdon's School for Young Ladies together." He glanced over at the woman with little real interest. "It's no wonder you don't recognize her. Lady Mirabella is known to few people in town. She grew up in the country and never had a season. The rumor is Traherne married her off as a child to settle a debt."

Basil elbowed Sebastian. "She doesn't look plain or fat to me."

Sebastian barely heard him. The world tilted, upsetting all sense of balance and order. A volley of emotions bombarded him. Nothing made sense. And yet it made perfect sense.

He watched his wife through a fog of incredulity. *His wife!* When she stopped to exchange pleasantries with someone, giving a smile that was a bit too saucy to be polite, his every nerve ending swelled with euphoria.

"This," he uttered after Selwyn left to rejoin his friends, "is most unexpected."

Pen guffawed, clapping him on the shoulder. "I'll say."

A sense of exultation took root in him. She was his.

She had been all along.

Basil eyed him. "You are acquainted?"

"Yes." He answered somewhat absently returning his gaze to Mirabella. *His wife.* "Although I did not know it was she." He watched her male companion take Mirabella's elbow in a manner too proprietary for his liking. The way she smiled up at Orford, with obvious warmth glazing her eyes, made jealousy course through him.

"She means something to you," Basil said with dawning awareness. "Does she return your interest?"

His gaze did not leave Mirabella. "I suppose you could say that."

Basil's mouth broadened into a smile of genuine delight. "Perhaps your worries all these years will have been groundless."

A seed of mistrust took root in Sebastian, usurping his sense of surprised elation. Mirabella's note just this afternoon claimed her return would be delayed. And yet, here she appeared, on the arm of another man. And she'd been in town for at least three days when he first spotted her at the opera. Perhaps even longer. She'd lied to him. Why? To spend a few more nights with her paramour?

"Well, there is no time like the present," Penrose quipped, raising his glass in salute. "Go introduce yourself and take your bride to bed."

Lust overtook Sebastian as that particular truth washed over him; the manly part of him stirred with impatience. He could have her in his bed this very night and take her as many times as he cared to. He would be well within his rights. But the haze of lust gave way to burgeoning anger. Reality tempered his baser instincts, forcing the return of his senses. His wife could not be trusted. She'd lied to him about her return. He wondered what other things she would be deceitful about. Who was she really? What were her intentions toward him? He had to find out.

Then, and only then, would he introduce himself and take his wife to bed, at last claiming what had been rightfully his all along.

Chapter Five

Bella laughed with delight when the sky exploded in a blaze of light and color.

"How fantastic!" Her face remained skyward, the wind breezing through her hair as Orford twirled her around the dance floor.

He smiled down at her. "Vauxhall's fireworks pale in comparison to the loveliness I behold in my very arms."

She laughed again, feeling free, reveling in the movement, the cool air and the spectacular show above them. "I wish this evening would never end." She felt a sudden pang. "That tomorrow would never come."

"You will have to go to him eventually."

"I'll thank you not to remind me of my duty just yet. I have a few more days of freedom before I must endure him."

When the music came to an end, Orford tucked her arm into his elbow. "Until then, I shall have you all to myself." He escorted her from the dance floor. "Perhaps our final time together."

Faint panic fluttered in her chest. "Nonsense, you are my cousin. We shall continue to see one another."

"Not if he sees how much I care for you. He could command me away from you."

"He would never do that." But she knew he could and very well might.

"Of course not." Orford patted her hand. "No doubt I'm worrying over nothing."

She knew he meant to be reassuring, but instead he had resurrected a nagging fear that her husband would be overbearing. That he would command her life, her friends, would dictate who she could and couldn't see.

"Let's rejoin the others. I see them over on the other side of the dance floor," he said.

She looked across to see their friends. Monty, Tabby, and Josette seemed to have made new acquaintances. Two young bucks hovered around Josette, which came as no surprise. The French woman was lovely and had perfected the art of flirtation. "I want to stand here and enjoy the last of the fireworks. Won't you be a dear and wave them over?"

"Very well," Orford said. "I'll go and signal to them." He gave her a quick peck on the nose. "I shall return, *ma belle*."

Smiling after him, Bella wrapped her arms around herself and gazed up at the explosion of light above her, trying to ward off a sense of aloneness.

"It is quite spectacular."

A shiver ran through her. She knew that voice. It had echoed in her memory for days. She turned toward it. "Stan."

"You know my name?"

"I heard your friend refer to you as such."

"I see. However, I do not know yours. It seems you have me at a distinct disadvantage."

Buoyed by his presence, she smiled at him. Another crackle of noise sounded above them, drawing her attention to the final blast of fireworks lighting up the sky. "How beautiful."

"My thoughts exactly." His voice, deep and self-assured, was almost without inflection. With his contemplative gaze fastened on her, he didn't seem to be referring to the fireworks. "You know my name. May I have the honor of knowing yours?"

His proximity, his overwhelming masculinity, made it difficult for her body to perform the everyday functions of life she normally gave no thought to, things like breathing or blinking. "Mirabella," she said. "Bella."

"A lovely name for a lovely lady." His eyes moved past her and seemed to darken. She followed his gaze to see Orford and her other friends coming toward them. Disappointment surged through her. It was wrong, but she wanted these last moments with Stan before she returned to reality. To Sebastian, her husband.

He offered his arm. "Would you care to walk, Miss—"

She took his solid arm, feeling its strength beneath her fingers. "Just Bella, if you don't mind. It's terribly incorrect, but I feel as though we are friends."

"Indeed."

He led her away from the edge of dance floor down one of Vauxhall's many leafy paths. They walked in silence for a few moments. Bella's body was alive to the sensation of having Stan beside her. What he must think of her to be walking alone with him down this secluded walkway where couples were known to steal more than kisses. "You no doubt think the worst of me, allowing you to escort me alone here."

He gazed at her, an inscrutable expression on his face. "I realize quite suddenly that I could never think ill of you."

Bella exhaled. She believed him. They walked along the path in an easy silence.

"Does your husband not mind?"

Her muscles tensed at the mention of Sebastian. Did he mind? Apparently not. He had never come for her, hadn't even bothered to consummate the marriage once she'd come of age.

She realized Stan was looking at her, awaiting a response. "I cannot say." She felt tears welling in her throat. "He...he does not concern himself with my activities." He frowned but said nothing to fill the silence. To her horror, Bella felt dampness on her cheeks. She brushed it away with her hand.

Halting, Stan faced her. His warm, large hand clasped hers as it rested on his arm. "You are distressed."

She forced a laugh, ignoring the way her heart ached with more unshed tears. "How silly of me. It is the way of an arranged *ton* marriage, I suppose."

His eyebrows drew together. "I am sorry for your distress. Truly."

She regarded him with astonishment. "It is not your fault. You have been nothing but kind."

He shook his head. "I thought it was so, but I've been so very wrong."

"No, you mustn't think such a thing." She reached for his hand with both of hers. His large hands instantly enveloped hers, wrapping around her smaller fingers, encasing them in warmth. Something splashed down on their joined hands. To

Bella's mortification, it was more tears. She never cried. She sank onto a bench. "I don't know what's come over me."

He sat next to her, his intense gaze riveted on her face. "Has it been so very terrible?"

"Bella?" Orford's voice sounded from the walkway. "I think I saw her come this way." Josette and Tabby's chattering voices murmured in response.

"Maybe she is down there." Monty's voice.

Bella rose. "I must go."

He stood with her. "Wait." The words were urgent. "There is something I must tell you."

"Bella!" Josette called.

"My friends are looking for me. I cannot stay here with you."

"Will you meet me on the morrow?" he asked, his expression intent.

She shook her head, well aware she must not see him again. "No, I cannot. It would not be right."

"Bella?" Orford's voice again.

"*Mon dieu*, I think I hear her over there," Josette's voice answered.

"One final time," he said. "I have something of utmost importance to share with you. I would never dishonor my wife. I swear it."

"The lending library," she heard herself say. "Eleven o'clock."

From the lending library, he took her to a park she had never visited before—a small but well-kept space with flowering bushes forming cheerful ribbons of color along the walking paths. Shades of yellow, white, and lilac streamed far ahead of them before disappearing into a copse of trees.

"Oh, it is lovely." Closing her eyes, she breathed in the mingled scents of lilacs and lilies.

Stan smiled, a lone dimple creasing high on his right cheek. "I hoped it would be to your liking. Fernwood Park is renowned for the beauty of its landscape."

They strolled up a small hill, following a well-worn path. He walked beside her, his posture perfect, hands clasped behind his back. Bella slid a quick glance at him underneath her lashes, her heart quickening at the way his fawn-colored breeches skimmed over those substantial legs. He wore a chocolate-brown tailcoat and the sun gleamed off his tasseled Hessians.

"In the Spanish countryside, they have the most beautiful flowers," she said, forcing her attention away from the effect Stan's nearness had on her. "Many are wildflowers, of course, but I think that is when things are at their most beautiful, wild and untamed."

Stan stopped to pluck a white bloom and handed it to her, their fingers brushing. The hot slide of his skin against hers sent warmth tingling low in her belly. Astonished by the strange sensation, she brought the bloom to her nose, inhaling its sweet scent, masking her bewilderment at how his slightest touch could affect every part of her. Even deeply private bits she hadn't really been aware of until now.

"Have you traveled widely?" he asked.

"Yes," she managed to answer. "Spain, Belgium, and France, now that the war has ended."

"Then you enjoy traveling." He took the flower and

tucked it behind her ear. His fingers brushed against the tender curve of skin, awakening the sensitive spot there, the flower's soft petals brushed a sensual sweep against her skin.

If she didn't know better, she'd think he was flirting with her. He *did* seem freer with her today than he had in the past. She shook the thought away. Although she didn't know the gentleman well, he did project an innate decency that left her unable to fathom him acting in an inappropriate manner. "I was at loose ends. I had nowhere else to go."

His dark brows knit together. "Surely you've always known you have a home with your husband."

Closing her eyes, she tilted her face upward, letting the sun's warmth caress her skin. The last thing she wanted to talk about was *him*. She spread her arms out to her sides soaking in the comfort of the midday rays. She twirled, savoring the feeling. "In Spain, we would picnic often in the country when the weather allowed. I relished running among the wildflowers, it made me feel so free."

"Do you crave freedom, Bella?"

Her chest constricted at the tender expression on his face. She stopped twirling and looked off, her gaze following the cascading color of flowers running down the hill. "Perhaps I do." Then someone like Stan could openly court her. "I'll never have a season. No gentleman with honorable intentions will ever pay me his addresses."

"You would have been the season's incomparable."

She smiled at the thought. "Do you think so?"

"Undoubtedly. The reigning beauty of the *ton* with all of the young bloods vying for your heart."

"And who would win me? The most handsome among them or the one with the highest title?"

"The one who loved you with all of his being." A fierce note edged his soft voice. "Who would treasure you as you deserve."

A wistful feeling tugged at her. "And, by now, there'd be a brood of children filling our home."

"Beautiful little girls with their mother's fire."

She pictured little girls with soft auburn curls. Only in her mind's fantasy, her sons had bronze skin and dark curls. And the greenest eyes. "Ten children."

That startled a laugh out of him. "As many as that?"

"For a start. I've always wanted lots of children." Her face warmed with embarrassment and yet it seemed right to do so with him. "I never had a real family. It was just me and the du...my father. He was never in residence. So I always dreamed of making my own tribe."

"A dozen children is it, then," he said softly.

"And I shall grow so very fat from bearing all of those babies."

He gazed at her, the sun shining in his emerald eyes, infusing them with golden accents. "And he will look at the mother of his children and still see the most beautiful woman he has ever laid eyes upon."

"Ah." Her heart moved a little faster at the seriousness of his expression. "His love will be as blind as that?"

"Undoubtedly. And he'll thank the Fates for having blessed an undeserving wretch like him with such an exquisite gift."

Her chest stretched with feeling. "It is a lovely dream."

"One day you shall have it."

"Perhaps, the children part and certainly a husband." But hardly adoring. She forced the melancholy away. "Tell me about your wife. I'm curious to know what sort of woman would capture your attentions."

An admiring warmth glazed his eyes. "In truth, I am just beginning to know her."

"Are you newly married?"

"In a manner of speaking."

And yet he was here, keeping company with her. "Was it a love match?"

"Our fathers arranged the union. We didn't meet until shortly before our nuptials. I admit to being angry and resentful at first." His expression turned tender. "But I'm coming to seeing the rightness of their decision."

Bella's heart did a clumsy flop at the obvious affection in his voice when he spoke of his wife. "You have come to care for her."

His lips curved upward, that lone dimple on his cheek deepening. "Yes, indeed. More so each day. I'm coming to realize how remarkable she truly is."

Jealousy slashed a jagged path inside her stomach. She'd misinterpreted his feelings. He obviously cared for his wife. "She is most fortunate."

His smile took a cynical curve. "I am not certain she would agree. And what of your husband?"

She shrugged and turned away to continue walking along the path. "Honestly, I don't know him. We were married when I was just a child. I had no hand in it. I barely knew what was happening at the time."

"Do you resent it?" Urgency edged his voice. "Has he restricted your freedom?"

The helpless anger she always felt at her husband's abandonment reared within her. "No, he has given me freedom quite by accident I think, through his neglect."

"Neglect?"

"I doubt he cares. Even for my innocence. He would not have sent me away and kept me away for so long if he did." She forced a harsh laugh. "He didn't even bother to send a suitable chaperone to ensure my decorum. I am a complication that he must endure to have what he truly wants."

Stan's entire body stiffened, a disturbing energy radiated off him. "And what is that, do you think?"

His reaction warmed her. How kind of him to be angry on her behalf. "My dowry, the kind of influence and consequence the nephew of a marquess could never have dreamed of."

The lines in his face deepened into a grave frown. "Perhaps once the two of you are acquainted, you will develop a better understanding of his true nature."

"You are a good and kind man." A feeling of tenderness welled up in her. "You could never understand someone such as my husband. Sebastian has made his true nature known simply by his absence. I haven't seen him since our wedding day."

The skin over his angular jaw stretched taut. "It is possible you have misjudged his intentions."

"Your generosity of spirit toward my husband is truly that of a fine gentleman."

He halted and planted his hands on his hips. "This has gone on long enough." He exhaled in a slow deliberate motion, as though he needed to draw strength. "Bella, there is something I must tell you."

Nerves twisted in her chest at his somber expression.

Suddenly, she felt wary. She didn't want to know what he had to say. "Enough serious talk." Anxious to change the subject, she eyed the picnic basket in his hand and forced gaiety into her voice. "What have you got there? I've worked up quite an appetite."

"I must tell you the truth...about my wife. About who I am."

"No." She shook her head forcefully. No truths mattered. After today, she would return to her husband. She wouldn't see Stan again. She didn't need to know anything about him. "Just for today, let us enjoy this afternoon. Reality will intrude eventually, but not just yet. Let us just enjoy a meal among the flowers and sunshine."

His tense expression softened. Following her lead, he said, "I believe my cook has prepared cold chicken, cheese, bread, and some tarts for dessert."

They found a spot to set up their picnic. Stan laid out a blanket and knelt to pull food out of the basket, organizing the items in a neat arrangement.

She watched, amused. "You certainly are very exacting with your placement of things. A picnic is not usually so orderly."

Appearing surprised by her observation, he looked toward the precise composition of the foodstuffs he'd just organized. "I do dislike disorder. I always have." He gestured toward the food. "Your feast awaits."

Biting her lower lip, she gave an impish smile. "I am in the mood to be positively wicked, decadent even."

Stan stilled, except for a lone twitch in the strong curve of his jaw. "Indeed? What exactly do you have in mind?"

She reached for a tart, biting into it with relish. "I think I will go straight for dessert. Can you think of anything more decadent?"

...

The next morning Sebastian relaxed as the hack driver turned in the direction of the lending library. For the first time in his recollection, he felt hopeful, even joyous. He was also as randy as a young buck. His body on edge, anticipating the moment he would find relief inside his wife's soft and welcoming flesh. Perhaps even by this evening.

Mirabella had been a revelation these last few days. It was more than her obvious beauty that drew him. His wife was unlike any woman of his acquaintance. She literally sparkled, infusing any room she entered with her glowing presence. And she was exceedingly bright, having soaked up a great deal of knowledge and experience from her travels.

During their picnic, talk had turned to her adventures on the continent. She'd proved an excellent conversationalist, witty and engaging, with an occasional hint of naughtiness in recounting her perceptions of her experiences. Bella talked of the museums she'd visited and her impressions of the different countries and people she'd met. He'd been so caught up in their conversation that he'd lost track of time.

She should have had the truth from him by now. He owed her that. Even though she'd stopped him, he'd had an obligation to press forward and reveal everything. Especially now that he knew his attempt to give her freedom had been perceived as abandonment and indifference. She thought him greedy and interested only in her title and wealth.

He would disavow her of that notion today by telling her

the glorious truth. He pictured Bella's face lighting up with happiness and relief. Perhaps she would throw herself into his arms. Maybe she'd accompany him back to his home—their home—on Park Street, where they would finally make use of his wife's adjoining bedchamber.

The moment the hackney pulled up to the lending library, gladness filled his heart to see her standing near the entrance. She was a vision in a straw bonnet with ribbons the color of sunshine and a matching spencer that caressed her curves. Underneath, Mirabella wore a simple cream dress. He smiled when she caught his eye, but her lips flattened and she looked away.

It had been difficult persuading his reluctant wife to see him again, but he'd promised her it would be their last secret meeting. He meant to keep that vow. After today he planned to parade his lovely wife all over town on his arm. Orford would no longer be needed.

Alighting, he walked toward her. She darted a look down the street behind him, giving every appearance of a trapped animal poised to make a run for safety. Perhaps meeting another man made her feel disloyal to her husband. He smiled to himself, thinking of again of how pleased Mirabella would be to learn the truth.

"Good day," he called out to her.

"This is a mistake." She held up a hand as though to stop him, or perhaps warning him to keep his distance. "I just came to tell you I cannot accompany you."

His heart swelled with compassion for her. "I must talk with you. Please, after today you will understand." He took her arm. "Come now, I know a quiet place where we can talk."

She avoided his gaze. "No, my husband expects me today. I must go."

He halted and his goodwill evaporated. Another lie. She had no plans to meet her husband. Not that she knew of. He stepped much closer to her than was proper. "Do you, indeed?"

"What are you doing?" She backed away, looking around to make sure no one had noticed them. He followed when she entered the lending library and hurried by the circular counter in the center of the shop. She passed a wall of books before finally turning into a narrow corridor that was empty of people.

Halting, she spun around to face him. "This cannot continue. I must not see you again."

Heat rose in his chest. "Why not? You seem content to allow other males to escort you."

She drew back. "What are you talking about?"

He stepped closer, his chest inches from hers, jealousy searing his gut. "Orford. Your friend who was with you at the opera and at Vauxhall."

Her cheeks reddened.

Was it because he stood so near to her, or had he hit too close to the truth about her constant companion?

"He is just a friend." Her eyes narrowed. "Who are you to question me? I already have a husband to answer to, and you, sir, are not he."

If only she knew. "And do you, my lady, answer to your husband?" he asked sharply. "Tell me, do you inform him of our encounters?

She paled, but her almond eyes blazed a lovely shade of gold. She pulled her shoulders back, looking every inch the haughty duchess she would one day become. "Move aside, sir. I have obviously misjudged you."

Instead of stepping out of her path as good manners dictated, his gaze fell to those plush lips, so pink and plump, his to savor. "Just a kiss," he murmured, unable to stop himself. She was his wife after all. There was nothing improper about it. "And then I shall let you pass."

She inhaled, her shock evident. "You, sir," she said scorchingly, "are no gentleman."

...

Bella took a reflexive step back when Stan moved closer. The potency between them flexed again, upsetting her balance. His eyes were intent on her face, vivid emeralds that easily penetrated her flimsy defenses.

"Allow yourself this one indulgence."

She felt woozy. His impressive form, with its carved wedges of muscle, no doubt honed by vigorous exercise, stood too near for her to think clearly. The shaving soap intermingled with the tang of clean male skin, coated her nostrils like an elemental calling card.

He stepped closer, a determined tilt to his strong chin. "Why deny yourself just a taste?" he murmured, his voice a warm, seductive purr.

His virility overpowered any remaining morsel of propriety in her. Blood rushed to her brain, hammering a relentless beat in her ears. Lord, she should not have agreed to meet him again. No good could come of it. She hadn't guarded her emotions all of these years just to open herself up to heartbreak now, when she'd finally resigned herself to doing her duty and joining her husband.

A traitorous thought slipped into her brain. Why not give in to temptation? Why should she go to Sebastian with her innocence intact? He didn't deserve it and likely wouldn't even notice. He had all he seemed to want—her fortune and the Traherne prestige. When the time came, he'd probably force himself to bed her in order to beget an heir. But it would not be an act of passion, nor of love.

Her eyes slipped to Stan's generous mouth and she couldn't help wondering what it would be like to kiss him. It could do no real harm since it wouldn't *ruin her* ruin her. Shouldn't her first introduction to passion be with someone she desired instead of out of duty to a husband who had little use for her?

"I shouldn't put you through this. The truth of the matter is—" He began, but she stopped him.

"Just this once," she said, feeling both arousal and fear.

His green eyes blazed. He stepped closer and this time she did not step away. A firm hand cupped her chin, a gentle touch angling her mouth for his ravishment.

Full lips came down on hers, soft and fleeting at first, scattering Bella's thoughts to the far corners of her senses. She sighed into his mouth and his tongue slipped inside, sampling her with deep, luxurious strokes. He tasted unabashedly male, mingled with a touch of sweetness, edged with the tiniest bit of tartness. Delicious. She'd known such kisses existed, had even seen Josette allow them from her beaus in the past. But she'd never dreamed, never imagined the wonder of it, the astounding pleasure that made one lose all sense of propriety. That made her forget she had a husband.

Stan wrapped his arms around her, pulling her closer until she was engulfed in masculinity. She pushed herself up against his heat, relishing the unfamiliar intimacy of a warm, muscled male body pressed against her feminine curves. She would allow herself this one taste of temptation before succumbing to duty—and an indifferent husband.

Stan groaned and kissed her deeper than Bella thought was possible. Losing herself in his lips and tongue, she brought her arms around Stan, caressing up and down his back, feeling the hard curve of muscle under his tailcoat. She pulled him to her, kissing him back, tasting and exploring…

"Mirabella Wentworth, is that you?"

Chapter Six

The words come out in a gasp of horror from somewhere behind Stan. Hot and flustered, Bella pulled away in a panic. Freezing in place, Stan let her go.

Bella's face felt as if it might burst into flames. She knew that voice. It was her mother's old friend, Lady Hervey. The *ton*'s sharpest tongue and biggest gossip.

"I thought it was you." Lady Hervey's weathered face was pointy with displeasure. "Such behavior is not to be born."

The hot flush of shame rushed through her as she met Stan's gaze. Anger darkened his face and he started to turn around. She clutched his tailcoat to stop him from turning around and revealing himself. It would only make things worse.

"Allowing yourself to be mauled by a stranger in a lending library of all places." Even the feather on Lady Hervey's ornate orange hat quivered in outrage. "Wait until His Grace hears about this. I am relieved your sainted mother did not live to see the shame you have brought upon her good name."

Indignation gouged Bella's chest at the mention of her mother by this petty woman. Her pulse at a full gallop, she raised her chin, pulled back her shoulders, and leveled a determined look at the witch. "By all means, go then and relay your information. Pray do leave us to our privacy."

One of Stan's dark brows shot up at the obvious impropriety of her comment, but that lone dimple high on his right cheek also creased with amusement.

Lady Hervey gasped. "Well, I never! You can be assured that no one in decent society will entertain you after they hear of this."

Tamping down a mix of anger and fear, Bella shot the old bag a rebellious look. "If you are what is considered decent society, then I have no desire to be entertained by the likes of you."

The other woman's chest shot out in outrage. "You are a shameless strumpet." Red-faced, she spun around and hurried away, muttering under her breath.

Bella's legs gave way, but Stan caught her, lending his steady strength. Good Lord, what had she just done? She was ruined. Lady Hervey would make sure of it. By nightfall, everyone would know Traherne's daughter had been caught kissing a strange man in the lending library.

Sebastian would know.

"Courage." Stan's firm grip still held her elbow. "You've done nothing wrong—"

"How can you say that?" She pulled away. "I must go. Promise me you won't follow."

He tightened his grip. "Once you hear what I have to say—"

"No!" She spoke sharply, panic threatening to overtake her. "All I want to hear at this moment is your promise."

He seemed about to say something, but stopped and abruptly released her. "Very well. For now."

She rushed away from him as nausea flooded her. She'd publicly humiliated her husband. He would surely hear of it. Would he beat her for cuckolding him? Did he even care?

After six long years, she was about to find out.

Bella sat in a leather chair in her father's study where the pungent odor of stale cigar smoke clung to the walls like ivy. She shifted in her seat, her stomach contracting. A chill encompassed the dark, wood-paneled chamber. It was dimly lit, with curtains partially closed along a lone window facing the street. Through the glass she glimpsed the immaculate Mayfair residences across the way, their quiet serenity at odds with the rioting in her stomach.

Running her hands over her scarlet gown, she smoothed the folds of her skirt, then fingered the gold trim along the scandalously low décolletage of her dress, the cut so deep her entire breasts were in danger of making a public appearance. On the Continent, nobody would give the cut of her gown a second look, but that wasn't the case here among the *ton*.

Sebastian and her father were on their way. She forced a deep, calming breath. Let them do their best. She was ready to face their recriminations, the two men who had all but abandoned her to the world, both so caught up in the Traherne consequence they'd barely bothered to acknowledge her existence. Running a look over her gown, she smiled grimly to herself. Well, they would notice her now.

Despite her bluster, she started when a noise sounded at the door. She jumped to her feet as the massive wooden door pushed open and was relieved to see the large, corpulent figure of His Grace rather than her husband.

She hadn't seen her father in almost three years, since a long-ago school break. He rarely put in an appearance at Traherne Abbey, his countryseat, and never visited the Richmond house. Even when Bella had visited on school breaks, he'd remained in town, apparently preferring its amusements to the company of his only child.

The duke appeared heavier now with more prominent jowls, his brown hair almost completely dusted with gray. Bella felt a jolt of longing. Whatever his failings, he was her father and she had missed him.

His Grace's black eyes took in her appearance, his obvious disapproval tinged with amusement. "That gown makes you look like a harlot," he said by way of greeting. "Do you think to distract your husband from his well-placed displeasure by displaying your wares like a common lightskirt?"

Her heart squeezed, but she forced a flippant reply. "Hello to you, too, Father. What a heartwarming greeting."

He ambled over to the sideboard to pour himself a drink despite the early hour. Some things never changed.

"Clever of you to distract him with your womanly assets." He chortled. "You are my spawn, that's for certain. I warned him you'd require a firm hand, but he refused to heed me."

"No doubt he was too busy spending your fortune."

"Never did know your place, did you?" Turning to face her, he raised the full glass up in salute. "You are well and truly his problem now." He downed the contents of his glass in one neat gulp. "I trust he will impress upon you a wife's proper role. It is past time you behaved with the decorum befitting a lady and a duchess."

Bella's throat constricted. Her father, her only real family, had not shown her a glimmer of warmth, just the usual careless disregard. "I am sorry to disappoint you by being born female, Your Grace."

Walking over to his desk, he leaned his hip against it and crossed his arms. "It is unfortunate your mother sacrificed her life giving birth to you instead of a son. Every man wants a true heir to carry on his line." He shrugged his shoulders. "But no matter. You will do well enough. In time, my grandson will give the title the consequence it deserves."

She swallowed hard; her father's words wounded her more than she would have liked to admit. Lost in her emotions, she barely heard the polite knock at the door.

"Here's Sebastian now." Her father looked expectantly beyond her to the door. "Enter."

Crossing her arms, she braced herself, hearing the butler announce her husband, followed by the sounds of rustling fabric and the footsteps of someone entering the room.

A rich, masculine voice followed. "I see you have reunited with Lady Mirabella, Your Grace."

She froze in confusion. She knew that voice. *Stan*. Had he come to protect her from Sebastian's wrath? Panic exploded in Bella's stomach. She had to make him leave before Sebastian arrived. She spun around, her heart vaulting in her chest. Stan stood on the threshold, his formidable presence imbuing the chamber with quiet command. He was dressed to perfection in a navy tailcoat that stretched across his broad shoulders with a soft blue striped waistcoat underneath. Charcoal breeches hugged his powerful thighs before disappearing into gleaming tasseled Hessians.

"Well, here she is." A thread of merriment was woven into her father's voice. "You should have taken her in hand before she disgraced us both."

Squinting in confusion, Bella darted a glance between Stan and her father, questions ricocheting in her head. How did they know each other?

Favoring her with a warm smile and a sparkle in those vivid eyes, Stan approached and offered his arm. She looked at him dumbly, unable to comprehend what his appearance in the duke's study meant. When she didn't move, he took her hand and gently placed in on his sleeve. Facing Traherne, he said, "Mirabella could never disgrace anyone."

His Grace's eyes widened. "Surely you've heard of her indiscretion at the lending library. Lady Hervey says she acted the wanton, allowing some varlet to put his hands all over her person. And that shrew is an insufferable gossip. Bella is ruined. Surely you see that you have no recourse except to banish her from your bed, to distance both of us from her wanton behavior."

"To the contrary, I would never banish my wife from my bed when I have just brought her to my side."

Bella's head swam. She could barely follow the train of their conversation. "What does your wife have to do with this?"

Her father looked at her, his forehead wrinkling. "Have

you taken to imbibing like a dockside strumpet as well as dressing as one?"

Brushing a gaze over Bella's revealing vibrant red gown, Stan's eyes lingered for a moment on the exposed mounds of her breasts. She reflexively brought her hand up to cover herself, embarrassed Stan should see her in such a scandalous gown. She'd worn it to provoke her father and husband, to show them she didn't care what they thought and would do as she pleased. But Stan's good opinion did matter to her.

He surprised her by bringing her hand to his lips. Warm, reassuring eyes caught and held hers for a moment. Heat pushed through her when his soft lips touched her skin in a tender caress. He replaced her hand back on his sleeve before turning back to the His Grace. "Pray do not insult my wife, Traherne."

The room shifted. When had the duke insulted Stan's wife?

"I credited you with more brains than you apparently possess, Stanhope. Can you not see it is Mirabella who insults us both with her behavior?" Traherne blew out an exasperated breath. "I don't care for proprieties, but they must be observed. You refused to bring your wife to heel and now she's allowing strangers to take liberties in full view of the *ton*."

Stanhope? *Stanhope*. Why was he calling Stan by Sebastian's name? Sebastian Stanhope. It finally dawned that "Stan" was a diminutive of Stanhope. Good Lord.

"Kissing one's husband is hardly scandalous," she heard the man beside her say, confirming what her mind was still trying to parse.

What an idiot she was.

His Grace frowned. "What the devil are you about, Sebastian?"

"The gentleman in the lending library with my wife was none other than myself." He flashed a slow, confident smile at Bella. "Perhaps I am guilty of enjoying my wife's abundant charms, but she is entirely blameless. I take full responsibility."

Fire flared deep in her. Stan was Sebastian. He'd known all along who she was—that they were husband and wife—yet he'd tempted her into what she'd believed to be an indiscretion.

"Is this true, Mirabella? Were you with Sebastian in the lending library?"

Fury clawed her chest and she gritted her teeth, not trusting herself to look at Stan…Sebastian. "This is the person who accompanied me to the lending library, yes."

Traherne barked a relieved laugh. "How is this possible?"

Sebastian placed a hand over Bella's, where it rested on his sleeve. "I summoned her home just as you suggested. We have passed the last few days becoming reacquainted again."

Her heart pumping, she pulled her hand out from under Sebastian's. It was all she could do not to break the vodka decanter over his deceitful head.

Traherne walked over to the sideboard to pour himself another drink, this time, apparently, a congratulatory one. He emptied the decanter into his glass. "Well, this is capital. That old biddy, Lady Hervey, won't have a chance to make mischief after all." He emptied the contents of the glass in one large gulp. "She always ran to your mother with word of my peccadilloes and my late wife was like Bella here. She was never one to let a perceived transgression go unnoticed, especially when it involved her husband."

Her pulse pounded so hard in her head, she thought her skull would burst open. "You are correct, Father." She cast a patently false sweet smile at Sebastian and was gratified to see a glitter of alarm in his mendacious green eyes. "I am not one to let a husband's offense go unpunished."

"Excellent, excellent," her father said in an absentminded way that showed his thoughts had moved on to other matters. "Well, I'm for the club. I have a luncheon date."

They'd been reunited for barely an hour and her father was already leaving her again. No matter. She'd reserve the full force of her emotion for Sebastian. It was exactly what he deserved.

...

Traherne had barely closed the door behind him before the decanter he'd emptied moments before came barreling through the air, aimed straight for Sebastian. He ducked, the alarming *whoosh* of air alerting him to just how close the crystal carafe had come to bashing him in the head. It sailed over and slammed into the wall ending its flight with a graceless thud on the carpet.

"Good God!" he exclaimed. "Are you mad? You could have rendered me senseless."

"As if you have any good sense to lose!"

"Surely we can discuss this like rational adults." Bending to pick up the carafe, he placed it on a lowboy. "Once you regain your wits, I'm certain—"

This time it was too late to duck. His arm shot up to protect his face from an incoming marble paperweight. Pain shot through his arm when it struck his elbow. "Blast it! Stop this nonsense at once."

Her expression feral, she scanned the chamber as if searching for something. Her wits, hopefully. She spun and grabbed for something on her father's desk. A letter opener. He lunged, reaching her just as her grip closed around the marble handle of the blade. Careful not to hurt her, he forced her wrists above her head, maneuvering the glinted edge so that it couldn't harm either of them.

"Let it go, Bella. You could hurt someone with that."

"Not someone, nitwit," she snapped. "You."

Her hold still tight on the weapon, she struggled against his superior strength. He held firm, certain she'd seize any opportunity to run him through. "Give it up. You haven't a chance against me."

Her breaths came in short, harsh gasps. "We'll see about that, you mutton-headed clod pole."

His own temper sparked. "Drop it."

"*No.*" He could feel the fury rippling through her muscles. Her cheeks were flushed with exertion, tendrils of curls had escaped her coiffure. She looked like sin in that scarlet dress that barely covered her, leaving a wide expanse of luminous pale shoulder and plump, creamy mounds exposed to his lusty gaze. And from this vantage point, the view was excellent.

His body's elemental urges surged, swamping him with the need to lay her across the desk, toss up her skirts, and feel her moist heat. He ached to pull down her bodice to see what color her nipples were. In his imaginings, they were the same delectable pink as her temptress lips.

"You're hurting me." Her soft tone snapped his attention

back to his steel grip on her wrists. Mortified at the thought of injuring her, he loosened his hold. She instantly tried to jerk her arms away. When that failed, she slammed him hard with her body instead.

The shocking shunt of her body against his—glorious soft breasts, stomach to belly, masculine parts against decidedly feminine ones—awakened his body to stunning alertness.

Triumph flared in her exquisite face, followed by an expression of clear malicious intent. He recovered his senses in time to catch her knee when it shot up, aiming for his bits. The unexpected movement upset her balance. "Blast you!" she cried.

His heart jumped when she fell away from him. He tightened his grasp around her bent knee, keeping it uplifted, steadying her. "Unmanning me will solve nothing," he said between harsh breaths.

She growled something in response, but his mind was too busy parsing their awkward position to comprehend her words. With her one leg hitched up, her feminine charms were snuggled against his thigh. Any hope of bodily control cascaded out of him. His vitals surged to attention, straining toward her inviting warmth.

Red shot through her face when she registered their indecent stance. She jerked back, but he held her firm. She teetered on one leg, totally at his mercy. Raging at him through clenched teeth, she growled, "Let me go, you *pig*."

His hapless body hardened against her enticing softness. "Not until you promise to behave."

She went rigid at the feel of his arousal against her inner thigh. "As if you know the first thing about proper behavior, you lying scab."

"I never lied to you."

"Ha! Another lie."

He did owe her an explanation, but with those fleshy orbs pressed into his chest and her femininity at his hip driving his body to bedlam, it was impossible to recall the cogent explanation he'd rehearsed. "That was never my intent—"

"Just what was your intent?" She struggled to wrench her hand away from his, the letter opener trembled in her grip. "Were you amusing yourself at my expense? Was it some kind of test to see if I could be seduced by a man who I did not know was my husband?"

Frowning, he tried to focus on her words and not the feminine heat snuggled against him. "No, of course not. I just wanted us to have a chance to become acquainted."

"You weren't spying on me to test my faithfulness?"

"Perhaps at first," he said with great reluctance. "Just for a moment."

Her eyes flared. "Why am I not surprised?" She jerked her knee, aiming for his vitals again.

He restrained her leg before she could unman him. "That changed almost immediately," he said quickly, needing her to understand the truth of matters between them. "I realized that I wanted to truly know you, that I enjoyed being with you. I wanted to court you the way a lady of your elegance and spirit deserves."

Her eyes watered and for a moment her expression softened. Then she blinked, recovering her anger. "Another lie. You are exactly the way I've always imagined you to be."

He started to protest, but then inhaled her scent, startled

to find her woman's heat comingled with the essence of orange blossom. He frowned. "Why do you never wear the same perfume?"

Her face scrunched up. "What?"

"At our first encounter you smelled of jasmine, the second time like lavender, and now…is that citrus I detect?"

"Not that it is any of your concern, but I like to change my scent to suit my mood."

That seemed like a disorderly way to manage one's toilet. He himself performed the exact same ablutions each day. "The lavender doesn't suit you."

She relaxed her defensive posture a little. "Why is that?"

"Something richer, with a hint of spice, would suit you better."

A thoughtful expression crossed her face, but then she seemed to remember that her open leg remained hiked up against him. If he adjusted his body slightly to the left, he could plunge headlong into her feminine sweetness. She went taut. "Release me." The words melted on a shaky breath.

He struggled to hold still, to keep from rubbing his member against her. "So you can plunge that pointed tool into me?" He felt the fight leave her. She relaxed her grip on the letter opener, allowing him to relieve her of it. He gently released her leg, the delightful turn of her curves sliding through his fingers.

Turning away from him, she sighed with a weighty sadness. "First, my father and now you. I should have heeded Josette's advice never to trust a man because he will always disappoint. Stan was a lovely dream while he lasted."

He felt an absurd jealousy of Stan. "For God's sake, I am

Stan. Don't you see? Nothing has changed."

"You're correct in that. Nothing has changed." She regarded him with open derision. "You are exactly what I expected you to be. The rest of it—*Stan*—was the illusion."

"Perhaps you should try living in the real world. You might find it suits you."

She gave a weary snort. "I've been living in the real world since I was three-and-ten. You and my father saw to that."

"No," he said resolutely. "Today, you begin your real life, as my wife, by my side."

Chapter Seven

His wife uttered not a word on the short ride from the duke's residence. Staring straight ahead, she ignored him, her lips pressed together as the fire in her cheeks cooled.

His chest squeezed at the obvious turmoil raging inside her. What a mess he'd made of things. He'd meant to allow her some freedom, but ended up wounding his wife with his years-long absence. He'd compounded that idiocy by not claiming her the moment he'd realized who she was.

His wife. His to love. His to build a true family with.

He'd devote himself to reassuring her of his true intentions. And, one evening soon, he would make her his wife in truth. His man parts swelled at the thought, the usual tight control he maintained over his bodily responses nowhere to be found. He crossed his legs to hide the obvious sign of his desire for her.

The indecent gown wasn't helping control his impulses. He'd understood immediately why she'd worn it. In defiance—likely to provoke both husband and father—to demonstrate she answered to no one. But that was before she knew his true identity. Once she understood the way of things, he doubted she would repeat today's performance.

He shifted in his seat, trying to relieve the pressure in his groin. His vitals were clearly anxious to unleash years of pent-up desire. Looking at Bella, taking in her high, gently sloping cheekbones and the generosity of her sweet mouth, thinking of her vibrant personality and quick wit, he was glad he'd remained faithful to her. She was a woman well worth waiting for.

They arrived at their Park Street townhome to find the servants lined up on either side of the staircase leading up to the entrance. Alighting first, he turned to help her down, proud to present his wife to the anxious staff. He noted how she smoothly pulled her hand away as soon as her feet touched the ground. The butler, Davison, and the housekeeper, Mrs. Nagle, stepped forward to greet them.

Sebastian made the introductions. "Davison, this is your mistress, Lady Mirabella."

The butler bowed low, showing his respect for the duchess she'd one day become. "My lady. It is my sincere pleasure to serve you. I shall endeavor to meet your every expectation."

"Thank you, Davison. I'm certain you will exceed them." She answered with the poise and grace befitting her station.

The housekeeper fell into a deep curtsy. "And this is Mrs. Nagle, our housekeeper," Sebastian said.

"Welcome home, my lady. We are pleased to have our mistress in residence."

"My thanks, Mrs. Nagle. I shall rely on your expertise

when acquainting myself with the household."

From there, Davison proceeded to introduce her to each member of the male staff. Then Mrs. Nagle did the same with the female servants. Bella repeated each name as it was told to her and took the time to exchange a few words with each one.

Sebastian was well pleased by Bella's graceful manner with the staff. She behaved every inch the duchess she would one day be and, if their mistress's scandalous gown shocked them, the servants were too well trained to show it.

Once the introductions were complete, Bella turned to Mrs. Nagle. "Perhaps you would be so kind as to show me to my chambers."

Sebastian stepped forward and offered his arm before Mrs. Nagle could respond. "Allow me, my dear, it would be my pleasure."

She looked at him with cool civility, her demeanor so unlike the vibrant, open woman he'd come to know. "I would not want to trouble you."

"Not at all, you would be doing me a kindness."

He noted a subtle tightening of her features, but she blinked it away.

"How can I refuse?"

...

Bella couldn't help appreciating the luxurious bedchamber in its muted shades of yellow and ivory. A large four-poster, canopied bed dominated the room and a bank of windows to the east looked out over a small but lovely, well-kept garden.

"It's quite nice," she murmured, conscious that the

housekeeper hovered nearby directing the footmen where to leave the bags Bella had packed that morning in anticipation of taking up residence with her husband.

Sebastian, blast his eyes, seemed pleased with her reaction. "My cousin, Willa, the Duchess of Hartwell helped with the changes. I wanted to make certain this chamber was fit for a duchess."

She smoothed a hand over the cool silk of the counterpane and willed herself to maintain her composure. She swallowed the grief in her throat, trying to brush away a sweeping sense of loss. Stan had never been real, yet she mourned as if someone dear to her had perished.

The housekeeper approached with a petite, young woman by her side. Curly, dark hair escaped her cap, framing the girl's narrow, friendly face and large brown eyes. "My lady, this is Louisa," said Mrs. Nagle. "She will be pleased to serve as your ladies' maid, unless you already have someone in service."

With a nervous smile, Louisa dipped into a deep curtsy. "My lady."

"I would be grateful for your help," she said warmly to the girl, hoping to put her at ease. "Perhaps you could begin with unpacking my things."

The girl flushed with pleasure. "Oh, yes, my lady. Straight away."

"In a little while, Louisa," Sebastian said from across the room. "Please leave us for now." He turned to the footmen and gestured for them to do the same.

Bella's heart pounded. She busied herself arranging her toilet items, moving her brush, tooth powder, and perfumes around on her dressing table. She pretended to ignore

Sebastian, who leaned against a bedpost, watching her with his arms crossed over his chest.

"You will have to speak to me eventually." He finally broke the silence. "Surely you have something to say."

She turned to face him, locking her eyes with his. "What would you have me say?" Her chest swelled with feeling. "That you made a fool of me? That I cannot bear to be in your company?"

"That would be a start."

His complete command of himself infuriated her. Did he never lose control? "Perhaps you should inform me how you intend to go on in this marriage. You clearly have no use for me now that you have access to my funds."

His green eyes regarded her with a calm confidence that unnerved her. "I think we shall get on quite well once the shock of this has passed."

She forced a harsh laugh and returned to unpacking her things. "If that is really what you believe, then you do not know me very well," she said. "But then again, we already know that."

He walked to her. "I am sorry for hurting you."

"It is of no consequence. All we have is a marriage of convenience."

He reached out and tucked a loose tendril behind her ear. She stiffened, acutely aware of his body standing too close to hers and of the way the scent of musk shaving soap and male heat tended to sneak over her and steal her senses.

"We have this," he said softly, his eyes intent on her face. "It is more than most married couples have."

Moving away from him, she said, "I don't know what you mean."

He closed the distance between them, the relentless hunter closing in on his skittish quarry. "I think you do." He reached out and smoothed the back of his hand down the column of her throat.

Her pulse scattered in all directions. "You are mistaken."

"Am I? The signs are all there. Your smooth skin is warm."

"Because I am angry."

His warm strong hand moved lower, to the top of her exposed chest, just inches from the top swells of her breasts. "Yet your heart races under my touch."

Lord have mercy. She clenched her teeth to keep from sighing out loud at the delicious trail of sensation his fingers drew on her skin. "A sign of my distress at your betrayal."

His hand moved lower, to the top curve of her breasts. "You are trembling."

"With anger. Because I cannot bear your touch."

"You have the most beautiful skin."

She almost fainted with pleasure when his audacious hands slipped even lower, inside her bodice, where his fingers brushed against the peak of her breast. Bella closed her eyes, unable to make herself stop him.

"Allow me to treasure you as you deserve. I burn for you."

She shook her head, helpless under his touch, her breasts swollen and eager. "I burn, too. With anger."

He chuckled, bringing his lips to her throat, showering it with small, tantalizing kisses. His fingers moved to cup her breast more fully. "We can bring each other great pleasure."

His mouth moved to hers, gentle and sure. He feathered light kisses over her lips. His tongue outlined her lips, sending her flying on a carpet of warm air. A gentle nip on her lower lip brought her back to earth; she gasped and his wily tongue took the opportunity to slip inside. He stroked in and out of her mouth, rubbing her tongue, going in deeper each time, taking more of her.

Sensation flowed, encompassing her. She tasted him back, a surprising sweet tanginess spiced with his unique taste. His hands tugged at her bodice. Her harlot's gown allowed him easy access. Damnation. She hadn't thought of that.

The shock of cool air bathed her bared breasts. He cupped her, his thumbs tantalizing the sensitive tips. "Beautiful," he murmured.

His lips left hers, moving down her throat, laying tender kisses across the top swells of her breasts as he worked downward, finally taking an engorged tip into his mouth. She cried out when the hot moist silk of his tongue stroked over her. She clutched his arms to steady herself. He wrapped them around her waist, drawing her into an embrace against his powerful form as he moved to the other breast and continued to feast on her. She pressed herself against his prodigious arousal and her entire body throbbed.

"That's it, my love," he said in a low, thick voice. "It is still I, Stan."

Stan was a lie, a fantasy that did not exist. The real man in his place had betrayed her and played her for a fool. How could she let him move her this way? She shoved him away with the force of that maelstrom of conflicting emotions. The reverse force of it propelled her onto the bed, landing on her back with her upper body propped on her elbows.

"There is no Stan." Feeling and fury choked her throat.

"He doesn't exist. He was kind, strong, and true. You possess none of those qualities. You lied to me and abandoned me."

Against his dark complexion and tousled hair, the green in his eyes deepened with touches of blues and grays, the colors of furious waves in a storm. "What is happening between us is very real," he said, his full lips moist from the intimate kisses. "I know you feel it as well, only you're a coward to acknowledge the truth."

"You would like that, wouldn't you? For me to give in?"

"We are married. We should make the best of it." His wild gaze ran over her and she realized how she must appear with her skirt hiked up well above her ankles and her bodice pulled down. She shot up to a sitting position, jerking her bodice up to cover herself. "I'm afraid that's impossible. You see, I've fallen in love with another man. I can't be unfaithful to my darling *Stan*."

He groaned in frustration. "I never told you my name was Stan. My friend, Pen, is the only person who refers to me by that rather abominable name." He pulled at his breeches to adjust them, drawing Bella's eyes to the sizeable bulge at his groin. It made her go warm, deepening the hungry need still throbbing inside her. She still wanted him, even after everything he'd put her through. Dragging the back of her hand across her lips, she tried to wipe his mesmerizing taste away. She thought back to when she'd first heard the name at Lady Claymont's rout, when Sebastian's flame-haired friend had found them together in the library. "Be that as it may, you lied by omission. There is very little difference."

Hands on his hips, he took a deep inhale as though he, too, needed to calm his body. "It was not a deliberate attempt to deceive you."

She experienced a small surge of triumph to know she had penetrated his usually unwavering self-control. "Then why didn't you make yourself known at the opera?"

"I didn't know who you were then. I swear it."

"When did you realize?"

"Not until Vauxhall."

"Vauxhall." She uttered a silent laugh of incredulity. "You took me down one of the secluded pathways, no doubt hoping to see if I could be seduced like a dockside tart."

"No, it wasn't like that."

"It must have proved an amusing gam, to see if your wife would unknowingly whore for you. Perhaps you and your friends wagered on it."

Temper flared in his eyes. "Of course we didn't."

"You almost won. Who knows what would have occurred in the lending library had Lady Hervey not appeared when she did."

"Mirabella."

Good. She wanted to push him to the edge of his blasted composure. "You were almost there. A few more minutes, and you could have had my skirts tossed up for the entire world to see."

He surged forward, leaning over her with a menacing glare. She fell back in a reflexive movement to avoid the collision of their bodies, landing with her upper body propped back on her elbows again. He planted one large hand on each side of her prone body. "Perhaps I should just toss up your skirts right now."

Alarm shot through her at the banked fury in his expression. "You wouldn't dare."

"Wouldn't I? You just intimated that I'm no gentleman."

Damnation. She'd neatly set her own trap by suggesting he'd behaved in a base manner. Now he seemed bent on acting down to her expectations.

"Should I prove you right or wrong?" he asked. "What do you suggest?"

His musky man's scent besieged her. The proximity of that sheer physicality was dizzying. "I suggest you take your idle threats and leave my bedchamber."

"But that would be almost gentlemanly of me."

"Not precisely. You're still acting like a lowborn ogre."

His expression shifted, like a door closing, and he straightened up. "As you wish." He moved away, his usual equanimity restored. "We dine at eight."

She almost regretted seeing his mask slip back into place, as though he'd just locked the most genuine part of himself away. "I am tired," she said. "I shall ask my maid to have a tray brought up."

"No, that will not do. We've been apart far too long." His impervious tone gave her no quarter. "Either you join me in the dining chamber, or I shall meet you back here."

"Very well. I shall see you at eight."

. . .

Even in the dining room, with footmen in attendance, the meal proved to be far too intimate an affair for Bella. Sebastian rose to his feet when she entered. She'd deliberately descended past eight in order to avoid partaking in before-supper drinks with him.

The sight of her place set next to Sebastian's at the head of the table made her stop short. "I prefer to take my rightful place at the head of the table." At the opposite end from him, as far away as she could get and still be seated at the same table.

"A wife's rightful place is by her husband's side." A nod from the master of the house prompted the footman to stand aside for Sebastian to pull out the chair next to his. "Sit. Please."

Unwilling to cause a scene in front of the staff, she took the chair he offered. As he retook his seat, she busied her hands by adjusting her skirts. She'd selected a more demure gown this evening, a pale peach with a modest neckline. The amused approval in his eyes suggested he'd noticed. After dismissing the footmen, he said, "I must say that gown is an improvement over this afternoon's display. Although, I would not object if you continued to wear your scarlet gown privately for me in the future."

She made a mental note to wear her most obscene gown when they made their first official public appearance as a couple. And her most chaste one for their moments alone in private. "I wish to discuss your marital rights."

His brows lifted with obvious interest. "Yes?"

"I hope you do not plan to claim them."

"Then your hopes will be dashed because I most certainly intend to claim them."

"Whether I am willing or not?"

"You seemed willing enough this afternoon."

Angry embarrassment heated her cheeks. "Do you intend to assert you rights even if I object?"

He sighed. "No. I would never force you. That is no way to begin our life together. It would hardly bode well for our future happiness."

She fidgeted with her soupspoon. "Good. I'm relieved we've settled that."

"Oh, it is hardly settled. I will give you time to adjust to your new situation, but I will not wait forever. I am no saint."

She supposed it was the best she could hope for. The footmen entered with the next course, spiriting away the soup she'd barely touched and laying out the meat and vegetable dishes. Bella sampled her Madeira.

"What are you drinking?" she asked, eying the clear liquid and wedge of lemon in his glass.

He followed her gaze to his glass. "Fizzy mineral water."

"Mineral water?"

"Yes, my friend Charles Plinth has developed a fountain that retains the sparkling quality of the water."

"It is portable?"

"The drink is delivered every few days and then returned to him for refilling." The lights in his green eyes sparkled. "It is my only real indulgence."

She realized just how little she knew about her husband. "You don't take port or wine with dinner?"

"I can't abide spirits of any kind."

Bella had never met anyone who didn't take spirits. It was unheard of, even among the poor. "You don't drink any spirits? Rum, wine, gin, ale, beer?"

"None at all. I like to keep a clear head."

"Is it difficult to abstain?"

"Not at all. I can't stand the taste."

They were quiet for a moment while the footmen withdrew.

"I should like to visit my modiste."

"Of course. You should have appropriate gowns. I can

accompany you first thing on the morrow."

She tensed. Her choice of a wardrobe was perhaps the one thing she still retained control of. "That won't be necessary. I'll ask Josette to join me."

"Josette?"

"She's a friend who has been traveling with me. Josette is French. She has impeccable style."

Sebastian gave her a measured look. "As you wish," he said in a noncommittal voice, turning his attention back to his food.

She picked up her fork and stabbed at a piece of mutton. "What I wish is to know how much I may spend."

"Beg pardon?"

"At the modiste. How much may I spend?"

"As much as you care to." He sliced his meat into precise pieces. "Simply have the bills sent to me."

Bills he would no doubt pay with her blunt. "And my other expenses?"

"You must do as you please. You have carte blanche."

Chapter Eight

"This is *parfait*," cooed Josette, running her hands lovingly over the expensive silk fabric.

Bella eyed the violet color from where she stood on a perch being measured by Madame de Lancy. "If you think so." She stepped down and picked up a fashion plate, eyeing a high-waisted gown with a ribbon under the breasts. "Madame, I would like gowns made of your thinnest fabric."

"*Mais oui*," said the French woman. "You intend to be daring in your fashion?"

"Absolutely. And this neckline is too modest. I want it to much lower."

Madame's eyes widened with surprised delight. "Of course, most English ladies are too provincial in their dress. You will be a leader in fashion."

Josette laughed. "Évidemment, *Madame*," she said to the modiste. "Lady Mirabella is soon to be a duchess. All will follow her fashion lead. The entire *haute ton* will visit you after seeing Bella's fabulous costumes."

"Perhaps I should offer Her Grace a reduced cost due to the custom her patronage is certain to bring me."

Bella glanced up from the fashion plate. "That is not necessary, Madame. Please charge me the full amount. The cost is not a concern."

The startled modiste beamed with delight. "*Certainement*. I shall have the gowns delivered at once."

Josette's brows lifted. Bella mirrored back the movement. "He says I am to have carte blanche. I intend to take him up on his generosity with my funds."

Josette laughed and dropped down next to her, giving the modiste a pointed look. "Won't you have your staff bring us tea, Madame?"

The modiste smiled, immediately understanding she'd been dismissed. She signaled her staff to leave. "Of course. I shall have it brought in," she said, closing the door behind her.

Josette turned back to Bella with an expectant look.

Bella frowned back at her. "What?"

Josette's catlike eyes slanted with mischief. "Tell me how you found the pleasures of the marriage bed, *ma cheri*."

Bella's cheeks heated. "There's nothing to tell. He did not visit my bedchamber last evening."

"*Non?*" Josette's eyes widened. "*Pourquoi pas?*"

Avoiding Josette's avid gaze, she shrugged her shoulders. "I made it quite clear he would not be welcome." She hated that part of her had been disappointed with his absence.

Josette's tinkling laughter filled the air. "*Mon cheri*, why would you deny your husband your bed? He is, how do you say, very much a man."

Bella's heart thumped. "What do you mean?"

A rap on the door interrupted Josette's answer. A maid entered with the tea. Josette waited until they were alone again to continue. "Monsieur Sebastian has a very strong masculinity. It is obvious. He will probably make an excellent lover."

"How could you know that?" Bella couldn't help being intrigued by the mysteries of the marriage bed.

Josette's eyes sparkled. "He seems to be very, ah, well equipped. Such a man would greatly satisfy his woman."

Bella's eyes widened. "Josette! Do you mean what I think you are saying?"

Josette leaned forward with a shrug to pour their tea. "You can tell his assets from those breeches."

Bella's body tingled. "Does that make a difference for a woman?"

Josette's eyes sparkled with devilment. "*Mais oui.* It is a magnificent feeling to be filled so fully." She handed Bella her tea. "You should not deny yourself. You are his wife. Why not enjoy the marriage bed?"

"He lied to me, Josette." Her throat tightened. "He abandoned me for six years. He only wants me in his bed now because my appearance pleases him. If I were homely, he would cast me aside again."

"*Trésor*, all men want to bed beautiful women." Josette bit into a biscuit. "Underneath their courtly manners, they are all beasts. They cannot help it. *C'est la vie.*"

"What of his lies and his abandonment? What sort of man marries a child? I was certainly in no position to consent to such a thing," she said bitterly. "You would have me forgive him everything and go meekly to the marriage bed?"

"Surely, you are not so naive as to blame him for the alliance." Josette sipped her tea. "Your fathers arranged the match. He was practically a child himself. What did he know?"

Bella put down her tea with an unladylike *clink*. "He knew enough to send me away while he lived here in high style."

"It is the way of the world. Men command us and we are obliged to obey," Josette said with a shrug. "We must make the best of it."

"He already controls everything else in my life." Pushing to her feet, she paced away from Josette. "How can I allow him complete reign over my person? It is the last thing that is still truly mine."

"So *dramatique*," Josette said with a dismissive wave of her hand. "Your beauty is a weapon. Use your charms to make him do your bidding."

Bella's eyes narrowed. "You make bedding my husband sound like a battle stratagem."

"It would be no hardship to bed Monsieur Sebastian. Use him for your purposes and your pleasure." Josette came to her feet. "Then we shall see who surrenders to whom."

The idea of Sebastian's powerful form pressing up against her bare skin made her flush all over. "He does make my body feel things that are a little frightening."

"That is desire, *ma cheri*. It is good to have with one's husband." Wandering to the mirror, Josette reached for a swath of violet silk and held it up against her body. She caught Bella's eye in the reflection. "If a man is happy in the bedchamber, he will give his wife whatever she desires outside of it."

"He does seem predisposed to be generous." She eyed the expensive fabrics and trims strewn about the room with little interest. "Perhaps he hopes the fripperies will distract me from estate matters."

"How you do go on." Josette looked wistfully at the violet silk. "A gown in this fabric will be exquisite for you."

"I agree. And you shall have one as well. We'll tell Madame to take your measurements."

Josette shook her head. "*Non*, my husband left me comfortable, but I cannot overspend."

"Nonsense." Bella moved to the bell to ring for Madame. "It is my treat. I'm certain Sebastian won't mind. We'll order you a ball gown in that delicious shade of pink as well."

After completing their business with the modiste, they went from shop to shop, ordering shoes, fans, hats, everything Bella would need for a complete wardrobe. She relied heavily on Josette's advice. When they completed their shopping, they stopped in at Gunter's for a shaved ice. Neither woman had ever been before and both were keen to try the lemony treat. They'd just been served when Orford appeared.

"What a fortunate surprise to happen across the loveliest ladies in town."

Josette shot him a wry look. "Hardly a surprise since I informed you of our plans. Are you determined to intrude upon our ladies' day?"

"Most assuredly," Orford said, winking at Bella.

"Why have you not at least brought Tabby and Monty with you?" Josette asked.

He pulled up a chair to join them. "Tabby is painting

and Monty is her latest subject so they could not be tempted away."

Bella reached over to pat his arm. "I, for one, am glad to see you."

He favored her with an affectionate smile. "Have you two been very bad today?"

Josette licked ice off a finger. "Very wicked."

Orford helped himself to a spoonful of Bella's ice. "Delicious." He scooped up another bite and offered it to Bella. "Have you? Do tell."

Bella took the spoonful in her mouth, rolling the lemony confection over her tongue to fully savor its taste. "We enhanced our wardrobes. Morning gowns, walking gowns, ball gowns."

"Indulged yourselves, did you?"

"Sebastian has given Bella leave to spend as much as she likes," said Josette. "So she begins today."

Orford took another bite of ice. "And so he should. I'm sure he's enormously grateful for her fortune. After all, before his marriage, Stanhope didn't have two shillings to rub together."

"Do you know that for certain?" asked Bella.

"It's why I've come to find you." He looked well pleased with himself. "I've done more digging."

"And?"

"Sebastian's father was on the brink of ruin when the two of you married." Taking another spoonful of her ice, he smacked his lips. "As you can imagine, the family's circumstances improved dramatically after your marriage. Before that they'd depended upon the limited generosity of the uncle."

"The uncle." Josette perked up with interest. "The Marquess of Camryn?"

"Yes." Orford wiped his mouth with a cloth. "Sebastian's brother is now the marquess. The uncle only had two daughters. One of those daughters is now Duchess of Hartwell."

"Of course, I knew he married me for the blunt." But hearing Orford confirm just how desperate for funds Sebastian had been pinched her heart.

Josette licked her spoon. "Now that you are truly man and wife, you will learn all about Sebastian *très bientôt*."

Orford's blue gaze focused on Bella with obvious concern. "Are you truly all right, my dear? He wasn't an ogre with you last evening, was he?"

"*Imbécile*." Josette shot Orford a quelling look. "Perhaps Bella prefers not to talk of such delicate matters."

"We are all friends here. We have discussed far more intimate topics." Orford looked intently at Bella. "I only wish to assure myself that you are unharmed."

She gave him a reassuring smile. "I am fine. Truly, I am."

"Idiot." Josette rolled her eyes. "Sebastian is her husband. The marriage act is hardly a cause for alarm."

Orford's jaw tightened. "He asserted his husbandly rights, then?"

A stony voice sounded behind them. "That is none of your concern."

Bella's heart stumbled as Sebastian approached with a bland look on his face. "Perhaps you should introduce me to your companions, my dear."

Her face burning, she said, "This is my friend, Josette. You made Orford's acquaintance at the opera, of course."

"Of course."

Josette beamed at Sebastian. "It is a pleasure to finally meet Mirabella's husband."

Orford lounged back in his chair wearing an insolent half smile. "Stanhope."

"Orford." Sebastian turned to Bella. "If you are ready, I'll escort you home."

She stiffened. He was already trying to curtail her movements. "I am still enjoying my ice. Surely you have matters to attend to. Orford will be happy to escort us home."

"Indeed. It would be my pleasure," said Orford.

"But completely unnecessary." Sebastian pulled up a chair. "I'm most happy to join you."

Now he intended to intrude upon her and her friends. Agitated, Bella popped up. "Actually, I am quite finished. If you insist on escorting me."

Sebastian's cool green eyes remain fixed on Orford, who stared back unblinking. "I do insist."

He escorted her to the coach. After helping her in, he followed and settled across from her, facing backward.

"Are you following me?"

Sebastian leaned back against the squabs with a cool demeanor that infuriated her. "Of course not."

She crossed her arms, her spine stiff. "Do you plan to limit my comings and goings?"

He stretched his muscled legs out in front of him, slanting them so as not to hit Bella's feet. "Not at all. Even if I did, I doubt you would heed me. You are free to come and go as you please."

They really were well-formed legs. Bella could not help noticing his powerful thighs. The pace of her pulse picked up. "Josette and Orford are my friends. I plan to continue to see them."

His considering gaze held hers for a moment. "Although you seem to have lamentable taste in companions when it comes to Orfus, your friends are yours to choose."

"His name is Orford and he is every inch a gentleman," she said, trying not to be affected by the vivid shade of his clear green eyes. Or how the heavy fringe of black lashes provided a perfect sultry outline for them.

"I beg to differ. A gentleman does not feed a lady in public or at all for that matter. Nor does he share her spoon in such an intimate matter."

"It's just Orford. It means nothing." She narrowed her eyes at him. "How long were you spying on us?"

"Spying? You were sharing bodily fluids with a man who is not your husband in a very public place for all to see."

"Sharing bodily fluids? Don't be ridiculous. Sharing a spoon is hardly intimate."

He leaned forward so suddenly it startled her. His intense proximity sent her pulse scurrying under her skin. He brushed his finger across her lips, his touch shooting through her like a cannon. The pull between them reared again, only now it was fiercer and wanton since duty and morality no longer kept it tightly wrapped. *You're married*, the voice in her head taunted, *you can do anything you desire.*

Her mouth opened of its own accord, her tongue flicking out to taste him. His sharp inhale suggested her boldness startled him as well. She couldn't stop her tongue from tasting him, running over the sweet saltiness, reveling in the mixture of soft skin and hardened calluses. The emerald shade of his eyes intensified, a muscle jerked in his jaw.

Longing welled up in her. She pictured his finger trailing down her neck, into her bodice.

Her gaze holding his, she wrapped one last lick around the tip of his finger, before opening her lips to release it.

He let his finger linger for a moment, then withdrew, brushing it across her lips once more, leaving shooting sparks in his wake.

"Touch is not the only kind of intimacy, Mirabella," he said in a low, gruff voice. He brought his finger into his own mouth before slowly drawing it out again. "There is also the unique, indescribable pleasure of the taste of a woman. I would not share that privilege with any other man."

Mesmerized by the trail of his finger, she forgot the mechanics of breathing. Her body felt like a glowing ember ready to burst into full flame. "Very well," she chirped. "If you feel so strongly about it, I shall cease sharing a spoon with Orford."

He sat back, eyes dark with possessive satisfaction. "When will your new gowns be ready?"

The sudden shift in conversation threw Bella off balance. "Some will be delivered in two days. The rest will follow shortly thereafter."

His brows lifted. "Two days. That's rather quick, is it not?"

Bella's smile felt delicious on her lips. "For the correct price anything is possible."

Instead of expressing irritation, he seemed amused. "Paid handsomely, did you?"

"Very."

If Sebastian heard the challenge in her voice, he ignored it. "Excellent. We're to Cam's house in a fortnight. You'll require something appropriate to wear."

Bella straightened, looking at him with alert eyes. "Your brother's house? The marquess?"

"Yes, they return from the country soon. The family is most anxious to meet my bride after all this time."

"Meeting your family sounds daunting."

"Nonsense. They all will no doubt be as entranced by you as I am."

"All?" She remembered he had four brothers.

"Yes, Cam and his marchioness. You will like Charlotte. She is not at all high in the instep. My brother, Sir Edward, is away in India so he will not attend."

"Your brother has been knighted?"

"Yes, he fought valiantly on the Peninsula and was rewarded with a knighthood."

His large family intrigued her, especially since she had almost no family of her own. "I see, and who else?"

"I believe my cousin, Willa, will be there. She's the Duchess of Hartwell. And her husband, the duke, I expect will accompany her."

"Your brother was her father's heir."

He appeared surprised that she knew that. "Yes, my uncle had two daughters and no sons, so Arthur became his heir."

"Arthur?" Bella asked, having a difficult time following all of the names.

"My brother's name is Arthur, but since he came into the title we call him Cam."

She nodded. "I see."

"And my other brothers, Will—"

"The artist."

He spoke about his family with obvious warmth. "Yes, and the youngest, Basil."

She could not help but notice that he'd left someone out. "And your mother?"

The warmth in his face cooled. "Yes, my mother, of course. She will no doubt be there." She sighed and settled back against the squabs. "I shall look forward to meeting them."

...

Late the following afternoon, Bella watched Sebastian ride away on another of his frequent outings. Her husband's physical pursuits certainly extended far beyond the customary daily constitutional. He spent an inordinate amount of time at the fencing and boxing clubs. At times, instead of riding his mount, he took brisk walks. She'd never seen anyone take so much exercise. But it kept him from home, for which she was grateful, especially today since she intended to take full advantage of his absence.

She made her way down to his study, which she had never visited before. Entering the chamber, she almost bumped into his secretary on his way out. "The master is away, my lady, if you are seeking him."

"I am not," she said. "Perkins, isn't it?"

"Yes, my lady, Henry Perkins, at your service." He was young and slim, with sand-colored hair, even features, and intelligent gray eyes behind round spectacles.

"Have you been with my husband long?"

"I have worked for Mr. Stanhope going on two years, my lady."

"What sort of work do you do?"

He blinked. "The usual, my lady. Correspondence, settling accounts...the Traherne holdings are vast, as my lady is no doubt aware."

"Are you on your way out?"

"I was. However, I would be pleased to stay and offer any assistance to my lady."

"My thanks, but there is no need for you to delay. Good evening, Mr. Perkins."

Taking her dismissal for what it was, he bowed and quietly quitted the room. Once he'd gone, she surveyed the surroundings, indulging her curiosity about the space where her husband spent a great deal of his time. The large orderly desk at the far end of the room must belong to Sebastian. A smaller workspace, where Perkins likely worked, sat in the far corner, stacked with books and papers.

Deciding to start there, she sat at the secretary's desk and picked up the first account book. She scanned it, going through row after row, page after page. When she finished, she picked up the next notebook and gave it the same methodical treatment. Book after book, she took notes on the figures until her eyes began to blur, losing all track of time until a tap on the door was followed by the appearance of Monty.

"Do you plan to stay closeted in here all evening?"

She rubbed her weary eyes. "Monty, this is a pleasant surprise."

His dark brows moved up. "You invited us for cards. Have you forgotten?"

"No, is it that time already?"

"It's half past." He gestured toward the documents and

books before her. "Find anything of interest?"

"Fortunately for me, Sebastian is attached to order. The account books appear to be neatly organized, one for each property and business concern."

"Convenient. What have you learned?"

"It all appears to be quite profitable," she said. "But I don't know where to look for the irregularities."

"Perhaps you're looking in the wrong place."

She eyed him. "What else should I examine if not the books?"

"Traherne's assets are quite vast and varied. It wouldn't be difficult to bury any malfeasance deep in the books somewhere."

"So where do you suggest I look?"

"Start at the end."

"Meaning?"

"Instead of seeing where the money starts, begin with where it ends up."

She perked up. "Sebastian. You want me to look at Sebastian's personal accounts."

"Tracing where his fortune comes from might be the less complicated way to pursue the matter."

Sitting back in her chair, she shook out her cramped shoulders. "So I need access to his bank account."

"Are you certain he's taking more money than the allowance allotted to him as your husband?"

"Before we married, he didn't have two guineas to rub together. Six years later, he is in possession of a great fortune. What does that tell you?"

"That perhaps he was just a boy when you married. He could have gone out and made his fortune."

"If he was inclined to make his own way, he wouldn't have agreed to marry me."

He put a hand flat against his chest. "I know better than to cross you on any subject related to your husband. He doesn't seem a bad sort, if you ask me."

"I didn't." Her sharp retort ended with a wry smile. "But I accept that you might have the truth of it. His personal bank account could be the key to finding out. Now I just have to figure out how to gain access to it."

"What difference will it make if you do prove he is taking extra money?" Leaning one shoulder against the door frame, Monty crossed his arms over his lean chest. "He assumes all control once His Grace passes."

"I've been thinking about that." She stretched her stiff neck from side to side. "If I can show my father that Sebastian is stealing from him, then perhaps he'll put estate interests into the hands of someone more trustworthy, for at least as long as he lives."

"Someone like you? That is the reason you've spent these last two years learning about farming and estate matters, is it not?"

She shook her head. "I know better than to expect His Grace to allow a female to run things. However"— she gave him an assessing look— "it would be almost as ideal if he chose someone who is honest, has a background in estate management, and wouldn't mind a little interference from me."

"Why are you looking at me like that?" Monty straightened, his neutral expression twisting into one of surprised disbelief. "You mean me? Surely, you aren't serious."

"Why not? You are someone I know and trust. Whatever your background, it's clear you know how to handle the running of an estate."

"Not one the size of Traherne, I can assure you of that."

"What does it matter?" Her enthusiasm grew as she warmed to the idea. "You and I can muddle through it out together. Plus, there are solicitors and estate stewards to help us find our way."

Beyond the study, the front door closed and the muted sounds of Davison greeting Sebastian in the foyer drifted toward them. Alarm registered on Monty's face. "Come away from there before he discovers you rifling through the books."

She was already up and halfway across the room. "Think upon what I've proposed," she said gliding out the door. "We would make a formidable team."

"You don't need me." He closed the door gently behind them and followed her down the hall. "You are formidable enough all on your own."

Chapter Nine

Sebastian quit his weekly card game far earlier than usual. Exiting his club, he motioned for his coachman to continue onward, deciding the walk home would do him good. While he still fought the overwhelming temptation to visit his wife's bed, he knew she needed time to adjust to her new situation and he intended to give it to her. Maintaining control with Bella so close, and knowing he had rights, was almost unbearable.

He'd stepped up his early morning runs and late-night rides, but that did little to ease those persistent carnal urges. His body seemed to have a mind of its own. Constantly on edge, it remained urgently aware of Bella's proximity.

He arrived home and bounded up the outside steps, anxious to see his wife, wondering how she'd passed the evening in his absence. Davison met him at the entrance to take his cloak. Sounds of laughter and conversation trailed down the hallway. He turned to the butler with a questioning look.

A shadow of disapproval crossed Davison's face. "Her ladyship is entertaining, sir."

His curiosity piqued, Sebastian followed the sounds and pushed open the door to the blue parlor, a smaller public chamber. Darkness cloaked the room save a lone candle near the wall where everyone gathered. They didn't appear to notice his entrance at first. Sebastian recognized Josette, the French woman, reclining on a chaise watching the proceedings. Bella stood close to the wall in profile, with a pleasant-faced, flaxen-haired young woman standing beside her holding the candle. A tall man with a high forehead and thinning, dark hair stood against the wall near the young woman, his arms crossed watching the proceedings.

The candlelight cast the shadowed profile of Bella's body against the large piece of foolscap attached to the wall. Surveying the scene, his glance ran over Bella and bounced right back, all reason deserting him.

She wore a flesh-colored gown that, at first glance, gave the illusion of sheerness, clinging adoringly to every curve, creating an image of feminine perfection he'd thought only an artist could conjure. The delicate fabric whispered over plump, upturned breasts, stroking over the soft inward turn of her belly and around full hips. Riveted by the vision of womanly bounty, all thought cascaded downward, centering on his rapidly swelling vitals. Then he realized how close Orford stood to his wife. His desire ebbed. Just behind her by the wall, Orford traced the outline of her shadow on the foolscap, standing so close his arm casually brushed against her as he worked. Sebastian tensed when Orford drew the outline of his wife's breasts, greatly exaggerating their size.

Covering her mouth, she laughed and shoved Orford with her elbow. "You rogue, that is not how I appear." She exuded vitality and playfulness. How relaxed she was with these people. Would she ever be like that with him?

Orford continued working. "As an artist, I must draw my subject as I see her. Besides, I must do something to compete with Tabby if I am to win."

The tall man leaning up against the wall cast a warm look at the pleasant-faced woman holding the candle. "Tabby is a true artist. You could not compete with her."

The woman they called Tabby blushed. "I had a good subject."

Bella planted her fists on her hips. "Are you suggesting I am not a good subject?"

Tabby shook her head. "Of course not. You are incredibly beautiful." She had a lovely. lilting voice and exuded a natural sweetness. Tabby cast a shy look in the tall man's direction. "It's just that Monty's physique makes him an excellent subject for a silhouette."

The French woman noticed Sebastian first. "*Monsieur*," she said, calling everyone's attention to his presence. "How delightful you have joined us."

He closed the door behind him. "A pleasure to see you again, *Madame* —" He paused, not knowing her last name.

"Laroux. But surely we should not stand on formality. Just Josette, if you please."

He turned to Bella. "I did not know you were entertaining, my dear."

"It's an informal gathering," she said coolly. "My dearest friends have come to keep me company."

"Still, had I known, I would have gladly stayed to greet

them. After all, your friends are mine as well." He ignored the way Bella's skeptical brow arched in response. Looking to the young woman they'd called Tabby and the tall man, he said, "Won't you introduce us?"

"Monty and Lady Tabitha Quartermain, Tabby."

Monty nodded in greeting while Tabby gave a timid smile. "Forgive us for intruding upon your home, sir."

He bowed, taking an instant liking to the young woman. She was not a beauty. Her face was thin with delicate brows and expressive hazel eyes, yet she had a pleasing way about her that spoke of serenity. "It is no intrusion. My wife's friends are most welcome here."

Bella gestured toward Orford. "And Orford of course."

"Orford."

"Stanhope. Care to join us?"

Breaking her pose, Bella shook the stiffness out of her shoulders. "I'm certain Sebastian finds Silhouettes to be a silly game."

Her subtle movements prompted Bella's soft mounds to quiver. Good Lord, the impact of that gown hit him again. He tore his eyes away from his wife's assets to settle a hard stare on Orford. "I hardly need to be invited to partake in entertainment in my own home."

Orford shrugged his lanky shoulders. "Your home. Of course, beg pardon." He gestured toward his drawing. "What do you think of my rendition of Bella?"

It was indecent and the bastard knew it. "I think you need to be taught some manners."

Orford's fine brows shot up in amusement. "By you, I presume." He laughed. "That's rich."

Monty coughed and stepped forward, putting a hand on

the oaf's arm. "Orford, perhaps we should take our leave."

Keeping his stare level with Sebastian's, Orford shook off Monty's arm. "Nonsense. Stanhope here feels someone needs to learn a lesson. And I quite agree."

Tension throbbed between the two men. Orford's cheeks were flushed and his fists clenched tightly at his sides. Sebastian kept his expression even, revealing no outward sign of his inner agitation. He would teach the buffoon a lesson to be sure, one Orford would never forget.

Bella stepped between them. "That is enough." Her brows knit. "Sebastian, Orford is our guest. They all are. I've invited them to spend the little season with us."

The thought of spending the next several weeks with this questionable group under his roof made his head throb. "I see."

Tabby hurried forward, her eyes wide with alarm. "Perhaps it is a bad idea. We should remove ourselves."

Bella uttered a sound of protest, but Sebastian interrupted her. "Nonsense, Lady Tabitha, you and your friends are most welcome here." He forced relaxation into his stance. "I'm merely suggesting a friendly bout of boxing. What say you, Orford, are you up to it?"

All eyes swung in Orford's direction.

"I'm more than happy to oblige."

"Shall we say Gentleman Jack's on the morrow?"

"It will have to be in a sennight, I'm afraid. I'm to Kent on the morrow to visit my mother."

At least he'd be rid of the smug whoreson for a few days. "Then we are agreed. We'll meet at Jack's upon your return."

"You should know Orford is something of a pugilist," said Bella.

His own wife was wagering against him. "Then I shall endeavor to acquit myself favorably in the face of Orford's considerable skills."

Josette came to her feet. "Well, now that that is settled, I, for one, am ready to retire."

Murmurs of agreement sounded all around. They exchanged good nights and Bella saw to her guests as they headed up the stairs; the sounds of closing chamber doors soon resonated down the stairway. Trailing behind them into the front hallway, Sebastian dismissed the butler and footman with a glance.

As the servants slipped away, Bella started to follow her friends up the stairs. "Well, I'm for bed."

"Is that one of your new gowns?"

Pausing on the stairs, she turned to face him. "As it happens, yes, it is." The movement pulled the delicate fabric across the soft mounds of her breasts, their shadowed peaks straining. "It's one of my favorites. What do you think?"

Sebastian's mouth went dry. "I think it leaves little to the imagination."

"It's quite the thing in Paris."

"I can see why."

"I trust you don't object."

Damn right he objected. Perhaps it wasn't outwardly indecent, but something about the sensuousness of the cut made it appear so. However, to admit it would likely provoke her into wearing something even more indecorous the next time. He raked his eyes over her form in a slow and intimate perusal. "Why would I object? I'm enjoying the view. You have such a lovely...form."

She inhaled sharply, a furious blush raced across her

cheeks. "That is disgusting." She clamped her arms over her chest. "Stop regarding me in that manner."

"What manner is that?"

"Like I am a tasty morsel you want to consume."

He gave her a dark smile. "Why? Those are the kinds of thoughts that gown provokes." He moved up the stairs toward her and brushed a kiss on her forehead, desire flaring in his loins. "It entices a man to want to claim his marital rights."

She stepped back, teetering on the stair, shock and alarm stamping her face. "You wouldn't dare."

He gripped her elbow to steady her, glad for the chance to relish the soft warmth of her skin. "A man can only resist so much temptation. And in that gown—"

She turned away from him and took a step upward. "That is quite enough. I am going to bed."

He followed, keeping pace one step below her as they progressed up the stairs, which gave him a perfect view of the intimate swing of her lush hips. "An excellent idea."

"Alone," she said archly over her shoulder.

"I am crestfallen, but I suppose it is just as well. I should save my strength for my bout with Orford."

She paused at the top of the stairs and faced him. "You were wrong to challenge him. He is very good with his fists."

"Is that concern I hear in your voice?"

She put her nose in the air as though she'd sniffed something unpleasant. "Not at all. It is an observation."

He leaned close. "Will you favor me with a boon if I best him?" His lips brushed her ear. "A kiss perhaps?"

"Why ever not." She gave a bored shrug. "Given Orford's skill, it won't come to that." He might have believed her show of indifference, but for the tide of color sweeping her cheeks.

His lips moved from that delectable little slice of skin at her earlobe and feathered across her heated cheek, tantalizingly close to her plump mouth. Her scent entangled him, the deep richness of cloves this time instead of orange blossom, jasmine, or lavender. Intoxicating.

The pull between them deepened, lengthened, the air pulsated with it. Her breath caught and her eyes fluttered shut as his lips teased near hers. Sensual anticipation pounded through his body, every pore overflowed with it. He could take her now, fill his hands with her breasts and satiate his senses with her softness. He could make love to her after too many years of doing without. No woman would do other than this provoking female, who was both within his grasp and just beyond it.

She'd gone still, her eyes dazed, her bountiful form leaning slightly toward him, as if she were waiting.

He forced himself to break the spell. Stiffening, he planted a swift kiss on her silken cheek. "Your faith in me is touching."

Her eyes flew open as he stepped past, her startled disappointment obvious. His breath shaky, he strode down the hall. It seemed he could still call upon the self-control years of restraint had honed.

Pausing on the threshold to his bedchamber, he turned to look at her. He met her gaze, noting the angry gleam that supplanted the look of surprise on her lovely visage. "I shall earn that kiss before I take it. Granted, pummeling Orford is its own reward, but it is nowhere near as sweet as the boon I plan to demand from you."

...

Early the following morning, Bella and Orford slipped into Sebastian's solicitor's office through a side entrance.

"This is most irregular," the clerk said, poking his shiny pate out the door, looking both ways down the narrow alley to make certain they hadn't been spotted.

It had taken a good deal of coin to persuade the man to give them access to Sebastian's financial and business documents. Yet the way he jumped at every sound, along with his glistening upper lip, suggested the clerk wasn't entirely comfortable with the deception.

"We'll make it worth your effort," Orford said in an imperious voice. "Do you have what the lady seeks?"

Appearing resigned, the older man nodded, the significant girth of his belly leading the way as he ushered them into a small, tidy chamber. "I have examined Mr. Stanhope's assets. Last year, he had an income of almost thirty-three thousand pounds."

Orford let out a low whistle. "He doesn't do anything by halves, does he?"

Bella sucked in a breath. That was a fortune. From what she'd been able to glean from her study of the estate books, Traherne's annual income was about forty-five thousand pounds a year, but the current balance in the Traherne bank accounts didn't reflect that level of abundance. The money was definitely coming into the ducal bank accounts, but it wasn't staying there. "Where do Mr. Stanhope's funds come from?"

"From what I am able to gather, he has a number of

business concerns." The clerk mopped his upper lip with a kerchief. "He invests in shipping and cotton mills that utilize the new mechanized power looms."

"I guess we don't have to ask where he gets the income to invest in those concerns," Orford said archly.

"Actually," said the clerk, paging through some documents on his desk, "he gets a good part of that income from three profitable properties that he owns outright."

"Sebastian owns three properties?" Bella frowned. "He never mentioned it."

"Ah, here it is." The clerk pulled a document out of the pile. "What is interesting is that he acquired the properties from Traherne."

Bella chest tightened. "Surely, they are entailed."

"No, these particular properties were not part of the entail. Mr. Stanhope owns them outright."

"How did he acquire them?" Orford asked.

"He paid for them and has the documentation to prove it," the clerk answered, rifling through the papers again and handing a document to Orford, who automatically passed it along to Bella's waiting hands.

She scoured the bill of sale, looking past the signatures of both her father and Sebastian, noting the figure Sebastian had paid. "Surely the properties were worth more than this."

"Yes, it does appear the amount he paid was well below their perceived value."

Disappointment stabbed at her belly. Sebastian appeared to be taking full advantage of her father's perpetual state of drunkenness. His Grace was likely signing away ducal assets without comprehending the long-term significance of his actions.

"There is one more thing." The clerk shuffled through the papers again. "Each month, a thousand pounds are removed from Traherne's main account."

Her stomach plummeted to her toes. "By whom?"

"It is an automatic transfer, authorized by Mr. Stanhope. It goes into a numbered account at Barclay's bank on Lombard Street."

Orford perked up. "Is that a different establishment from where the majority of Traherne funds are kept?"

The clerk nodded. "It is."

"You're saying it is a numbered account in a separate bank. I take it that means there is no name attached to it."

"Yes, just a number," the clerk said. "You'll have to visit the bank to determine who the signatory on the account is."

"Yes, thank you. You can be sure I will do that."

...

Several mornings later, Sebastian ushered Bella into his curricle for a drive well before the fashionable hour to be seen in the park.

"Was it really necessary to depart so early?"

"I thought it best to decamp while your friends were still abed."

He wanted her alone, away from her blasted friends so he could court her as she deserved. It was likely the only way to win his way back into her affections. The constant presence of her friends in the house made it difficult to progress with Bella. Enduring them the entire little season would require all the patience he could muster. They were always around, at every meal, in the evenings playing Whist or Silhouettes or listening to Josette play the pianoforte. How was he to reconcile with his wife—and work his way into her bed—with a crowd of people constantly underfoot? She seemed particularly edgy today. Perhaps she was angry over the way he'd toyed with her on the stairwell.

She clutched the side of the curricle as he made a turn, but that didn't keep her soft thigh from pressing hard against his, making him acutely aware of her feminine heat. "We hardly needed to leave so early since they rarely wake before noon."

He kept his eyes ahead. "Have you traveled with them for long?"

She stiffened, obviously sensing his disapproval. "We have been together for the past two years."

"How did your jolly group come together?"

"Josette, I met in France just after the war. Orford is a distant cousin whom I have known since I was in apron strings. Our mothers were very close. He chanced upon us in Spain."

"How fortuitous." He doubted that blackguard did anything by chance. "He decided to stay?"

"I believe he remained with us because he is sweet on Josette. He was also out of funds."

Sweet on Josette? Could she really be that blind? Orford only had eyes for Bella. "So you fund this merry band of travelers?"

"It was my portion to do with as I pleased."

"Don't you ever care to strive for more?"

"There are some who believe there is no higher to climb than duchess for a mere female."

He found it hard to believe she had no compelling

interests beyond cavorting with her friends and buying indecent gowns. "Has it never occurred to you to use your fortune and sharp mind for the betterment of yourself and others?"

"You don't know anything about me."

"I know you could put your keen mind to better use than flitting about from one shop to another and donning one scandalous gown after another."

She exhaled a short, contemptuous breath. "So this is about my taste in gowns."

"You demean yourself by wearing them. Such behavior is beneath you. You are not the flighty, mindless girl you pretend."

He felt her tense beside him. "You should not presume to know me. We are practically strangers."

"Fair enough." He pulled on the reins, slowing to allow a cart to pass in front of them. "Tell me then about your other friends. Monty, for instance."

She seemed reluctant at first to continue any conversation with him, but finally she said, "We also encountered Monty in Spain where he was studying Moorish architecture."

"And is he also without funds?"

"Not at all. Funds are not a problem for Monty. In fact, he insisted on paying for the villa we stayed at in Spain over the summer."

Interesting. "Family funds?"

She shrugged with apparent lack of interest. "Monty is something of a mystery to us all. We know very little of his background."

"Do you not wonder what he is hiding?"

"No, I do not. I know what I see. Monty is a gentleman,

good and true. Anyone can discern that."

"And yet he hides the truth of his identity."

"You don't know anything about him."

"Neither, apparently, do you." He guided the animals around a corner. "Is Miss Tabitha's background a mystery as well?"

She shot him a disdainful look. "Not at all. Tabby was with me from the start. We were at Miss Langdon's School for Young Ladies together."

"What is her story?"

Bella looked away. "There is nothing to tell."

"How about the fact that she is ruined?"

She stilled. "What do you mean?"

"I knew there was something familiar about Lady Tabitha. It came to me last evening. That's the Quartermain chit who ruined herself and then refused to marry the gentleman in question. Dominick Howard, I believe his name is."

"You know nothing about Tabby. I will not allow you of all people to cast aspersions on her character."

"Me of all people? Have I done something to upset you?"

"Why do you ask?"

"You seem particularly agitated."

Her gaze slid away in a manner that left the impression she was hiding something. "Nothing beyond the usual."

He let it drop. They were away from the heart of London traffic, heading out into more open road. "I've no need to cast aspersions on Miss Tabitha. All of society has already done that. My question is, why are you in league with a woman like that?"

"A woman like that? I'll tell you what manner of woman Tabby is." Color rose in her delicate cheeks. "She is the sweetest, most gentle girl. She is too good for this world."

He softened his voice. "She would not be the first girl to allow her head to be turned by a gentleman. But why did she not consent to marry Howard? She had already allowed him to take liberties with her person."

"I assure you Dominick Howard is no gentleman. Tabby despised him from the start. He forced himself upon her to compel her into marriage."

His insides iced. "Are you suggesting that Howard raped Lady Tabitha?"

"I'm not only suggesting it. It is a statement of fact." She shot him a challenging look. "Unless you doubt Tabby's word."

"I do not," he said softly.

"She was devastated." She blinked and then widened her eyes as if to keep tears at bay. "I feared she would never recover after he…did that to her."

Poor Tabby. He could not imagine such a fragile creature enduring that kind of violation. "What of her family? Surely, they sought to avenge her honor."

"All they wanted was to make the scandal go away. They tried to force her to *marry* him. Can you imagine?"

"I cannot."

"She couldn't bear to let that man put his hands on her again, to give him unlimited rights to her body."

"Of course not. The very idea is abominable."

"I feared she would lose her mind from the strain of it, so I convinced her to come away with me to the Continent instead."

Warmth flowed through him. His stubborn, courageous wife had saved Tabby when no one else had bothered. "Lady Tabitha is the reason you requested to go abroad after leaving school."

"It was the only way I could think of to save her."

"Howard should have been brought to account for his mishandling of a lady." He struggled to control his temper. "That her family would try to force such an alliance is beyond the pale."

"I couldn't agree more." She shot him a pointed look. "Young girls should not be forced into marriage to further a family's ambitions."

Something twinged in the vicinity of his heart. "Is that why you came to her assistance? To help her avoid the fate that befell you as a girl?"

She looked regretful. "I would never compare you to a monster like Howard. Still, forcing matrimony on young girls is wrong."

"Quite right."

Silence hung in the air for a moment.

"It is not as though Tabby was one to defy her family's wishes. She'd been promised to another, Baron Edgemont, since girlhood. Even though he is a stranger to her, Tabby was willing to follow her family's wishes and marry the baron."

"The baron renounced her?" he asked softly.

"We did not wait to find out. We fled to France." She paused and eyed him. "Is this inquisition quite over? Have you learned all you need to know about our houseguests?"

"Not in the least. But my runner should be able to fill in the gaps soon."

She gasped. "Your runner? Pray do not tell me you have hired someone to investigate my friends?"

"They're under my roof and spend a great deal of time with my wife," he said mildly, directing the team into a turn with a firm hand. "It is only natural for me to want to learn more about them."

"It is not natural to spy on one's friends. You overstep."

"I am sorry you think so, but I will not be deterred."

"But I've answered your questions about them."

"Yes, and if anything, what little you know about your companions gives rise to only more questions."

"That's abominable!" She glared at him, the heat of emotion making her cheeks flush a lovely shade of pink. "Maybe you are hiding something of great importance from me. Perhaps I should put a runner on you."

"You needn't waste the money. If you have any questions, I'm happy to answer them."

She opened her mouth, as though quite ready to say something, and then clamped it shut again. "I have no questions…at the moment."

...

Louisa's eyes were full of admiration. "Oh, my lady, as I live and breathe, you are a vision in that gown."

Bella considered herself in the mirror. Her sky-blue gown's modest décolletage was edged with silver trim. Louisa had pulled her hair up, threading thin silver ribbon throughout her curls. She did look her best. She would present an image of restraint and elegance for her first meeting with Sebastian's family. Nerves twisted at the thought of this evening's gathering at the marquess's home. What did she know of family? She'd never had one.

A knock startled the thoughts out of her mind. Louisa pulled open the door and Sebastian entered.

"Are you ready to face the family?" He looked immaculate in his elegant formal wear. The stark white of his cravat highlighted the olive shades in his skin. His dark green satin coat brought out the clear green of his hooded dark eyes. His evening clothes were perfectly fitted to his rugged physique.

Her pulse accelerated, as it always did in his presence, even though she feigned indifference. "How did your bout with Orford go this morning?" Orford had returned from visiting his mother, so the two men had finally faced off at Gentleman Jack's.

He spread his arms, the fabric of his jacket stretching taut over muscled arms. "As you can see, I survived quite intact."

She turned back to the mirror to allow Louisa to make some final adjustments to her hair.

"That is just as well. It would not do for your family to see you all banged up."

"Your concern is truly touching."

She turned to face him. "I am ready."

"Excellent." His eyes filled with warm approval. "You look lovely."

His appreciative gaze sparked a warm feeling in her. "I'm pleased you approve."

"How could I not? I shall be the envy of every man this evening." He smiled, flashing the dimple in his right cheek. "You are the very image of beauty and decorum."

She narrowed one eye, a kernel of anger stirring in her breast. "Did you come in here to assure yourself that I dressed appropriately for your family?"

"Your tendency toward scandalous gowns certainly shows your loveliness to its full advantage, but we both know they are not appropriate for polite company." He turned to the mirror to adjust his cravat pin. "After all, isn't that why you wore the scarlet gown at our first official meeting as husband and wife?"

"Why don't you give me a few more minutes? I'll don my cloak and join you in a moment."

As soon as the door closed behind him, she started tugging her dress off, knowing even as she did so her temper was driving her to make a regrettable decision.

Louisa flew to her side. "My lady! What are you doing?"

Bella shook with anger. "Help me take this off. Bring me my scarlet gown."

"But, my lady, the master said—"

"I am mistress here. You will do as I say or find yourself another position."

Paling, Louisa began to unbutton the back of the blue gown. "Yes, my lady."

Bella forced a sharp inhale and gentled her tone. "Be so kind as to bring me the scarlet gown." Louisa hurried to the dressing room. "And bring me my evening cloak as well." Bella called after her. "I will wear it before I leave my bedchamber."

She regretted her impetuousness the moment the front

door to the Marquess of Camryn's impressive townhome on Curzon Street opened. Entering the foyer with Sebastian, Bella could hear laughter and conversation coming from somewhere nearby. She stiffened at the thought of facing all of those people in her scandalous gown.

Sensing her anxiety, but mistaking the cause of it, Sebastian gave her a reassuring smile. "We are a rather boisterous family. Pray don't let it alarm you."

She pulled her cloak more tightly around her when the butler stepped forward to take it from her. Seeing her hesitation, Sebastian moved over to do it himself.

"They won't bite," he murmured in her ear, his breath brushing against the sensitive skin. He moved his hands to her shoulders to take her cloak. "Don't worry, I shall stay by your side."

She resisted the desperate urge to cling to her cloak when he lifted it away from her shoulders—then swallowed hard, took a deep breath, and waited for her husband's reaction.

Chapter Ten

The footman's eyes widened before he smoothed his expression and resumed an unseeing gaze. She sensed Sebastian stiffen behind her. Her cheeks burning, Bella cursed her quick temper and even quicker tendency to act without thinking.

"Thank you, Smythe." Sebastian handed the cloak over to the butler, his tone giving no indication that anything was amiss. Bella gulped a breath, gathering her courage to turn and face her husband.

"We thought we heard you out here," a cheery voice called from down the hall. A golden-hued man in formal dinner dress strode toward them, flashing a wide smile. He was very tall, quite a bit taller than Sebastian, with untamed tawny hair and a strong, lithe form.

Sebastian's tight voice flowed around her. "Cam."

So this was the marquess. His smiling eyes went immediately to Bella, his curiosity apparent.

"Lady Mirabella, I presume? Since my brother seems to have misplaced his tongue, allow me to make myself known to you." He executed a sharp bow. "Arthur Stanhope, Marquess of Camryn, at your service."

She curtsied, praying her breasts would not pop out of the flimsy bodice. "A pleasure, my lord."

His eyes sparkled. "Just Cam, please. After all, you are my sister now." He turned to Sebastian. "She's a vision. I see why you've kept her all to yourself."

Sebastian shot his brother a wry look. "I'm certain you do."

"I must say I have never known my brother to be at a loss for words. Of course, such beauty would render any man speechless." He offered Bella his arm. "Come and meet the family."

She placed her hand on his arm, warmed by his friendly demeanor, especially considering the chillingly silent presence behind her. Forcing her herself to breathe, she kept her shoulders back, resisting the impulse to hunch over and cover herself.

A tall, willowy woman came toward them with a welcoming smile. "Lady Mirabella. We are so pleased to know you at last."

"Allow me to introduce my wife, Charlotte," Cam said.

The marchioness was a surprise. At first glance, one could mistake her for being almost plain, except for stunning, soft blue eyes that enlivened her face. Cam clearly was besotted with his wife.

"We've been so looking forward to making your acquaintance," Charlotte said, taking her hands.

Sebastian's cousin, Willa, Duchess of Hartwell, soon

joined them. The dark-haired, dark-eyed beauty seemed far more reserved than Charlotte, but it soon became apparent that the two women were great friends. And the teasing affection Willa showed Sebastian bespoke of a warm familiarity between the cousins.

Taking Bella's arm, Sebastian steered her toward the others. The fresh musk scent of his shaving soap wafted over her, the heat and strength of his arm radiated under her hand. His expression was stone-like, his hooded eyes clear yet guarded.

Despite her embarrassment over her gown, Bella enjoyed meeting Sebastian's brothers. Basil, the youngest, was quite the charmer. His eyes flitted over her gown with obvious interest before coming back to meet her eyes with an appreciative grin. Will, the artist, was quiet and more circumspect, with a distracted air about him. While their personalities were vastly different, Sebastian's brothers were remarkably similar to each other in appearance. It struck Bella how physically unlike Sebastian they were. Although by no means short, her husband didn't share his brothers' height, and his strapping physique and olive complexion were a marked contrast to their slim, shapely forms and light coloring. The lone trait they all shared was those singular eyes and that unique amber-green tint.

At last they came to stand before a dainty, fair-haired woman in her middle years. Sebastian bowed. "Ma'am, I present my wife." He turned to Bella. "My mother, Mrs. Matilda Stanhope."

Sebastian's mother took Bella's hands in hers, her smile warm and genuine. "I am so pleased to meet you." She looked at her son with obvious affection. "Sebastian, she is lovely."

"Indeed." He answered with formal courtesy. "I am the most fortunate of men."

To his credit, Bella couldn't discern any irony in his tone. Focusing on his mother, she dropped into a curtsy. "It is my pleasure, ma'am, to make your acquaintance."

Seeming not to notice Bella's disgraceful gown, Matilda helped her up. "Let us dispense with such formality. I hope you will come to call me Mother as Charlotte does, or just Matilda, if you prefer."

His mother's sparkling amber eyes, although different in color, were like Sebastian's in that they were infused with both strength and kindness. Realizing Matilda was nothing like the shrew she'd imagined, Bella took an immediate liking to her.

Her husband cleared his throat. "I'll leave the two of you to become acquainted." He stepped away, his abrupt departure bordering on rudeness. If his mother noticed, she did not show it. Instead, she took Bella's arm. "Come, let us walk about the room so that I may come to know you better."

...

Joining his brothers by the hearth, Sebastian immediately knew that he was in for it.

Cam didn't bother hiding his amused smile. "Well, Sebastian, I daresay your wife will enliven the family."

"And we're not exactly dull to begin with," Basil added.

Sebastian's gaze followed his wife's turn about the room with his mother. That gown was an abomination more suited to a courtesan than to a lady. Her plump breasts were almost completely bare to his brothers' gaze.

Basil saluted him with his glass. "She's a diamond of the first to be sure. And that gown." He shook his head. "Lord."

"I'll brook no insult to my wife."

"Easy. I meant no offense." Basil held up his hands, palms outward, in a show of supplication. "Quite the contrary, you are to be congratulated on your good fortune. With a wife like that, a man would never be tempted to stray."

Cam sipped his drink. "Not that Sebastian is the type to tomcat anyway."

Sebastian released a long breath. "As much as I abhor being the source of your amusement, you'll no doubt be pleased to know she is wearing that gown to provoke me."

"It is a most provoking gown," said Cam.

Sebastian's mouth twisted into a wry smile. "After I expressed admiration for the appropriate gown she intended to wear this evening, she changed into that bit of fabric, which can scarcely be considered a gown."

"Admiration or approval?" asked Cam. "I can tell you from experience, if she is anything like Charlotte, your wife will not appreciate being told what to do."

"I am her husband. She will do as I bid."

"That seems to be working rather well so far," said Cam, laughter in his voice.

"You do always try to organize and control everything around you," Will said.

Basil nodded his agreement. "Unfortunately for you, Lady Mirabella does not seem particularly biddable."

"I like order," Sebastian said tightly. "There is nothing wrong with that."

"Except that marriage can be a disorderly business," Cam said.

"That can be a good thing," Will said. "I often have a firm idea in my mind for a painting. Yet, once I begin, the brush sometimes has a will of its own and I'm left with something far better than my mind conceived."

"I don't see the relevance. My wife is not a painting."

"If she were, you could paint a more modest bodice on her," Basil said, his eyes twinkling with laughter.

Sebastian calmed an urge to give his brother a well-deserved douse on the chops. His body was already so tightly wound, he felt liable to snap at any moment.

Cam put a warning hand on Basil's shoulder. "Enough."

"What? I'm just advising him to relax and enjoy his wife." Basil gestured toward Bella. "He's fortunate to have her warming his bed."

Sebastian couldn't disagree. If only she was warming his bed. "You're giving me advice on how to handle a wife?" he said to Basil. "You're hardly the marrying kind."

"I might be if there were more facsimiles of your wife around—beauties in possession of great charms and an even greater fortune. If only she had a sister."

Sebastian's gaze moved back to Bella. Her scandalous gown barely contained those creamy, full breasts, which quivered whenever she moved. He took a long swallow of his mineral water. Perhaps he'd go for another run later this evening.

Cam eyed him. "She is warming your bed, isn't she?"

"That is none of your concern."

Cam's brows shot up in undisguised surprise while Basil whooped a laugh. "I suppose we can take that as a *no*."

"Take that as you will."

Basil's mouth trembled with amusement. "That explains why you are in such ill humor."

"Perhaps I should dress your hide," Sebastian said in sharp warning. "That would restore my good temper."

Eyes dancing, Basil leaned forward, speaking in a quieter voice. "A good strumming would do a better job of sweetening your countenance."

"What's the problem, Seb? Cam asked. Surely you are drawn to her."

Basil scoffed at the question. "What red-blooded man wouldn't be?"

Sebastian squelched another urge to cuff his youngest brother for his impertinence. "She needs time to accustom herself to her situation. As do I."

Cam cast a look at Bella who, along with Matilda, chatted now with Charlotte and Willa. "I doubt you need the time."

"I've never seen Sebastian so out of sorts." Basil's grin widened. "I think we've finally found the woman who can tempt a saint."

...

After supper, the ladies retired to the sitting room leaving the gentlemen to their cheroots and port. Bella gradually relaxed as the evening progressed. Matilda, Charlotte, and Willa were friendly and accepting. Relishing the warmth of Sebastian's family, she was grateful and relieved that no one mentioned her gown or treated her ill because of it.

She asked to be directed to the ladies' refreshing room. Camryn's townhouse was quite large and she took a wrong turn somewhere on her way returning to the parlor. Turning back, she tried to retrace her steps using the hum of conversation as her guide. Rounding a corner, she found herself in the servants' hallway. About to turn back the way she came, Bella heard an unmistakable voice—Sebastian speaking in quiet tones that sounded almost intimate.

Curious, she followed the murmur of conversation to what appeared to be a pantry area, a large closet full of linens and silver. Sebastian stood looking in, his immense shoulders blocking out most of the view into the room. Moving closer, but still undetected, Bella could see his companion was a young servant. The girl's face glowed with adoration as she looked up at him. She had a very pretty face, beautiful even, with large, expressive eyes and a creamy complexion.

"Lovely," Sebastian said, followed by a string of quiet words Bella couldn't quite make out.

The girl blushed and moved toward Sebastian but then stopped as though she felt awkward. He let out a low laugh, and pulled her toward him into a hug, brushing a light kiss on the girl's forehead.

"No need to be coy. We know each other too well for that. Come, we haven't much time before I'll be missed." He took the girl's hand in his and led her down the narrow servants' corridor, his large, masculine body dwarfing her delicate form.

Shocked, Bella stepped back, her shoulder hitting the edge of the wall. Her heart pounded in disbelief and she barely felt the sharp pain that cut into her skin. Sebastian and a servant in his brother's household? There could be no other explanation for his laying hands on the girl. No one came to this area of a home except for servants. Masters and guests certainly didn't, unless it was for a less-than-honorable purpose.

Spinning around, she stumbled back in the direction of the drawing room, every breath a painful stretch in her chest. How naive she had been. No wonder he never visited her bed. Why should he with such an exquisite servant girl at his disposal?

As she neared the salon, the murmur of conversation reached her. Forcing air into her lungs, she smoothed her skirt, straightened her spine, and did her best to appear unaffected as she rejoined the others.

Later, on the ride home, Sebastian was unusually quiet. Sitting across from him in the dark, Bella sensed his contemplative eyes on her. He'd rejoined the party about fifteen minutes after the scene in the pantry. Visions of him pulling the young girl into his arms replayed over and over in her mind. Each time it did, her anger mounted.

"You've made your point with that gown. Do not wear it again."

The sense of command in his voice aggravated her distemper. He dared take that tone with her, demanding a proper wife, while he cavorted with servants? "I warn you, I cannot abide being told what to do."

"Be that as it may, you will heed me on this." His face was shrouded in shadows, his expression difficult to decipher, but she did not miss the rigidness in his voice. Yet, even in anger, Sebastian seemed in complete command of himself, which made her even more furious. Did the man never lose his composure?

"Fine, I will cease with this gown." She smiled into the darkness. "After all, it is tame in comparison to the gowns

I ordered from Madame de Lancy." He stiffened in a way that made her scalp tingle. "I cannot wait for you to see me in them."

Holding utterly still, he did not respond. Heat spread across her chest like wildfire. "I think I shall wear one when I am with Orford. He is sure to appreciate me in it."

Sebastian surged forward out of the shadows. Her heart jumped and she instinctively shrank back against the squabs. Instead of reaching for her, his hand went to the door. That's when she comprehended that the conveyance had halted.

"We are home," he said in a voice that suggested he had not heard her inflammatory remarks. He helped her out and up the front stairs where a candle still burned for them. Davison greeted them with the news that her friends had departed for Vauxhall.

Uttering an uncharacteristically terse thank-you to the butler, Sebastian took Bella's arm to escort her above stairs. His rigid posture, the intransigent set of his expansive shoulders, the very deliberate *click* of each boot step, all belied that otherwise calm exterior.

He *was* angry. Furious even.

The hair on the back of her neck tingled. She'd never seen him truly out of sorts. His demeanor brought to mind that ominous lull before a catastrophic natural disaster strikes.

He hastened his steps, practically dragging her up the stairs, pulling her arm, moving quickly. When they reached her chamber, he did not leave her as he usually did. Instead he stepped in behind her.

"Thank you, Louisa, that will be all," he said to the sleepy girl, who'd waited up for her mistress. "Go and seek your bed."

As soon as he closed the door behind the maid, Bella spun around to face him, her heart clamoring. "I did not give you leave to enter my bedchamber. Please show me the courtesy of departing at once."

He pulled off his cravat and folded it in a slow, deliberate manner, as though he hadn't heard her. Removing his tailcoat, he placed it neatly over the back of a chair.

Alarm trilled down her spine. "Why are you disrobing?"

Unbuttoning his waistcoat, he said, "Take off that dress."

"I beg your pardon?"

He advanced toward her, the muscles in his thighs flexing powerfully as he did so. "You heard me."

Hugging herself, she stepped back from him. "I will do no such thing. Leave or I will scream."

Cold anger glittered in his eyes. "Take if off or I will take it off for you."

Chapter Eleven

Bella froze, her heart clanged such a frantic beat, she could barely hear herself think. When she didn't move, he reached for her.

Jumping back with a squeak of surprise, she batted his hands away. "All right, all right. I will do as you ask." She blinked back tears. "I need my maid to help me with the buttons."

"No need. Turn around."

Trembling, she did as he demanded. She felt his fingers at her back making quick work of the buttons. Panic set in, robbing her of breath. The front of the dress gaped open and Bella pulled it down and stepped out of the skirt, leaving it on the floor. She straightened, clad only in her thin chemise and stays.

Snatching up the offending garment, he strode to the fire and hurled it into the flames. With a poker, he shoved the gown inside and watched for a moment as the voracious blaze devoured it. Turning to face her, his gaze flicked to her body and froze. He swallowed, the sinews moving in his throat.

The fine, thin chemise did little to hide the curve of her breasts or the delicate peaks that strained against the flimsy barrier. Some hard emotion she didn't understand shone in the darkest part of those emerald depths—something intractable. "Take it all off."

"What? I will not."

"Fine." He began to pull off his linen shirt.

The sight of Sebastian's expansive bare chest crowded out all cogent thought. It was impossibly wide, its thick contours well defined, his arms slabs of carved muscle. All dusted with springy dark curls against smooth bronze skin. Even the hard curves of his otherwise flat belly spoke of strength.

Her mouth went dry. The sheer mass of his powerful form contrived to make him much more beautiful than any statue, which would seem puny and insignificant in comparison.

His harsh tone dragged her back to reality. "Lie down on the bed and spread your legs."

She gasped. Did he truly mean to take her like this? Fear and panic welled up inside of her. The man might be her husband, but she didn't know him at all. Yet, by law, he could do whatever he pleased with her, including taking what he wanted by force. Bella's voiced cracked. "Surely you don't mean to use me like some strumpet."

"Why not? You dress like a whore. Why should I not treat you as one?"

"You would know a great deal about whores," she said bitterly. The awful helplessness of the situation hit her. How insignificant she was. Despite the money and supposed consequence of being a future duchess, in the end, she was nothing but a piece of property. She belonged to him. Like the chair in the corner or the linen shirt he'd just discarded, she was just another piece of chattel.

Her gaze darted to the door, to any possible escape. "How dare you treat me in such a despicable manner?"

"It is interesting that you choose to act in an outrageous manner and then are surprised when someone actually treats you outrageously in return."

"Do you think I will cower before you? You are a man of no consequence save your connection to me and all that is rightfully mine."

A shadow of surprise glimmered across his face. Then that face of composure cracked into a savage countenance that prompted goose bumps to erupt across Bella's skin. He advanced in on her, his voice dark and threatening. "Lie down on the bed."

Stumbling backward against the bed, she plopped down on her bottom, her mind racing to find an escape, but her thoughts collided with obstacles in every direction they turned.

She looked to the lantern by her bedside. Perhaps while he rutted over her, she could slam it down on his head. She blinked and a tear fell. Looking down, she shook her head, disbelieving that she could be in this despairing predicament. "Please don't."

He drew an audible breath. For a long moment neither of them moved. Finally, Sebastian's hand came under her chin to tilt it gently up until she found herself looking into the dark storm of his eyes.

"I would strongly suggest you dispense with any gown that is beyond the bounds of decency. I will not ask it again. If you need to have a new gown made up for His Grace's rout, please do so immediately." He referred to an upcoming gathering hosted by her father to mark her first official appearance in society. He strode over to his discarded clothes and picked them up on his way to the door. Pulling it open, he paused before stepping over the threshold.

"Do not mistake my leniency for weakness. You may be a future duchess, but I am master here. You would do well not to forget it."

...

Bella paused outside the breakfast room and took a fortifying breath to steel herself against seeing her husband following last night's debacle.

He'd left the house again after departing her bedchamber, slipping out under the cover of darkness, moving quickly and with purpose. From her window, she'd watched her husband fade into the inky shadows and wondered if he'd gone to seek comfort in the body of Camryn's young maid.

A quick look around the sunny breakfast room confirmed Sebastian's absence. She exhaled, but shock immediately replaced relief when her gaze landed on Orford. His darkened left eye was swollen almost shut, his lower lip split. The injuries appeared even more pronounced against the canvas of his handsome face.

Bella's hand flew to cover her mouth. "Gad, what happened to you?"

Monty turned from where he stood filling his plate at the

sideboard. "It turns out your husband is a skilled pugilist."

"No!" exclaimed Bella. "Sebastian did that to you?"

Orford's answering smile froze when he winced in pain, touching his hand to his split lip. "It's nothing."

"It is *not* nothing." She ran a light finger over his swollen eye. "Are you all right? I can't believe Sebastian did this."

Josette nibbled on a roll. "He is full of surprises that husband of yours." She gave Bella a knowing look. "As I guessed, Monsieur Sebastian is very manly."

Tabby shuddered delicately. "Gentleman should not fight. It is uncivilized."

"Apparently, he is quite renowned at Gentleman Jackson's," Monty said, slipping into the seat beside Tabby.

"You went along as well?" Bella asked him.

"Purely as a spectator. I'm not one to pass up a good bout." Monty chuckled. "I learned few gentlemen care to face your husband. He is considered quite fearsome."

Orford's face darkened with displeasure. "Blood will tell, I suppose."

The two footmen attending them stiffened. Reaching for her chocolate, Bella surreptitiously observed the servants' reaction. "What do you mean?"

Orford shot her a sympathetic gaze. "Of course, you will have heard the rumors."

This time there was no doubt the two footmen exchanged a quick disapproving glance. She noted, not for the first time, that even the male staff members displayed an uncommon devotion to the master of the house. Nodding to them, she said, "Thank you. You may go."

Once they'd exited and closed the door behind them, she returned her attention to Orford. "What rumor is that?"

"That Stanhope is not really the marquess's brother at all."

"What matter of nonsense is this?" An unexpected surge of protectiveness welled in her. "Of course Camryn is Sebastian's brother."

Orford put a comforting hand over Bella's. "They say your husband is a natural."

"What is that?"

"It is understood among the *ton* that he was merry-begotten."

Bella's blood froze. Sebastian a bastard? "How can that be?"

Nothing made Josette's eyes sparkle more than salacious gossip. Leaning forward, she spoke in hushed tones. "They say the mother enjoyed a liaison."

Bella's eyes widened. "His mother and another man?" She couldn't imagine the gentle woman she'd met last evening cuckolding her husband.

Josette laughed at her friend's obvious shock. "*Mon cheri*, it is nothing. She had already given her husband two sons. Do not be so provincial."

Tabby glanced nervously toward the door. "It is not well done of us to speak ill of our host. Really, he appears quite the gentleman."

"You would think so, Tabby." Monty favored her with an indulgent look. "You are too good by half to appreciate the baser nature of human behavior."

Bella was stunned. "And her husband, Sebastian's father, he didn't mind?"

Orford lifted an elegant shoulder. "Who's to say?"

"I see." She sat back in her chair feeling strangely out of

breath. "Who is his sire?"

"The talk is that he was an Italian of no consequence," said Orford. "Probably a peasant."

She pondered that, thinking of Sebastian's dark curls, the olive tones in his complexion, how much his appearance differed from that of his brothers. It made sense.

Orford brought Bella's hand to his lips. "I'm sorry, my dear, your husband's bloodlines are even less impressive than they appear."

She suppressed an impulse to defend Sebastian. Why, she couldn't fathom, especially after his beastly behavior last evening. It had not been the behavior of a gentleman. It had, in fact, been base.

After the meal, everyone agreed to Tabby's suggestion they visit the British Museum to see the Elgin marbles. Bella declined and pulled Orford aside as the others prepared to depart. "Anything new on the mysterious account at Barclay's Bank?"

He shook his head. "Unfortunately, it has not been easy to find a clerk who is amenable to our particular form of persuasion."

"Keep trying; we must find out whose name is on that account."

"Who else could the money be for besides your husband?"

"A mistress. A parcel of by-blows. Who can know for certain? There are any number of possibilities." She wanted all of the details about Sebastian's secret account, the one to which he diverted one thousand pounds of Traherne money each month. "I must have inconvertible evidence of Sebastian's pilfering when I take this matter to His Grace."

"Not to worry, I'll keep trying." He gingerly touched his split lip. "It's my pleasure to assist with this matter."

Shortly after her friends' departure, Bella received a note from Willa, Duchess of Hartwell, inviting her to take tea. Eager to avoid running into her husband, she immediately sent her acceptance back to Sebastian's cousin. At the appointed time, she donned a russet-colored dress, which brought out the color of her hair and eyes, this one with a neckline that was just fashionably low, not scandalously so.

Hartwell House stood in the finest part of Mayfair not far from Camryn's equally impressive address. A dark-skinned butler she presumed to be from India showed her to a parlor, where the duchess rose to greet her. Camryn's wife, Charlotte, the marchioness, was with her.

The duchess wore a stunning red day dress that complemented her porcelain skin and remarkable beauty. Her large brown eyes were warm and friendly. "We are so pleased you have come," she said, inviting Bella to take a seat. "As you can imagine, Charlotte and I are most curious about Sebastian's wife."

"You will find us to be terribly inquisitive," Charlotte said with a laugh, her lovely blue eyes sparkling. "But we are fond of your husband and are anxious to see him happily settled." She wore a simple pale blue day gown with a high waist and a satin ribbon that tied under the modest swells of her bosom.

The duchess poured a cup of tea for Bella. "Sebastian is so obviously taken with you."

"Taken by me, Your Grace?" Bella accepted the tea. "Surely not."

The duchess filled a plate of food for her. "You must call me Willa. After all, we are family now."

"And I am Charlotte," said the marchioness. "Of course Sebastian is taken with you. It was obvious to all of us last evening."

Both women gazed at her in an expectant way that made Bella's cheeks heat.

"Sebastian's feelings are often difficult to decipher, but his eyes followed your every movement last evening," Willa said handing her a plate.

Probably because he worried her top would be lost. "I had not noticed."

Charlotte sipped her tea. "Sebastian is not like other men. He never looks at women, certainly not in the appreciative way he regards you."

Looking into the open, friendly faces of her new relations, Bella realized she quite liked them. Of course, they were wrong about Sebastian and other women. Willa and Charlotte were gentlewomen of the highest rank who'd have no inkling if Sebastian was indeed a thief with a propensity to use servant girls to satisfy his baser needs.

Willa filled her own teacup. "It is not as though he hasn't had the opportunity. That quiet way about him entices many women to his side, but Sebastian rejects every advance as far as I can tell."

"Is that why they call him the saint?" asked Bella.

"Not just that," said Charlotte. "He is a gentleman in every way. Chaste, charitable, and I am certain he is a kind and indulgent husband."

"He also has a keenness of mind and sweetness of temper," said Willa. "He is gifted with humor and perception. He is the utmost gentleman."

He'd hardly been a gentleman last night. "He does seem to worry about his consequence."

Charlotte and Willa exchanged a glance.

"Not at all." A frown marred the duchess's lovely face, her displeasure obvious. "He is the last to think of such things."

"It is only natural," she said in easy conversational manner, "for a man to choose a bride based upon breeding and the standing she brings to the alliance."

Charlotte's face softened. "You are mistaken. Sebastian cares nothing for titles. He declined the one that was offered him."

"I'm afraid I don't understand," said Bella.

Willa patted Bella's knee as though she were a child. "Because of his good standing and, no doubt, his marriage to you, the Lords offered to bestow the title of viscount on Sebastian."

Stunned, it took a moment for Bella to understand Willa's words. "Sebastian received a title? Through an act of parliament?"

Charlotte bit into a strawberry. "It is the way of men. They see Sebastian is married to a future duchess so they want to elevate him to a title that would make him worthy of his wife."

Naturally. She swallowed down her bitterness. Marriage to her had proven even more advantageous for Sebastian than she'd thought. "He hadn't mentioned his ennoblement."

Charlotte patted her lips with a linen cloth to wipe away

any remains of strawberry juice. "That's because he refused it."

Bella's eyes widened. "Beg pardon?"

Charlotte settled back in her chair, her amusement obvious. "He turned down the title."

"That's impossible."

"Not at all," said Willa. "He rejected the offer of a title out of hand, saying he quite preferred to remain a mere mister."

Charlotte chuckled. "It was quite the shock. No one has ever turned down a title before."

"But why didn't he take it?"

Willa shrugged. "Cam and Hartwell tried to convince him to. They told him to think of his future offspring, but he wouldn't hear of it."

A noise in the hallway drew their attention. Willa rose. "Aunt Matilda and Mother are here," she said, putting an end, for the moment, to Bella's questions. Of which she now had many more than before.

...

Bella's head was still swirling when she returned home and hurried to her rooms. Sebastian had turned down a title. Why, when position and fortune appeared to be so important to him? It made no sense at all.

She learned from the servants that he'd spent the day at home, most of that time in his study, receiving business-related calls. Still unnerved by the events of last evening, she was glad for the chance to avoid him. Still, the reprieve was short-lived. Almost immediately, she received a summons from Sebastian to join him in his study.

"What does he want?" she asked Davison when he delivered the missive.

"He requests your presence, my lady. He mentioned there are matters to be discussed." She watched Davison bow out of the room. While the butler was most attentive, she couldn't help feeling he was really her husband's man. He, like all of the servants, demonstrated an extreme loyalty to their employer, who they clearly saw as Sebastian. Even though they were likely paid with Traherne funds. She sighed. It was the way of things. She might as well accustom herself to it; a woman owned next to nothing once she married.

Her mind returned to her impending appointment with her husband. What to wear? She finally settled on her most severe gown, with a high collar and long sleeves to the wrist, left over from her finishing school days. Her hair, she pulled back into a severe manner, fashioning a bun at the nape of her neck.

Nerves jabbing at her stomach, she made her way to the study. The door was ajar allowing murmurs of conversation to drift out into the hall. His business associates must still be with him. She turned to go, but a decidedly feminine sound coming from the study stopped her. Curious, she advanced to the door and peered inside.

Her maid, Louisa, stood before Sebastian. They were in front of his desk, with just inches separating them. Bella couldn't see Louisa's face, but she had a clear view of Sebastian's. A warm smile lit his face as he looked down on the girl. Bella's stomach lurched. He laid a hand on the girl's shoulder and murmured something Bella couldn't hear. Yet their actions spoke volumes; his casual physical contact with the servant girl, their proximity to each other, the easy, fond expression on her husband's face. Pain twisted in her chest. Sebastian and another servant. Perhaps Louisa was yet another reason he didn't visit her bed.

She pushed the door open. "You asked to see me?" she asked, her voice unnaturally loud.

Looking at her, Sebastian slowly removed his hand from Louisa's shoulder, as though laying hands upon a servant was nothing to be remarked upon. His eyes skimmed over Bella's dress, a glimmer of amusement flashing there before his gaze turned inscrutably polite.

"Yes, thank you for coming." He motioned for her to come forward. "That will be all, Louisa." The maid hurried out, dropping a quick curtsy to Bella, her eyes downcast. She closed the door behind her.

Sebastian gazed at Bella for a moment. He was in shirtsleeves, his enormous, muscled forearms lightly dusted with dark curls. He wore no cravat so that his collar opened at the neck, revealing curls of dark hair licking at his throat. "Are you contemplating joining a nunnery?"

Tearing her gaze away from his impressive form, she realized he referred to her severe gown. "There are no nunneries in England, as you well know."

"True. Perhaps off to join a mission of mercy then?"

"I thought you would find this mode of dress more to your exacting taste."

"I see. So you must either play the lightskirt or a spinster governess. Is there no middle ground for you, Mirabella?"

"Is there no place but the middle ground for you?"

A slight smile curved his lips. "Well said. Please sit." He gestured toward the chair in front of his desk.

Advancing, she grasped the back of the chair instead. "No, thank you. I'd prefer to stand."

Courtesy dictated he remain standing as well. "As you will." Clasping his hands behind his back, he walked to the hearth. His breeches clung to the firm, well-rounded muscles of his rear. Bella swallowed hard and jerked her gaze away when he turned to face her.

Clearing his throat, his clear green gaze met hers. "I wish to apologize for last evening."

Bella's eyes widened. He'd behaved badly, but she hadn't expected a show of remorse. She'd baited him, insulted him, even shamed him before his family. "Oh."

"My behavior was abominable." His full lips pressed into a grim line. "It was wrong of me to insult you in such a manner. You are my wife, and, as your husband, it is my place to honor and protect you. It is certainly not to debase you. Allow me to assure you such a sordid scene will never happen again."

She released a breath, her mind still focused on her maid. "What was Louisa doing in here?"

"Beg pardon?"

"Why was my maid in your study?" Bella crossed her arms over her chest. "Does she report my comings and goings to you?"

His grim countenance eased. "Of course not."

"Then why was she here?"

He regarded her with puzzlement. "She is in my employ. I make it my concern to check on the welfare of the servants."

"Is she your—" She flushed, unable to finish the thought.

"Is she my what?" He regarded her for a moment before his eyebrows rose in understanding. "My peculiar?

Of course not. She is just a servant. Although I am flattered by your interest."

"I am not interested. Not in the least." The words tumbled out. Too quickly. Mortified, Bella closed her eyes. She opened them to find penetrating eyes focused on her.

"There is only one woman who interests me in that way."

She fought the urge to cover her face in shame for showing jealousy over a servant. "Yet you don't make demands of that sort on me—" She clamped her mouth shut again, wishing she could keep her tongue in her mouth and control her feelings the way Sebastian did.

He came around to the front of his desk and rested his hip against it in a manner that caused his thigh muscles to bulge. "What is it, Mirabella? Pray do speak freely."

Pressing her lips together, she gave him a mutinous look and shook her head, not daring to open her traitorous mouth again.

"Is this about me demanding my marital rights?"

Bella tightened her arms across her chest. "I accept your apology." She spun around, anxious to quit the room. "If that is all—"

Suddenly he was behind her, all warmth and hard masculinity. "No, that is not all." His breath tingled through her hair. Large arms came around her. He seemed to hesitate before pulling her back against the rocklike length of his body.

"Surely," he murmured in her ear, "you cannot think I am immune to your charms." It was so hot in the room with him holding her. Her heart contracted. She longed to sink back into him, to be encompassed by his virility, to surrender to him. Determined to fight it, she shook her head against the feeling. Caring for her husband might very well lead to despair and disappointment.

She pushed away from him. She felt his hesitation, but then he released her. "If that is all—"

"It is not." He returned to his desk. "Please indulge me for a few more minutes."

She forced a breath and her shaky legs carried her back to the chair he'd offered earlier. This time, she gratefully sank into it.

Crossing his arms over his wide chest, he leaned his hip back against his desk again. She immediately realized her mistake. Sitting put her at eye level with the contours of his groin area. Josette's words about his manly assets swirled in her mind. Swallowing hard, she forced her gaze up to her husband's face. As usual, his expression was inscrutable.

"Since you brought up the subject of the marital bed."

"I did no such thing."

"Of course not. Please forgive my impertinence."

Eager to escape this line of questioning, Bella started to rise from her chair. "Now that we've cleared that up—"

"Still, you are my wife and it is not outside the bounds of propriety for me to assert my husbandly rights."

She plopped back in the chair with an unladylike thud. "Why don't you satisfy yourself with your ladybird?"

"I have no mistress."

She snorted. "Please. You must think me an incredibly silly chit to believe that."

His dark eyebrows drew together. "You must think me completely without honor."

"It is not a question of honor. Many husbands have...a friend such as that."

"I do not."

"Perhaps not at the moment." She squinted her eyes at him. "When did you give her up? Your last mistress, I mean."

"When we married."

"When I came to live here a few weeks ago?"

"No, when we married. I parted with my mistress on my wedding day."

"So you've resorted to occasional dalliances with ser... whoever is at hand...instead of having a formal arrangement with one woman."

"No. I have not known a woman in that way since we married."

Six years ago? She laughed. "You must think me a fool to believe such a Banbury tale."

"It is no tale. There was nothing to be done for it. We had married. There was no honor in betraying my wife."

It took her a stunned moment to process his meaning. She searched his face for signs of mendacity, but his clear eyes returned a strong and steady gaze. She shook her head in disbelief. "Six years? Are you telling me you've gone without a woman for six years?"

His unwavering eyes held hers. "Yes."

"What is the matter with you? Do you not like women? Oh." She felt dizzy. This was a complication she had not foreseen. "I saw men such as that in Paris."

A line formed between his dark brows. "I don't follow."

"Men who are drawn to...their own kind."

His chuckle was a low baritone, the sound warm and amused. He knelt in front of her, his enormous hands brushing her flanks. "I assure you, my taste is for women. One woman in particular." His hands slid higher until they rubbed the outsides of her hips.

Her nerve endings quivered with excitement, as though they'd been awakened from a long hibernation. "What are you doing?"

"Convincing my wife of my desire for her." He leaned in to kiss the side of her neck, sending pleasurable sparks through her body. "I assure you, I am most anxious to end my years of abstinence."

"Oh."

He nipped at her neck. "My little hoyden is speechless for once."

She gripped the arms of her chair while his soft lips and hot touches of tongue feathered against the rampant pulse throbbing in her neck. His mouth moved up her neck, tasting her along the way, taking a sensual soft bite every now and again.

"I should like to take my boon now," he murmured against her prickling skin.

"Hmm?" she said, too distracted by his drugging ministrations to follow his words.

His lips moved up her neck, tasting her along the way, taking a sensual soft bite every now and again. "My bout with Orford. A kiss was to be my reward."

Yes. *Yes.* "Then I suppose I'll have to allow it," she said in as distant a voice as she could muster.

After what seemed like an eternity, his mouth finally reached hers and fastened on to it. Soft and warm, his lips caressed hers with tender movements. Beyond any pretense, she parted her lips almost immediately, hungry to taste him.

His tongue rubbed hers with confident, insistent strokes. He tasted indescribably good, tangy, sweet, yet masculine.

She'd never experienced such sensory pleasure; every part of her awakened and vibrated with life. She finally forced herself to break the kiss. Gasping for breath, she searched his face. "Have you really been faithful to me?"

He bent to nibble on her ear. "Yes."

"Oh!" Acute pleasure shot through her at the sensation of his mouth on the tender flesh of her lobe. She gulped and forced him back, her hands on his chest. "But why?"

He was clearly a virile man, perhaps the most so she had ever met. To go so many years without a woman seemed unnatural. And utterly romantic. "Tell me."

He sat back on his heels, his beautiful eyes fastened on hers. With a deep sigh, he pushed to his feet and walked to stand in front of the hearth. After a moment, he turned to face her, a grave look on his face. "Do not think I am at ease with what I did to you, Mirabella. I allowed our fathers to take an innocent child and force her into a lifetime attachment to a stranger."

Her heart thumped painfully. "Why did you do it?"

He rubbed the back of his neck. "I was ten and nine. I had never heard of anything so disagreeable, forcing marriage on a child. But your father owed mine. With our union, the gaming debt was settled."

She must have misheard him. "I don't understand."

"My family would have been ruined if I hadn't agreed to the alliance. It was well before Cam inherited the marquisate. There were no funds for the education of my younger brothers and long-time servants would have been put out without a pension. I could parse no other way to save my family from certain destitution."

The world tilted. He seemed so far away. "A gambling

debt that *you* were forced to pay the price for?"

A look of puzzled alarm firmed on his face. "Surely, at some point, His Grace informed you of the circumstances of our marriage."

Tears blurred her eyes. "A wager." Air gushed out of her lungs. She shook her head. "Dear Lord, it cannot be."

"I assumed you knew." His face softened. "Your father owed mine a significant gaming debt. The resolution was our marriage. I resisted, but not strongly enough. My family gained the invaluable connection to yours and Traherne's debt was satisfied."

"But why would His Grace need to resort to that to settle the debt? Traherne is very profitable."

An expression she couldn't interpret crossed his face. "It has not always been so. Traherne's purse was considerably less robust when we married."

"My father wagered me away like one of his mounts or a fistful of guineas?" She blinked away tears. "Tell me it's a lie."

He came to kneel before her, taking her cold, lifeless hands in his large warm grip. "It is the regrettable truth. I resolved at that moment to soften the blow of this marriage for you in every way."

"You sent me away."

"No," he said fervently. "I vowed to give you your freedom, to restore whatever bit of your youth that was within my power."

"I was alone."

"When you wanted to travel, I agreed because it was what you deserved." Tenderness infused his voice. "What you did not deserve is what we did to you."

She raised her hand to her strangled throat. "I mean nothing to my father. He wagered me away."

"On the day we married, I vowed to treat you with complete honor. That included remaining faithful to my wife." He tilted her chin back to him so she that she gazed into his emerald depths. "I cannot regret it. However it happened, you are my wife and I am grateful. I look at you and I know you were worth waiting for."

Bella's chest squeezed with some unknown emotion. A sob escaped her throat. He brushed a tender kiss on her forehead. "I am here, Bella. Let me cherish you as you deserve."

Tears streamed unabated down her cheeks, as though they would never stop. He leaned over and lifted her in his arms. Weightless in the air for a moment, she settled blindly on his lap, large, comforting arms drew her close against a wide protective chest.

Her heart burst with pain for the little girl whose father cast her off on a stranger, for the times she aimlessly traveled the world with no real family ties to speak of. Grief rose up and consumed her. Gentle hands stroked her hair and cheeks, the curve of her back, murmuring words of comfort, showering her with soft kisses. She nestled into the smooth contours of his enormous chest, feeling the hard turn of muscle beneath it, her tears sopping his linen shirt.

She rubbed her lips against the bare expanse of his sinewy throat and the warmth of his bronzed skin. He swallowed hard, the muscles of his throat working.

"Bella."

Ignoring the warning in his tone, she kissed the hard curve of his jaw, relishing the feel of the unyielding bone beneath it. She ran her hand across his cheek with a light touch, exploring the stubble that scratched against her skin. The musk scent of shaving soap enlivened her, awakening her body to his maleness.

He closed his eyes, nudging his cheek into her hand with a shuddering breath. "Bella, we must stop."

"Why?" She kissed along his temple, to his brows, her hands stealing around his neck. "We are married. Haven't we waited long enough?"

Chapter Twelve

Sebastian knew something of heaven and hell because at the moment he was experiencing both. Ever since her arrival, Bella had constantly challenged his hard-won equilibrium. He'd spent years honing the ability to keep his impulses in check, yet his wife provoked emotions far beyond anything he'd experienced before.

She was all soft curves and welcoming woman in his arms. His senses were attuned to her arousal, the headiness of it like an opium addict who has abstained from his drug for far too long. He longed to make love to her, to take her as his own, to plunge years of need into her lush, accommodating body. For a moment, he thought to let her have her way with him because it was what he wanted, what his body ached for.

Sensing the awakening of her body, how roused with need she was, caused lust to shoot through him. He clutched the chair arms to his sides, not trusting himself not to lose complete control and ravage her like the beast in him clamored to do. "You are not yourself."

She pulled his shirt from his breeches and over his head. He was not so righteous that he did not lift his arms to assist her efforts. "Wrong, I am finally being myself. You have no idea how wicked I can be."

He couldn't wait to find out.

"So strong," she murmured fanning her pale hands across the breadth of his bare chest. Her tapered fingers appeared even more delicate against the crude expanse of his bronzed skin dusted with dark curls. She bent her head to taste him there and he almost jumped out of his skin.

"You have to stop or I will lose all control."

She paused and gazed at him, eyes bright with sensual agitation. "Sebastian Stanhope, losing all control?" She reached for his breeches and brushed her hand intently against his hardened male flesh. "I should like to see that."

He was so aroused he almost came right when she touched his vitals. Clenching his teeth, he gripped her hand. "Duchess, be careful of what you ask for."

Her untutored fingers worked at unfastening his breeches. "Duchess, hmm? As the daughter of a duke, I am accustomed to being accommodated. And, at present, I want you. Immediately."

He closed his eyes and groaned, slamming his head back against the soft leather of the chair, hoping to pound some sense into his addled brain, fighting for the control that had served him so well all of these years.

"Blast it! How is this done?"

He peeked one eye open to glimpse Bella's flushed cheeks and how she bit her lower lip, a tiny frown of concentration on her forehead. He dared to peer down to her hands, where she appeared to have trouble opening his breeches.

The sight of her delicate hands so close to his arousal was too much. Any reservoir of restraint cascaded out of him. Surging out of the chair, his arms closed around her. Now that he had her, he would never let her go. Certain he wouldn't be able to contain himself long enough to make it to the bedchamber, he went to the carpeted floor with Bella in his arms, her easy curves eager against his body. "This is not the way this should happen," he uttered harshly, even as he swooped down to ravish her.

She was laid out on the carpet like an earthy sacrifice, cheeks blazing, her rapid breathing pushing the swells of her breasts against that God-awful spinster's gown she'd squeezed her curves into. He flipped her over onto her stomach straddling her behind and made quick work of her dress. He spread it open, unveiling the pale smooth expanse of her nape and shoulders. He nipped the back of her neck, tasting the delicious blend of sweet femininity and salty earthiness.

Before she could react, he flipped her over again, working on her stays and pulling them open; her chemise followed until, except for her stockings and slippers, she at last lay bare before him.

He paused to take in the lushness of her womanly form, the roundness of her peaked breasts, the indentation of her belly button, the soft, downy hair that began just below her stomach and exploded into a riot of heavenly dark curls between silken creamy thighs. His enthralled senses inhaled every part of her, feasting on the elemental things he had missed all of these years. "You are so lovely."

She laughed, the imp. The sound throaty and inviting. "Are you just going to stand there? Perhaps you have forgotten how it's done."

"You are a bold piece." She caught her breath when his hand closed over the soft swell of her breast, savoring its quivering warmth. He thumbed the rigid point. It had been so long.

Her hand came over his, her voice pleading. "Sebastian, I want you to lie with me. Please."

Still cupping one breast, he pressed a gentle kiss on the other and inhaled the sweet scent of her skin. "It will pain you."

"Meeker women than I have withstood it," she said, breathless, arching her unbearably soft breast deeper into his hand.

His body shaking with need, he felt through the tangle of her sweet curls, relief flooding him when he felt the moist honey of her readiness. He knew he should slow down and keep himself in check so that he didn't hurt or frighten her, but his manly urges crowded out all cogent thought. On a plaintive groan of long-suppressed need, he freed himself and poised his swollen flesh at the entrance to bliss.

He looked into her exquisite face to find it empty of all guile. Cheeks flushed, her expression was open and emotive as it had been in those first days before she'd realized his deceit. Her golden-brown eyes were brilliant with expectation.

He nudged in a little at a time until he came up against the barrier that proclaimed her a maiden. A surge of masculine satisfaction rifled through him at the confirmation that no other man had ever taken possession of her. Blood roaring through him, he pushed past her maidenhead until he was fully encased, surrounded by the welcome of her sweet, snug heat. He stilled and savored what he had missed for far too long—the essential essence of a woman, the soft breaths and lilting murmurs of pleasure, the scent of feminine arousal. What a glorious woman.

She urged her hips against his. Liquid fire shot through his vitals. He began to move in slow, deliberate movements; her dark wet tightness caressed his swollen gland with each thrust. Her body responded, curving into his. He quickened his pace. Waves of pleasure and pressure intensified, building almost beyond his capacity to bear it. His body's natural instincts took over and he lost any hope of finesse in this first loving of her.

He stroked hard and strong, throwing off years of restraint, of economy, of suppressed physical longing until everything fell away and there was only her. Ecstasy burned up through his legs into the small of his back. A squeezing, pulling sensation gripped his ballocks and the unbearable tension finally released. He saw black before spinning away into the achingly brilliant bliss of reaching his peak with the incomparable woman who was his wife.

...

The following evening, for her first official showing in society, Bella selected a royal-blue silk gown with a stylishly deep décolletage that was in no way scandalous. The appreciative glint in Sebastian's eyes as he escorted her out to the dance floor suggested he approved. "How do I look?"

"There is no lovelier woman in the room."

She moved into his arms for the start of the waltz. "And yet I had to beg for the flattery. How ungallant of you."

"I was loath to compliment your appearance for fear you'd retreat back to your chamber for a gown more suited to an opera singer."

She suppressed a smile. "This costume is exceedingly appropriate for the performance I plan this evening." She pulled her shoulders back in a way that emphasized her full breasts, an asset gentlemen—especially her husband—seemed to appreciate.

The deliberate subtle arching of her back had the desired effect. His eyes went to the pale swells on prominent display above her bodice. His throat moved a little. "And what performance is that, may I ask?"

Batting her eyelashes, she said, "Why, that of the perfect wife and daughter, of course."

"Wench." His expression sobered. "Are you certain you are in good health after last evening?"

A sense of well-being flowed through her. "Supremely."

The tense lines of his face relaxed. "I'm glad to hear it. I fear I was not gentle enough with you."

"Not to worry. I'm no fragile hothouse bloom."

"So I noticed."

She smiled, feeling almost giddy in his arms. Being bedded by her husband had been an astonishing experience, more intimate and pleasurable than she anticipated. She still had lingering misgivings about his financial activities, but at least for this evening she intended to put them aside for a bit. With so many curious eyes observing their every interaction, she was grateful for the security of his embrace. Even though it was a smallish affair by ducal standards—

dinner and dancing for fifty, rather than the hundreds typically included in more lavish affairs—she felt the strain of people's interest in her.

Gazing about, she took in her surroundings. Thousands of candles provided brilliant lighting throughout the public rooms, which were overfilled with mahogany furniture atop gleaming oak floors. The ballroom itself was mostly empty of furnishings except for chairs and benches lining the perimeter of the room intended for chaperones, matrons, and those who preferred to play the part of spectator. Elaborate tapestries graced the walls and a series of niches around the ballroom held ancient statues. She marveled that all this would one day be part of her inheritance, yet she had never seen any of it before now.

Her eyes fell upon a group of people congregated near a statue. Like most guests in the ballroom, they watched with open curiosity, doing little to disguise their interest in her and Sebastian. "They're all staring at me as though I were some exotic zoo animal."

Sebastian kept a firm hand on her torso, guiding her in the dance movements. "A beautiful woman always draws her share of attention."

"I'm sure my looks are secondary. They all want to gawk at Sebastian Stanhope's mystery wife."

"It's more likely they're curious about Traherne's heir. A duchess in her own right is a rare thing indeed."

When the music came to an end, they reluctantly parted since manners dictated each should dance the next set with someone else. A few gentlemen lingered nearby, poised to approach her for a turn on the dance floor, but His Grace beckoned her to his side before they could.

"Come," he said, settling heavily into a simple chair too small for his large frame. The other guests cleared a respectable space around them. "Sit beside me. I'm getting too old to dance."

"Or too foxed," she said drily.

He barked a laugh. "Girl, you are your mother's daughter."

"Am I?" She knew so little about her mother. "Why did you never remarry?"

"I loved that woman. It's the only thing that made her constant nagging bearable." He swallowed a good portion of his drink. "I wouldn't have found another woman half so fine."

Bella looked in the deep lines of her father's face, the bleary eyes and broken blood vessels in his cheeks an overt testament to years of overindulgence. She felt the same tug of longing she always felt in those rare moments she was in her father's presence. "What was she like?"

"Very like you, with the same fire and beauty." Glassy eyes assessed her. "You remind me of her."

Her parents had been a love match? She'd never known that. It pressed home how little she knew about them. "You loved her."

"I did, very much. Each time I visited you, it brought the pain of her loss back again." He held up his glass. "Drink helped, but not much."

Emotion swelled in her chest. Her father had loved her mother. So much so, that any reminder of his wife had pained him. "Yet you forced my marriage to Sebastian. You did not allow me to find a love match."

"Balderdash. I've seen the way the two of you look at

each other." He chuckled. "It took you long enough. For a while there, I feared I'd miscalculated."

"Miscalculated?" Emotion closing her throat, she looked unseeing to the swirling blurs of color on the dance floor. "Losing a fortune at cards hardly required a clever stratagem on your part."

He guffawed. "I had other means of settling the debt. Sebastian happened to be the most expedient." He finished off his drink. A footman instantly appeared with a replacement. "Even then, your husband had a reputation for his clever mind and firmness of character."

She searched his face. "Are you suggesting that you purposely chose Sebastian for me?"

"He has four brothers. His father tried to get me to take any one of the others. I refused."

Breathlessness assaulted her. "Why?"

He shifted heavily in his seat. "Fortune hunters were already lining up for you. I selected a gentleman who would treat my daughter with care while also overseeing the dukedom with a clever hand."

"Perhaps too clever a hand."

"What are you getting at?" He peered at her with bloodshot eyes. "Speak plainly girl."

"You give him complete control over Traherne funds."

"Yes. I trust him implicitly."

"Do you not worry he might avail himself to more of the ducal coffers than he should?"

He frowned at her. "Why would he do that? After my demise, he'll have access to it all anyway. Whatever he amasses goes to his offspring, who will also be your children. Any way you look at it, it all stays within the family." He nodded. "Fortunate thing it was that he married you."

"Indeed." The funny thing was, she was beginning to feel lucky to be bound to Sebastian.

"I'd moved heaven and earth to make you my legitimate heir," the duke went on. "Your future needed to be assured even if I died before you reached your majority."

Her mind whirled into light-headedness, shaking loose everything she'd always believed about her father. The duke hadn't been absent and careless. At least not totally. He'd wanted to secure her future and keep her safe.

They were silent for a moment, both with their eyes on the dancers. "Are you content with Sebastian?" he asked.

The wanton part of her certainly was, so much so that it frightened her. "We are still learning to…accommodate each other."

"Excellent. He saved my arse, Sebastian did."

"How so?"

"We were in the direst of straits when you married. Without Sebastian's good sense, we'd have been forced to sell off everything that wasn't not entailed."

"But…I thought that as my husband he takes an allowance from Traherne coffers."

"Coffers he helped fill to overflowing."

"Oh." And was now apparently helping to unfill? What a paradox her husband was. Was it possible Sebastian was taking the money because he felt entitled to it?

"Not that he is in need of an allowance." He barked a gruff laugh. "His own personal fortune likely rivals mine now. And on top of that, he'll receive a generous settlement from the estate once you give birth to an heir."

"He will? How generous?"

"It's in the original marriage contract." His attention was diverted by Orford's approach. "Ah, here's your cousin."

Orford approached with a bow for the duke. "Your Grace."

"Come to take my girl for turn about the dance floor, Orford?"

"With Your Grace's leave."

"You have it." The duke pushed up from his chair with considerable effort. "I'm off to the cards room." He shuffled off without a parting word to her. For once, instead of feeling wounded and abandoned, Bella mostly felt bemused. That was the longest conversation she could remember having with her father. And the most enlightening.

She fell into the routine of the party. Dancing with Orford and a number of other gentlemen, and engaging in polite chatter with the ladies in between sets. It relieved her to have a chance to mingle with Willa and Charlotte. When their husbands came to claim them, she made for the refreshment room hoping for a moment alone before another gentlemen approached her to partner for the next dance.

"The absent wife returns."

She turned to find Jacintha Belfield leaning against the door frame. She recalled meeting the countess at Lady Claymont's musicale. This was the woman Sebastian had avoided that evening. "Lady Hawke."

Languid, pale eyes assessed her, lingering over her features. "So you are Sebastian's wife."

She straightened. "I am."

Lady Hawke pushed off the wall and prowled toward her. She was a lovely woman with blond hair to complement those silvery eyes. Physically Bella might be considered the greater beauty, but Lady Hawke radiated an unnerving sexual confidence. "No longer the chubby little girl he was forced to marry so long ago."

"So it would seem." The hair on Bella's arms stood on edge. Most of the guests here were not privy to the details of their long-ago nuptials. "Are you well acquainted with my husband?"

"Intimately acquainted, since well before your rather... unexpected nuptials."

Her blood iced. Intuitively, she understood this predatory creature had enjoyed carnal knowledge of her husband. "Is that so?"

"Yes, he wasn't much more than a boy himself at the time. As you can imagine, Sebastian is not one for surprises; it upsets his sense of order." She smiled. "I comforted him as best I could."

Hot humiliation flooded her. Sebastian had discussed her with this woman. She could see them together in bed, mocking the homely child he'd been forced to marry. Doubt about his faithfulness rocked her. According to Josette, it was impossible for any man to go without a woman for an extended period of time. And Bella had been apart from him for years. Lady Hawke's presence in his life would explain his prolonged lack of interest in other women. Perhaps Sebastian's claim of years-long abstinence had been a ploy to get into her bed so he could meet the terms of the contract that required the begetting of an heir.

"There you are, Lady Mirabella. I've come to claim my dance." Sebastian's friend Penrose stood before her, offering his arm. "May I have the pleasure?"

She favored him with what she hoped appeared to be an effortless smile. "Of course." To Lady Hawke, she said, "Do enjoy the rest of your evening."

Penrose escorted her to the dance floor. "You should not pay heed to anything she says."

"Beg pardon?" Numb with uncertainty, she moved into place in the ladies line.

The row of gentlemen opposite them bowed to the ladies, who curtsied in return as the music began. Moving into the dance, she stepped forward and placed one hand in his as they proceeded into a circle.

"Lady Hawke is not always entirely…reliable."

Stepping back and sashaying forward again, they linked both hands and took a turn. "I see."

Penrose's eyes remained intent on hers. "She can be most indiscreet."

Her heart dropped. Pen obviously knew Sebastian was sleeping with that ravening creature. His attempt to defend his friend only confirmed her worst suspicions. "Whatever could she have to be indiscreet about?"

"I'm sure I don't know." He cleared his throat. "Still, as such, it would be…unwise of you to heed her."

They parted again and reunited. Shoulder to opposite shoulder, they curved a circle around each other. She fought to keep her voice even. "I assure you, I pay no heed to my husband's indiscretions."

His eyes darkened as each of them stepped back again. She moved through the dance steps like an automaton, a serene smile stamped on her face, even though her insides felt as if someone was hacking at them with a scythe. Stealing a look around the room, she wondered if any other women present had also been intimate with her husband. Down the line, she watched him dance with a lovely young girl with wheat-colored hair. The expression on the girl's face — one of rapt admiration — was one Bella had seen before, on Louisa and the servant girl from Camryn's townhome.

Penrose followed her gaze. "That is my sister, Adelaide. I assure you she's harmless."

"She's a beauty." She placed her gloved hand in his to follow the other couples promenading down the center. "Is Lady Adelaide betrothed?"

"Not as of yet. But she has taken well this season. My mother has high hopes."

"I should have a care then, if I were you, not to leave her unattended with my husband." She spoke the damning words lightly, as though Sebastian's indiscretions did not matter in the least to her.

Surprise stiffened his features. "I trust Sebastian implicitly, most especially with Adelaide," he said with icy courtesy.

"One can only hope your trust in him does not come at the expense of your sister's reputation."

He inhaled in obvious shock as they stepped away from each other. He bent in a bow, she in a curtsy, as the interminable dance came to an end. She cut a straight line for Orford who was busy charming a group of maidens. No surprise there. Despite his lack of fortune, Orford's looks, easy charm, and connection to the duke would no doubt ensure he married well. But, for now, she needed him. "Come," she said, taking his arm. "Let us go outside. I am in dire need of some air."

More than one eyebrow lifted at Bella's proprietary hold

on Orford's arm. "Lady Mirabella," said one rather horse-faced young woman. "Surely you can spare us a handsome gentleman."

The room—hot and airless—seemed to close in on her. "Of course. My husband is just over there. I can spare him, and I am certain he would be happy to oblige," she said sweetly as she pulled Orford away.

He came willingly, surprised amusement lighting his face. "I, too, am always happy to oblige."

"Good, I need to get out of here." Her lungs felt paralyzed. Behind them, one of the harpies made a comment about "kissing cousins." Thinly veiled snickers followed. She didn't miss the way the eyes of many guests tracked their movement toward the terrace doors. Once through them, she paused to fill her lungs.

Orford frowned. "What is it? What's amiss?"

"I just met Sebastian's mistress."

"Oh dear."

"Yes, oh dear." She hurried down the stairs. "As you can imagine, it was delightful."

"Slow down," he said, following her. "You'll stumble over your gown. Where are we going?"

"Away from probing eyes. I'm tired of being stared at like a museum exhibit."

"What is she like?"

"Who?" She eased her pace once they reached the darker reaches of the garden. "Oh, the mistress. Have you met Lady Hawke?"

His eyes widened. "Truly?" He gave a low whistle. "Lucky bastard. I'm impressed."

She shot him a dark look. "You would be."

"She's a diamond of the first water. Any man would want to dock her."

"You're making me feel so much better."

"Darling, I'm sorry he has hurt you so." He took her hand. "Unfortunately, it is not uncommon. Many gentlemen have mistresses."

She rubbed her throat, trying to ease the choking sensation. "I'm not going back in there. Take me home. I can't abide being here a moment longer."

He hesitated. "Everyone saw us leave the ballroom together. Tongues will wag."

She gave a mirthless laugh at the hypocrisy of it. "Leaving with my cousin ignites a scandal, but it's perfectly acceptable for my husband's mistress to be in attendance this evening?"

"It is the way of things."

"I don't care." She spotted the garden gate and started toward it. "Are you coming?"

"Gladly, darling." Falling in step with her, he took her arm. "He's a fool. If you were mine, I would never stray."

"But she's not yours." A low-pitched voice that was dark with warning sounded behind them. "And she never will be."

Chapter Thirteen

She spun around, her heart thrashing. Partially eclipsed by shadows, Sebastian stood with legs planted apart, his stance rigid.

Orford turned as well, in an utterly relaxed motion. "Stanhope."

Ignoring Orford, Sebastian's stony gaze fixed on her. "Going somewhere?"

She pulled her shoulders back. "Yes, we are leaving."

"Through the back gate?"

"Bella is fatigued," said Orford.

Sebastian's eyes remained planted on her, their expression inscrutable. "I'll gladly escort my wife home."

"No need," she said too quickly. "Orford is happy to oblige."

"I'm sure he is. However, you are not departing through the back gate. Half the guests saw you leave the ballroom with him."

Heat flashed in her chest, burning all the way up to her throat. "I see. The *appearance* of decorum is all that matters to you."

"It will create a scandal, as you well know."

"I don't care."

"I do." He finally looked to Orford. "I should like to speak with Bella alone."

Orford stiffened. "I will not desert a lady."

"My wife is not alone. She is with her husband."

Bella returned Sebastian's obdurate gaze. "Do leave us, Orford. I should like to talk to my husband."

"If you are certain." Orford's glance bounced to Sebastian and back to her. "Shall I stay out on the terrace in case you have need of me?"

"She won't need you."

Bella looked to Orford, favoring him with a tender smile that spoke of her fondness for him. "Thank you, dearest, but do go and rejoin the others. I'm certain your prolonged absence has disappointed the ladies."

"If you are certain."

"I am. This shan't take long. I'll join you presently."

After Orford took his leave, Sebastian spoke. "Pen tells me you spoke with Lady Hawke."

"Yes, I had a lovely conversation with your mistress."

"You understand full well that she is not my mistress."

"I know nothing of the sort." She crossed her arms over her chest. "Surely you won't deny bedding her."

"I have known her in that way, yes. But she is no longer my mistress."

"What is she to you then?"

"She was my first experience in carnal matters. My only

in fact."

Air whooshed out of her lungs. She pointed toward the house, to where Lady Hawke prowled somewhere inside. "That predatory creature was your first woman? The only one you've—"

"Yes."

"Impossible!"

"It's the truth. She has been rather dogged in her pursuit recently." His unwavering gaze held hers. "But, as I told you, the liaison ended once we married."

He spoke with such earnestness, such certainty, that doubt nagged at her again. "I don't know what to think anymore."

"I am a man of my word."

Her heart pumped. She wanted to believe him. "Why do you leave the house at all hours of the night?"

His brow furrowed. "What does that have to do with… you think I go to a mistress?"

"If not Lady Hawke, someone else. If there is no ladybird, where do you go?"

"You will think it foolish."

She arched a brow. "I doubt it can be as disagreeable as the thought of you dallying with another woman."

"True enough." He relaxed his stance. "Very well. I take exercise."

"I was not aware the boxing and fencing establishments kept such irregular hours."

"They don't. I walk and sometimes I run."

"Run?" She'd never heard of such a thing. "Where do you run to? Why do you not take your mount?"

Amusement glimmered in his eyes. "I don't run

anywhere in particular. The point is not the destination, it is in the running itself."

She shook her head. "I don't comprehend. What is the purpose?"

"It makes my blood pump through me, my heart races so hard it feels like it is going to burst."

She grimaced. "That sounds dreadful."

"At first it is, but it relieves my body of tension. It wears my physical body out in a positive way and brings me great relief."

"Relief from what?"

"A man has certain…needs." He cleared his throat. "With my wife abroad, I could not satisfy them in the usual manner."

"Oh. I so want to believe you."

Stepping closer, he cradled her face in his large, warm hands. "You must put your faith in me at some point, Mirabella."

"I want to." Emotion inflated her chest. Putting her hands over his, she savored their slightly roughened texture. "Trust doesn't come easily for me."

"I suppose I deserve that."

"My father wagered me away, and then you left me to my own devices—"

"And once you came home, I was not exactly honest with you."

"Most of the men in my life, who are supposed to have a care for me, have been…something of a disappointment."

Taking a deep breath, he rested his warm forehead against hers. "I shall work hard to earn your trust. Will you give me the chance?"

She swallowed, trying to ease the ache in her throat. "I will try."

"In the future, if you have concerns or suspicions, you must come directly to me for an explanation before assuming the worst."

"Yes."

"Do I have your word?"

"You do." The secret bank account flashed through her mind. This was the moment to ask him about it, but then he kissed her and she forgot about everything except the way his warm tongue tasted against hers. Slipping her arms around his neck, she pressed against his muscled frame, feeling the strength of his arousal. All she could think about was making love with him again. "Sebastian?"

"Hmmm," he murmured, nuzzling her neck.

"Is taking exercise really how you have managed to go without a woman for six years?"

"That…and there are other ways a man eases his needs."

Bella's cheeks heated. "I see."

His hands ran down the length of her back over the curve of her backside. "I doubt it," he said against her lips.

"Josette was married. She is very French. And very free with her thoughts and knowledge on the subject of the marriage bed."

"I see. What else does she say?"

"That I should go willingly to your bed. She felt certain you would acquit yourself well."

"And what do you think?"

"That more experience is required to render a fair judgment."

His smile flashed white in the darkness. "I shall do my

best to oblige you."

She searched his face, which was half hidden in the night shadows. "I've been yours all along. Why did you not assert your husbandly rights long before now?"

"You belong only to yourself." His fingertips traced over her cheekbone. "I would never presume to own you."

"Most men believe their wives are chattel."

"I know better." His lips moved to her ear. "That leaves seduction as my only recourse for winning you over."

The pace of her heartbeats increased. "That sounds very wicked."

"Doesn't it?" he said, tonguing the outer rim of her ear.

She almost squealed from the sensation, so deliciously intense it was unbearable. "But proper Sebastian is never wicked."

His tongue flicked inside her ear. "I plan to be exceedingly so in the next few minutes."

"We're in my father's garden," she said, breathless with excitement.

"Let's hope Lady Hervey doesn't make another unexpected appearance." He slipped his hand inside her bodice. "Because that would truly ignite a scandal the *ton* won't soon forget."

...

"Is it straight?" Bella tilted her head. "Perhaps a little higher on the left." She instructed two footmen positioning the massive painting that had just been delivered.

"Very impressive." Sebastian walked up behind her, dressed in a casual style for riding, gloves in hand. "Is that one of Will's works?"

"Yes, isn't it magnificent?"

"Absolutely." He wasn't looking at the painting though, but rather straight at her with clear green eyes that flickered with more than just polite interest. His smooth caramel skin shone against the bright white of his shirt. Stone-colored breeches skimmed masculine hips, and the strong thighs she now knew flexed masterfully when he was in the throes of passion.

Her insides stirred with pleasure. The past few days had passed in a happy haze. Josette had not been mistaken about his virility. Sebastian came to her bed every evening, staying through the night. Sometimes they awakened in the drowsy dark of night to make love before drifting back to sleep, only to take their pleasure again in the morning before rising to begin the day.

Everything would be perfect if not for her lingering doubts—the secret bank account and the Traherne properties Sebastian had acquired for half their value. Yet she'd begun to believe there must be a reasonable explanation for his questionable business practices. More and more, she couldn't conceive of Sebastian behaving in a deceitful manner. She would ask him soon, but resisted the idea of doing so immediately. She didn't want anything to disturb the cloud of bliss she'd floated on since they'd become lovers as well as husband and wife. Even if it was all just an illusion, she wanted to enjoy this dream for a bit longer.

She turned her attention back to the painting. "Your brother sent it over as a wedding gift. Is it straight, do you think?"

Sebastian studied Will's latest work of a young lady

walking in the park. She appeared to have been captured in motion, her gleaming hair swaying in the breeze, eyes lively and alert. At the same time, the lush colors and generous strokes imbued the painting with certain sensuality. "It appears so."

Bella dismissed the footmen with a firm thank you. "I debated whether to place it in one of the public reception rooms, but I opted for the family sitting room so we can enjoy it at our leisure every day."

"An excellent choice." He came to her and pulled Bella into his arms, lowering his mouth to nuzzle her neck.

She sighed happily, giving him better access to a sensitive spot he'd become quite expert at tending to. "Sir, this is most inappropriate. Our guest will be here at any moment."

"Orford does seem to be constantly underfoot."

"I'm not speaking of Orford or any of our other houseguests. Your mother is coming for tea."

He released her. "I see. Well, enjoy your visit." He walked into the foyer, calling for the butler. "Has my mount been readied?"

"Of course, sir. I'll have him brought around." Davison gestured to the footman who silently slipped away.

Surprised and disappointed by the abrupt deprivation of his masculine attentions, Bella followed. "Where are you going? Your mother will arrive at any moment."

He pulled on his gloves, the polite mask on his face devoid of any genuine expression or emotion. "I'm sorry, my dear, you'll have to entertain my lady mother on your own."

"What engagement is so pressing that you cannot be here to receive your mother?"

"I am riding with Pen in the park."

Pressing her lips together, she glanced at Davison. "Leave us please." The butler bowed and left. "You mentioned nothing of this plan to ride with Pen when I informed you of your mother's visit this morning."

"I don't direct your movements, Duchess." He dropped a kiss on her cheek and made for the door. "Nor do you manage mine."

She blew out a breath. "This is your mother we are discussing, not some visitor of little significance. We have not received her here. It is well past time that we do."

He pulled open the front door. "I don't stand on ceremony with Mrs. Stanhope and neither should you."

She followed him out. "You are beyond exasperating. It is shameful to treat one's mother with so little respect."

Several loading wagons crowded the front of the house. The outside footman gestured down the block. "Cleatus took your mount just a ways down, sir. Her ladyship is taking delivery of the new furniture."

Sebastian turned to Bella, eyebrows raised. "Indeed?"

She returned an answering look. "You gave me carte blanche. I took the liberty of ordering a few items."

Sebastian surveyed the dozen or so workmen heaving the heavy furniture. "A few items? It appears you've decided to furnish several townhomes at once." He turned to walk toward the groom who waited with his mount up the street.

Bella fell into step beside him. "If I didn't know better, I'd think you purposely avoid your mother."

Maintaining his stride, he maneuvered around the workmen unloading the wagons. "My relationship with my mother is best left alone. It is not a subject I discuss."

She cast him a sidelong glance. Perhaps Sebastian's lack

of warmth toward his mother related to Orford's story about the truth of his parentage. Did her husband think less of his mother because of her supposed indiscretion with another man? Even if it were true, Matilda was still his mother—his true parent—and she seemed inordinately fond of him.

"Do you know how lucky you are to even have a mother? Never mind that Mother Matilda is the sweetest, kindest—"

"Enough." He strode away toward his mount. "Give my regrets to Mrs. Stanhope."

Frustrated, she walked back toward the house to find his mother's coach just arriving. Greeting her mother-in-law, she ushered her inside where they settled on a sofa and took tea in the front parlor.

"I am sorry Sebastian could not attend us this afternoon," she said as their visit drew to a close. "He had a previous engagement."

Smiling, Matilda reached over to pat Bella's hand. "No need to explain, my dear."

She swallowed, uncomfortable with the lie, but feeling compelled to continue it in order to spare Matilda's feelings. "I am certain he regrets missing this lovely visit."

Matilda's measuring gaze fell on her. "Sebastian does as he must. There is no need to feel any discomfort on my behalf. I understand, truly, I do."

"Well I don't." Emotion swelled in Bella's chest. "He should realize how fortunate he is to have a mother at all, especially one as lovely as you."

"You really are a dear." Matilda offered that gentle smile of hers. "No one can replace your true mother, but I do hope you will come to regard me with some affection."

Bella gripped Matilda's hand, the long-held pain of

missing a mother's tenderness flared in her. "I am grateful. I don't understand why Sebastian is not. Why does he treat you so?"

"You must ask your husband."

"Ask me what?" Sebastian stood on the threshold.

Matilda's face softened, warmth infusing it. "Sebastian, what a lovely surprise."

He executed a quick bow, the kind one would give an acquaintance. "Madam."

Bella's eyes rounded. "I thought you were riding in the park with Pen."

Maintaining a formal posture, Sebastian took a seat on the sofa opposite them. "We cut our ride short. I thought you might require some assistance in directing furniture placement."

Matilda's eyes shone with obvious maternal adoration. "I saw the items being delivered when I arrived. Are you redecorating? That is delightful. Which chambers do you plan to change?"

Sebastian accepted a glass of lemon mineral water from a footman. "It is my wife's project. You'd best direct your inquiries to her."

A brief moment of vulnerability shone in Matilda's face before her composure slipped firmly back into place. "Of course," she said turning to Bella. "You must tell me everything, my dear." Anxious to ease the obvious tension in the room, Bella obliged and they spent the remainder of the visit discussing the changes she hoped to make to the house.

When the visit came to an end, Bella escorted Matilda out onto the doorstep while Sebastian remained behind in the entry hall. "Forgive me if I overstepped earlier," Bella said to her mother-in-law.

"You have not," Matilda assured her as the footman handed her up into her conveyance. "You never could. Sebastian is as happy as I have ever seen him and I believe you are the reason for that."

Bella warmed at the thought. After seeing Matilda off, she returned to find Sebastian waiting for her. "I attended tea with my mother," he said. "I hope you are pleased."

"At least you shared your presence, if not your affection."

He pulled her into the nearest doorway, closing the door behind him. "If it is affection you want, allow me to show it to you in the fullest."

Her heart accelerated. "Sebastian, someone might come upon us."

His mouth trailed down her throat. "Such a pity. I should like to take you right here."

"Truly? Is that done?"

"Most assuredly." His lips captured hers. The kiss was long and thorough, both tender and erotic. "I would turn you over that chair and take you from behind."

"From behind?" She licked his lips and he opened for her. She delved inside the sweet cavern of his mouth, the taste of lemon swirled. "Would I like that?"

"I believe you would. Very much." His tongue moved into her mouth for an unhurried, heated kiss. "First, I would toss up your skirts and look at that part of you that no other man will ever see."

A rush of heat engulfed her. "And then?"

"I might taste you there until you reach your pleasure."

"Sebastian!" The idea shocked her, but her womanhood clenched with excitement at the promise of such wanton delight. The image of Lady Hawke flashed in her mind, intruding like a bucket of cold water being dumped on her. Had he done that with his paramour?

He detected the change in her. "What is amiss?"

She shook her head and kissed him again. "Nothing."

He pulled back, his penetrating gaze on her. "No lies, remember? You promised to tell me of any misgivings."

"Did you do…that with Lady Hawke?"

His expression stiffened and she watched as he visibly tried to relax it. "Why does it matter?"

"She was your only woman before me. And she seems so…experienced in these matters."

"Her sexual prowess is undeniable. And, yes, there was very little of a carnal nature that we left unexplored during our liaison."

Pain ached in her chest. She could never compete with a sensual predator like that silver-eyed temptress.

He held her tight. "Where do you think you are going?"

"I'm sure to bore you."

"You could never bore me," he said softly. "What I experienced with Jacinda was purely physical."

"Are you saying you didn't enjoy it?"

"Oh no, I enjoyed it." When she tried to pull away, his large hands tightened around her waist, holding her fast. "I was a university buck with no experience when Jacinda introduced me to bed sport. Any randy boy would have been in raptures."

"I see." She knew she sounded petulant but didn't care. "Your paramour's charms are undeniable, but you resist them only because you feel honor bound to remain true to your drab, little wife."

He chuckled. "My *former* paramour. And you are anything but drab, as you well know." He held her chin with a gentle touch, forcing her to look him in the eye. "Any bawd could play Jacinda's role. No one can fill yours. What we have between us is beyond the carnal. You are my love."

Her heart jumped. *His love.* Did he love her? He lowered his mouth to hers and kissed her with deep, tender strokes. Sensual agitation swept her body. "What is to stop us from locking the door?"

He smiled against her mouth. "Nothing at all."

A tap sounded and the door swung open revealing Orford on the threshold. "There you are, my dear."

Disappointment panged through her. She forced a smile when Josette and Tabby materialized behind him.

Josette's knowing look flitted from Bella to Sebastian. "I hope we do not interrupt."

Sebastian inclined his head. "Of course not."

Tabby's eyes went immediately to Will's painting. "How lovely." She hurried past Josette and Orford to view it up close, examining it almost with reverence. "Magnificent. Look at the fullness of the strokes. It appears almost as though the artist did not give it much thought, but the overall effect suggests that is not true at all."

Bella stole a glance at Sebastian and held his eyes for a moment. "It is a wedding gift from my brother in marriage, William Stanhope."

"Remarkable," said Tabby. "I am such an admirer of his work."

Sebastian dragged his eyes away from Bella. "Perhaps we should invite him to take supper with us one evening soon."

Tabby's eyes lit up. "That is most kind of you, sir. I would enjoy meeting your brother above all things."

"Shall we take a turn in the park?" Orford asked. "The weather is ideal. If you are otherwise engaged, Stanhope, I shall be happy to escort the ladies."

Sebastian cut an amused look in Orford's direction. "That is most generous of you. I do have to meet with my man of affairs so I reluctantly leave these lovely ladies to you."

"Are you certain?" asked Bella. "Can you not accompany us for a quick walkabout?"

Sebastian brought her hand to his mouth, letting his warm lips linger against her skin longer than courtesy dictated. "I'm certain." His eyes held hers. "Until later, my lady."

Her heart fluttered. She could hardly wait to be alone with him. She felt a pang of guilt for wishing her friends were no longer staying with them. She wanted Sebastian all to herself, without interruption or the obligation of seeing to guests.

A few minutes later they stepped into the overcast afternoon. Orford turned to offer his arm to Bella, but Josette looped her arm through Bella's first. With polite nonchalance, Orford turned and offered Tabby his arm instead. They took the lead, strolling ahead, with Bella and Josette trailing behind. Monty—who had taken his leave two days prior—was missing from their group.

"Where did Monty say he was off to?" asked Bella.

Tabby looked back over her shoulder. "Something about attending to estate matters. He's to return in a sennight."

"Estate matters?" Bella looked at Josette. "He has a

property that needs tending? Is that finally a clue about Monty's true identity?"

Josette shrugged. "The gentleman prefers mystery. That is his affair." She gave Bella a knowing look. "I am more interested in this glow you have about you these days."

Heat filled Bella's face. She looked ahead at Tabby and Orford, grateful that they'd pulled far enough ahead not to overhear the conversation. "What do you mean?"

"Your husband has introduced you to the pleasures of the marriage bed, no?"

Bella smiled. She could talk to Josette about almost anything. "You were right," she admitted. "It is very nice."

Mischief sparkled in Josette's eyes. "And nature has endowed him, has it not?"

"Josette! I cannot discuss that with you." She dipped her chin. "Not that I have anything to compare it to, but I will say I haven't been disappointed in any way."

"That is excellent. Now you must keep him interested."

"Keep him interested?"

"*Bien sûr.* There are many ways for a lady to please her man in the marriage bed."

There were? "Tell me all of them." She was determined to learn everything about the sensual arts. Anything to banish that she-wolf Lady Hawke from Sebastian's mind. Josette happily proceeded to oblige Bella's curiosity, in the most excruciating detail, leaving Bella both shocked and fascinated by the time they turned into the park.

A group of young bucks and ladies had set up a game of skittles. Pausing to watch, Orford and Tabby turned back toward them. "Are you up for Skittles?

Josette clapped her hands with delight. "Oh, let's do."

They joined the group. After several games, Bella found a bench to rest on for a moment, and Orford joined her. They watched with amusement as Tabby and Josette struggled to outdo each other.

"Kind, gentle Tabby is a tiger," remarked Orford. "Who would have guessed it?"

Bella smiled. "She has the heart of a competitor."

"And you, Bella, where is your heart these days?"

Watching her friends at play, she brushed back a tendril that had escaped her bonnet. "It is with my husband."

Orford stilled. "I sensed that was the case."

"I know you will think I am foolish." Emotion roiled in her chest. "In truth, I am confused. He seems all that is good and kind and yet—"

He finished the thought for her. "You cannot forget about the monies he takes from Traherne."

"I know I shall have to confront him, but perhaps he has a reasonable explanation. Everyone seems to hold him in the highest esteem."

Orford sighed. "I did not want to burden you with this, but it seems I must, if only to protect you."

"What do you mean?"

"There is a clause in your marriage contract that awards a generous portion to Sebastian once you beget an heir."

"Oh, yes." She waved a dismissive hand. "I am aware. But if he were interested solely in the money, he would have taken me to the marriage bed years ago."

"According to our friendly solicitor's clerk, there is an expiration date on that clause. If you haven't born a son within the next twelve months, that portion of the contract is void."

She pushed the hovering doubts from her mind. "It seems foolish for him to have waited all of these years only to press his advantage now, at the eleventh hour."

"You must harden your heart against him before he devastates you with his debauchery."

"Debauchery?" She stood, not wanting to hear more. "Really, Orford, you go too far."

He came to his feet as well. "It is more than just the money he has stolen from you." He threaded his hands through his artful curls, which he set each night to achieve the high style of the day. "He is not true to you."

"Yes, he is. I asked him of bawds. There are none. You can inquire all about London. No one has ever heard of my husband keeping a peculiar."

"That's because he dallies with servants."

Her heart slammed to a stop. "Beg pardon?"

"He dallies with them and when they get with child, he sends them away."

An ache stirred in the recesses of Bella's belly. "You must be mistaken."

"There is a young maid in the Marquess of Camryn's home. They say she is a beauty that he got with child. She is just six and ten."

A young servant in Camryn's house. The image of the lovely young serving girl in Sebastian's arms rushed back in a powerful burst of memory, stealing the strength from her body. She sank back down on the bench with quivering legs, feeling numb, foolish, and betrayed all over again. "How can you know this?"

He sat beside her. "I make it my business to protect you. I've made discreet inquiries. They say Stanhope came and departed with the young girl."

"Took her away?" Bella fought to breathe. "To where?"

"There is apparently a place he takes them when he is done enjoying their favors." He took her hand. "I am so sorry, darling."

"Them." Flicks of light danced in her vision. "There are many of them?"

"He is said to have taken several bastards there."

Bella pushed to her feet, trying to firm her trembling legs. "I must return home."

"You mean to confront him?" Concern creased his forehead. "There is nothing to be gained from it."

"Perhaps not. Are you coming?"

"Of course, dear." He offered his arm and his unrelenting support. Summoning Tabby and Josette, he signaled it was time to depart. Bella set a brisk pace for the walk home. Her husband had asked her to come to him with any concerns about his fidelity and she fully intended to. She herself had witnessed his instances of inappropriate intimacy with servant girls, as well as the mysterious robustness of his bank account. It could not all be happenstance. The time had come for her to face the reality of her circumstances.

She returned home to find Sebastian in the ballroom with his fencing instructor. She watched for a moment, both fuming and aching. He moved swiftly—not quite with grace, for his powerful physique did not have the lean elegance for that—but with relentless assuredness, as though he had no doubt of the outcome. He'd removed his shirt and wore only black breeches.

His eyes warmed when he spotted her and called the action to a stop. Chatting in French with the instructor, he cut the lesson short.

"Do not let me intrude," she said stiffly.

"It is no intrusion. Pierre was preparing to take his leave in a matter of minutes any way."

The fencing instructor acknowledged her as he gathered his things. "Indeed, my lady, I have another appointment." He hurried from the room, closing the door behind him.

Sebastian moved toward a towel on a nearby bench and toweled off his face, neck, and chest. Bella swallowed. Even now, she found him physically arresting. To her, he was all that was beautiful in a man. He guzzled his lemon water, the sinews of his throat moving as he swallowed. He watched her watching him. Putting the glass down, his clear eyes flickered with intent. "May I be of service?"

"No, not in that way." The words escaped in a harsher tone than she'd intended.

"Have I displeased you in some way?"

"I don't know. Have you?"

He walked toward her, slow and deliberate, his eyes assessing. He came to a stop behind her. "You haven't even removed your pelisse." His soft breath brushed her ear. "Allow me."

She acquiesced, allowing him relieve her of her outer garment. "I was anxious to see you."

He nuzzled her ear. "I am gratified."

She shivered. "But not for this." When his hands moved to the back closures of her dress, she made no move to stop him.

"How disappointing," he murmured, his lips brushing the back of her neck. "I shall endeavor to convince you otherwise."

Her dress loosened, and she could feel him working on her stays. A cool rush of air caressed her skin as the bodice drooped open in front. He pushed it down her arms in a slow, deliberate motion, the warmth of his strong hands skimming the sensitive bare skin. The gown picked up momentum and rushed to the floor, as though it too couldn't resist doing Sebastian's bidding.

She swallowed. "You said I should come directly to you if I had any questions."

"Yes." Moving around until he faced her, he loosened her stays and pulled them off, leaving her clad in only her shift, stockings, and slippers.

"You say you have been faithful."

Kneeling before her, his hands did a sensual slide around her hips to caress her bottom. He nuzzled her womanhood through her thin shift. A clenching heat scorched her insides.

"Most assuredly." He pulled away and raised her foot to slip off her shoe. His hands slid with slow purpose up her stocking, coming to a stop when his fingers brushed the bare skin of her thigh. He rolled the stocking down.

She lifted her foot to allow him to pull the stocking off, the silk whispered down her leg. "You claim there are no ladybirds."

He repeated the same motions on her other leg. "None."

"Not even servants."

He rose to his feet. "Of course not." He looked around. "The floor will not do. It will cause you too much discomfort. Come." He led her to a bench at the side of the cavernous room. She went, hungry for the truth but at the same time famished for him. Facing her, he lifted the hem of her shift.

She raised her arms to allow him to pull it off over her

head. "I have heard otherwise."

His eyes gleamed with appreciation at the sight of her bare body. He ran his hands over her shoulders, down to her breasts. He cupped the tender globes with warm, enticing hands, his thumbs caressing the points. "Have you? From whom, may I ask?"

Her eyes shuttered as her head fell back. It was as if the sun's strongest rays pulsated inside of her. She hated herself for being a slave to the explosive sensations he incited in her. Struggling for sanity, she forced hers eyes open. "Does it matter who informed me?"

His hands left her breasts. He removed his breeches in quick, efficient movements. His member emerged pointing, swollen and demanding. He sat on the bench and tried to turn Bella to face him. She resisted, anxious to hold on to her anger. Chuckling, and with her back still facing him, Sebastian eased her down onto his lap, slipping inside her from behind.

"If I am to be impugned, I should know my accuser." His large hands wrapped around her hips. He eased her up and down his hardened flesh, showing her the motion.

She caught the rhythm almost immediately and began to move of her own accord. Up and down, caught up in the delicious slide of sensation. She struggled to follow the conversation. "Orford says there is a servant girl in Camryn's household who is with child."

"Susan. Yes, I know of her situation." His breathing quickened as he worked inside of her. "The question is, how does Orford know of it?"

"What does that matter?" Jealous anger sparked in her again. She moved faster and harder. "I saw you with her."

His hands massaged her shoulders as he stroked in and out of her. "Did you?

She groaned from his ministrations and with frustration. And came down harder on him. "Yes, you were embracing her."

His hands crept around to her breasts. He kneaded them with a gentle touch. "And from this you deduce I am the father of her bastard?"

She yanked up off him and stood up, turning around to face him. "Do you deny it?"

He gazed over her body with eyes the color of a turbulent ocean before a mammoth storm. "Yes, I do deny it. On my honor, I am not the father of Susan's child." His hand slipped around her waist, warm and certain. He eased her back onto his engorged, glistening flesh. Her body leached onto his, clenching around his hard heat. This time she straddled him so they faced each other. Perspiration trickling down her back, she picked up the primal movements again. Massaging her bottom, he helped her move. "But you took her away."

He slid his long fingers to the sensitive place between her legs. Her body trembled as waves of exquisite sensation peaked and surged. "Yes, I helped her. She and her bastard need assistance." He watched her face, his eyes intent on hers, his voice rough with exertion. "Otherwise, she'll end up selling her body and the babe could end up in an even more dire situation."

"And there are others?" she asked panting, accelerating her movements atop him.

A primordial sound escaped him. He arched into her and held for a moment, as if trying to regain some semblance of control over his body. "Yes," he rasped. "I help those who are in need of my assistance."

She gave him a moment, savoring the fullness inside of her, and then began to move with more urgency—back-and-forth movements that became increasingly demanding and insistent. She could barely manage any words. "And they are nothing to you?"

His answer was almost a groan as he moved with her. "Not in the way you mean, no."

"Why do you help them?" Before he could answer, sensation rushed in and she spiraled away on a blinding swell of pleasure. She felt him follow her and they peaked together. He convulsed and stilled for a final time, pouring himself into her.

She realized she'd wrapped her arms tight around him. His cheek pressed against the swell of her breast. They were bound together.

"I help them because they are bastards," he said. "As am I."

Chapter Fourteen

Bella froze, unsure she'd heard him correctly. Drawing back, she searched his face.

He returned her gaze, unwavering. "Surely you will have heard the rumors."

"I didn't credit it."

His hands smoothed over her back in gentle motions. They were still intimately connected. "Even though I look completely different from my brothers?"

She cupped his strong face. "You have the same eyes."

"True. Come now, you've asked for the truth. Are you not stouthearted enough to hear it? Have you changed your mind?"

"I have not changed my mind."

"I first heard the term bastard at the age of nine from some children at a harvest celebration." A reluctant smile curved his lips. "When Cam and Edward learned of it, they taught those boys a lesson they did not soon forget. But I asked my father afterward and he became very angry. He said I was a cross the Lord had sent for him to bear. Matilda came to my rescue. She took me away before he could beat me."

Her heart stung for him. She longed to hold him close, to comfort the child he had been. "Did your mother always protect you from his temper?"

His hand slid from her back around to caress one of her breasts. "Always. Cyrus was not a warm man with any of his sons, but he saved a special disdain for me. I cannot remember a time when I did not feel his blatant disregard." He toyed with the tip of her breast in an almost absentminded fashion, his unseeing gaze locked on the faraway place of his childhood. "But Matilda favored me. Even my brothers understood I maintained a special place in her affections. And when I was older, I realized why."

Running her hands through his mass of sable curls, she leaned forward to place a tender kiss on his temple. "Why?"

"It became obvious to me" — pain tinged the clear green of his eyes— "that I must be the product of a love affair with a man who was not her husband, a dark-skinned man of average height such as I, not a tall, fair-haired man like Cyrus."

"Perhaps your mother sought some warmth. You say your father…Cyrus…was a cold man."

"Not with Matilda. He adored her." His hand moved to her other breast, weighing it, shaping it. "That's the irony of it. He was entirely devoted to her. I'll never understand how she could betray him."

She ran her hands over the smooth musculature of his brawny shoulders. "One never knows what really occurs in a marriage. Perhaps he strayed."

He snorted. "Not Cyrus Stanhope. You could not have met a more pious, upstanding gentleman."

"He gamed with my father. He could not have been perfect."

"It was the only lapse I can remember." He leaned forward to kiss her breast. "And thank God for that, for it brought you to me."

"I must say that explains why you avoid your mother."

He exhaled, toying with a stand of her hair. "I find I cannot look at her without thinking of her dishonorable behavior. And she always gave the appearance of being completely devoted to my father. People would scoff at the notion she could stray. But here I sit, living proof of her deceit."

She thought of Sebastian's mother, a woman who emanated kindness, generosity and, above all, decency. "I cannot imagine your mother cuckolding her husband. She does not appear the type."

"Would you like to see where I take them?"

"Hmm?" she said absently, distracted by the way the sun glinted across his dark curls. "I'm very grateful to your true father, whoever he is, because he is the reason you are here."

He smiled, running his hands up her bare flanks. "Have you forgotten the reason for your anger? The servants."

She had forgotten. She leaned forward to give him a lingering, openmouthed kiss, savoring his masculine taste with its lemony tang. "I am still quite angry about all of your servant girls." He remained inside of her and she moved experimentally just for the fun of it, and in an effort to draw him away from the dark memories of his parents.

He laughed, his eyes shining with appreciation. "You minx." Kissing her with firm finality, he lifted her gingerly off his softened male flesh and bent to retrieve her shift before standing. "Get dressed. I have something to show you."

She flashed him a deliberately naughty look. "I can't wait."

Pushing to his feet in one powerful motion, he laughed again and helped her pull her shift over her head. "It's nothing like that, but it will answer all of your questions."

...

They took the carriage to Bloomsbury in Central London, an area unfamiliar to her.

"What is that?" she asked pointing to a large building off the main square.

"That's the Gray's Inn Society. It was originally built as a place for barristers to live." He looked beyond Gray's Inn. "But that is what we are here to see."

Their carriage came to a halt inside a large circular enclosure, which contained three sizable buildings. The generous courtyard in the middle was brimming with children laughing and running. Some older children were in an organized line walking into one of the structures. They all dressed in similar clothing, a uniform of sorts.

"What is this place?" Bella asked, stepping down from the carriage. Sebastian waved the footman away to help her down himself.

"Its official name is the Stanhope-Wentworth Home for Foundlings. People here call it the foundling home."

"Foundlings?" She stopped abruptly, the amazement

plain in her voice. "It bears our name. Do you finance it?"

He offered his arm and urged her forward. "*We* do. Hence the name."

"You use Traherne funds here?" Hope flowered in her heart. Perhaps this explained the monies he'd taken from ducal coffers.

"In a manner of speaking. I use the allowance the estate grants me as your husband. It had accumulated since we married." Disappointment stabbed at her. These children, then, were not the reason Sebastian was withdrawing a thousand pounds from estate accounts each month.

Walking across the courtyard, they were waylaid by an urchin. "Mr. Sebastian, Mr. Sebastian. Will you come and play cricket with us?"

He smiled at the red-haired boy, kindness shone in his face. "I will, Billy, but it must be later. For now, my lady desires a tour of the home. Can you offer a bow for Lady Mirabella?"

The boy dipped awkwardly. "How do, my lady."

Bella smiled. "It is lovely to know you, Willie."

He grinned back. "Enjoy your tour," he called running back to join his friends.

"They know you."

"I try to visit weekly. We have almost two hundred children residing here at present. Many more, the youngest babes, are sent to live with wet nurses in the country until they reach the age of four or five."

"But this must cost a fortune."

"I do have my own funds, my dear. I've partnered with Cam in a number of factories. I have other business ventures that have returned handsome rewards."

Such as the properties he'd purchased from the duchy for a scandalously low price.

He gestured to the two buildings on either side of the courtyards. "The children are housed in these two buildings. Boys in one, girls in the other."

"How do they come to be here?"

"They are almost all baseborn. Sometimes the parent brings them; sometimes it is other family members. We don't ask any questions of them. We record the date of arrival. If a parent leaves a token or special remembrance for the child, we catalog it. We also note what they were wearing when presented to us."

"How long do they stay?"

"At fourteen, the boys are sent to apprentice in various trades so they will be able to make their own way. Some who show an aptitude for learning are sent to school."

"And the girls?"

"At age sixteen, they are sent to apprentice as servants for at least four years. Most stay on with their employers once the apprenticeship comes to an end."

"My maid, Louisa, she is one of your foundlings?"

"Yes, Louisa came to us older than most, at age eight, but she was a quick learner and anxious to please. She apprenticed with Charlotte's lady's maid. Afterward, I placed her in our household to serve you."

"And the footmen?"

"Foundlings all, as are most of the staff except for Davison and Mrs. Nagle."

"That explains their extreme devotion to you." It took a singular man to save so many from a wretched life on the streets. She pointed to the third structure at the far end of the courtyard. "And that?"

"That holds the rest of the answers you seek. Come," he said steering her toward the far building.

They entered to a large open room. While not exactly spartan, the chamber's furnishings were practical and unembellished giving the room an air of clean simplicity. There were no children present, only young women, although some still looked like girls, appearing no more than thirteen or fourteen years of age. It did not appear obvious at first glance, but both girls contained the round figures of impending motherhood. Bella's eyes went to a sewing circle where the women appeared to be working on uniforms she'd seen the children in the courtyard wearing. All of their bodies were ripe and rounded, showing obvious signs of what had brought them here.

"They are all increasing."

He followed her gaze. "Yes. This is the home for unwed mothers. They stay here until their babies are born. The children are sent to wet nurses in the country, and their mothers attempt to return to the work they left behind."

A rustle of fabric and soft lilting laugh turned Bella's attention to one of the women who had risen from the sewing circle to retrieve more fabric. With her dark luminous hair and eyes, the girl possessed exceptional beauty. Recognition clicked in Bella's brain as her eyes slid to the obvious signs the girl was increasing, her thick stomach at odds with an otherwise slim form.

"Susan." The servant girl she'd seen in Sebastian's arms at Camryn's townhome.

"Yes."

"Was she one of your foundlings?"

"Yes. And now, regrettably, returns with her own foundling."

"She's so lovely." She said it without jealousy. Susan's beauty was obvious to anyone with eyes.

His face dimmed. "Yes, that is what made her a likely target for some scoundrel. I thought Susan would be safe when we placed her in Cam's home." He made a sound of disgust. "She refuses to reveal the father. We only know that he is a gentleman. Even now she protects the scapegrace."

She sucked in a breath. "Someone of quality did this to her?"

"Clearly not someone of quality, but yes, a supposed gentleman."

"Have you asked Cam if he knows anything?"

"He and Charlotte are just as baffled. They were away in the country when the girl got with child."

Susan spotted them, her remarkable face brightening at the sight of Sebastian. She hurried forward, still graceful despite the large burden of the child she carried. "Mr. Sebastian. How good of you to visit."

"Susan, you look well."

The way Susan flushed and cast her eyes downward made her look achingly young and fragile. "Despite my shame, I am thriving here. Thank you for bringing me."

"There is someone I want you to meet." He touched his hand to Bella's lower back. "Susan, this is my lady."

Susan turned her attention to Bella, and dipped into a low curtsy. "My lady." She gave a shy smile. "We are all so pleased Mr. Sebastian's lady wife has come home at last."

Bella felt a rush of protectiveness toward the girl. She possessed an innocent, childlike quality so at odds with her stunning beauty. It was a combination a ruthless rake could easily take advantage of. The very idea infuriated her. "May I ask when your babe will come?"

"I am six months gone with child, my lady."

"Susan, am I the father of your child?" Sebastian asked abruptly.

Red suffused the girl's face, her distress apparent. "You know you are not, sir. You would never take such liberties." She cast an almost accusing look at Bella. "Everyone knows Mr. Sebastian is too good to do something like that."

"I do know it," Bella assured her before hitting him with a hard look. "That was unnecessary."

"Perhaps," Sebastian said idly. "But I felt it best to put the issue to rest. One never knows when Orphus will make another accusation."

Bella bristled. "You are well aware that his name is Orford. And he is only looking out for my best interests."

"I think he is looking out for his own selfish interests."

"Orford?" The sharp tone in Susan's voice caught their attention, forcing Bella and Sebastian to abandon their bickering. "Cary Orford?"

Surprised, Bella said, "Why yes."

"Do you know Orford, Susan?"

Obvious anger pointed Susan's features. "Did he accuse you of fathering my child?"

"He suggested the possibility to my wife. Your refusal to name the father has given rise to unfortunate rumors about my character. Some believe you protect the gentleman out of a misplaced fondness for him."

"I am not fond of my child's father." Bitterness laced Susan's voice. "And Mr. Orford knows it."

The hair on Bella's neck tingled. "How exactly do you know Mr. Orford, Susan?"

Susan chewed her lip. "He said no one would believe me."

Bella's chest constricted. "Orford?"

An angry energy simmered beneath Sebastian's controlled surface. "I believe you, Susan." He laid a gentle hand on the girl's arm. "Pray tell us the truth."

Her dark eyes glistened with unshed emotion. "Mr. Orford is the father of my child. He told me I was special. He brought gifts and promised many things. He said my pleasing appearance could bring me a much better life than that of a serving girl."

The words barely penetrated for Bella. It sounded like ocean waves were breaking in her ears. Orford? How could it be? The revelation hit her like a wallop to the stomach. He wasn't only a liar, but a cad who took ruthless advantage of innocent girls. "How did you make his acquaintance?"

Susan brushed away tears in a quick rough motion. "He came to call on his lordship, but the marquess was away to the country. I'd returned from an errand. Mr. Orford was leaving from the front stairs. He spoke to me all nice like. Asked a lot of questions."

"What sorts of questions?"

"He wanted to know all about you, sir."

"What precisely?"

"Whether you took Cyprians to your bed." She flashed an apologetic look at Bella. "Pardon the language, my lady."

Bella swallowed down the heat burning her chest. She couldn't wait to get her hands on Orford. "It is quite all right. Please go on."

"He came around a lot after that. Always seemed to be there when the housekeeper, Mrs. Peters, sent me on an errand. He began to turn up on my day off. It started with walks, but then we went for a picnic and he…I…" She shook her head.

"It is all right, Susan, you don't have to share all of the particulars with us," Sebastian said.

Susan's eyes met his and she seemed to find strength in his steady gaze. Taking a breath, she continued, lowering her voice so as not be overheard. "Afterward, he said I could be the finest courtesan, that the best gentlemen would want me." Her voice trembled. "He would handle the money matters, he would take half and give me half. Said he deserved some coin for his efforts."

"Naturally," said Sebastian, his voice dry.

"I thought he had a care for me." She knuckled away the tears in her eyes. "Mr. Orford wanted to set me up in a house and bring gentleman callers there. He expected to continue to enjoy my favors while I did…that…with other men who would pay."

"And when he learned you were with child?" Bella asked gently.

"He was so angry. He said he didn't want a babe off a whore. Mr. Orford told me he plans to marry a great lady very soon."

Fury curled Bella's fists, her nails digging painfully into the flesh of her palm. No longer able to contain herself, she erupted. "Why that scoundrel! I will take care of Mr. Orford." She pulled an obviously surprised Susan into a fierce embrace. "He will not be allowed to get away with this. I promise you that."

...

Noting Bella's strident steps in the direction of their waiting coach, Sebastian surmised his wife had decided to cut the tour short.

"You should have broken his perfect nose when you had the chance at Gentleman Jack's," she said without breaking her stride. "It would have served him right, the blackguard."

"You're quite right. I should have. I only restrained myself because I knew it would upset you."

"If only you had knocked out some teeth while you were at it, marred that handsome face of his."

He'd be happy to oblige. When he had the chance, he planned to pummel Orford within an inch of his life. "You are a bloodthirsty thing, aren't you? Remind me not to get on your bad side." He caught her in his arms, interrupting her determined gait. "Handsome? So you think Orford is appealing?"

Clearly not in the mood for games, she wriggled loose. Pity. His body stirred at the fire in her eyes and the intense energy undulating off her.

"Aren't you going to say I told you so?" she snapped. "You've always taken Orford for a cad." She halted in front of the coach and allowed him to hand her up.

He climbed in behind Bella, settling across her in the backward-facing seat. "No need to. You just did."

She eyed him. "How can you be so calm? Aren't you beyond furious? He ruined that poor, sweet girl."

"Control is something I have had to cultivate my entire life." He allowed a grim smile. "Being the bastard son, it was imperative that I be perfect."

Her face softened. "Truly?"

Sebastian shifted his gaze toward the window. "I felt if I excelled in everything, then, perhaps, my father would be better able to bear my presence."

Her tone lost all of its anger. "Did it help?"

"No, it seemed to make him angrier. I think he would have gained satisfaction in my being a colossal failure."

"He was cruel. I wish I had met him. I'd have at him for treating you so."

"My Amazon warrior." He smiled at her. "Perhaps this is not the ideal time to discuss this matter, but I received word of important news while you were on your walk with your friends."

"What is it?" she asked without particular interest, still appearing distracted and shaken by the revelation about Orford.

"It concerns the man who attacked Tabby."

Her gaze sharpened. "That beast Dominick Howard? What of him?"

"It seems he offended one person too many. Howard succumbed after a duel yesterday morning near Primrose Hill."

"How did it happen?"

"A dispute over an insult to a man's mount."

"He died as a result of a disagreement over horseflesh? Surely you jest."

"And it might interest you to know who finished Howard off."

She learned forward. "Who is this hero who cut down that useless cur?"

"None other than Baron Edgemont."

Her eyes widened. "Tabby's long-ago betrothed?"

"Satisfying his honor, I expect. Howard did him a grave insult in ruining his intended."

Bella sat back against the squabs in a huff. "Trust a gentleman to make a woman's pain all about him and his honor."

"He didn't publicly shame Lady Tabitha by naming her as the reason for the duel. Hence, the claimed insult against the baron's mount. Apparently, Howard said something untoward about the steed."

"I don't care how it happened. At least Tabby will be forever spared from Howard's disgusting attentions." Her expression turned contemplative. "I should tell her before she hears of it elsewhere. Poor Tabby. To learn of this and Orford's deceit at the same time."

The coach pulled up to their townhome and Bella alighted quickly, rushing up the stairs. She paced into the foyer, pulling off her pelisse, and handing it off to Davison, who passed it to a waiting footman. "Welcome home, sir, my lady."

Sebastian handed his overcoat to the footman. "Thank you, Davison. Is Mr. Orford in residence?"

"He is, sir. He and Lady Tabitha just called for tea in the garden."

Bella charged off in the direction of the garden with Sebastian following. They found Orford sprawled in a chair, his legs propped up on a footstool. His handsome profile tilted upward to bask in the gentle sunshine, bringing to mind a lazy, self-satisfied cat.

Tabby sat across from him at her easel, frowning in

concentration as she brushed watercolors across her canvas.

Squinting against the sun, Orford turned his head at their approach, greeting them with a languorous look. "Here are our generous hosts." Seeming to take in the tension in Bella's stiff posture, Orford's questioning eyes sought hers. "Is anything amiss?"

Red flushed Bella's face. She reached over and shoved his feet off of the stool, unsettling Orford's relaxed position. He startled into a sitting position. "I say, Bella! What the—"

Fury made the golden highlights in her almond-colored eyes spark in the sun. "You are worst sort of lying cad."

Tabby's brush froze in the air. "Bella, whatever is the matter?" Her gentle face paled at Bella's obvious fury. "Whatever Orford has done, surely it cannot be that bad."

"You are wrong about that, Tabby. You have no idea what this rogue is capable of."

Orford's eyebrows shot up. "Rogue?" He flashed a disdainful look at Sebastian. "What has your husband done to convince you of my debauchery, perhaps to detract from his own?"

"Shut up, you idiot," fumed Bella. "How dare you impugn his good name with your false rumors? Sebastian has more decency in his little finger than you have in your entire worthless self."

Tabby stood up. "Bella, please calm yourself."

Sebastian went to her. "Lady Tabitha, what Bella has to say to Orford is not appropriate for a gentlewoman's ears." He offered his arm. "Do allow me to escort you inside."

"Go Tabby." Bella's harsh gaze remained fixed on Orford, color high on her cheeks. "What I have learned about Orford's character is most distressing."

Tabby's quivering mouth flattened with determination. "I am no innocent, as we are all aware. I shall stay."

Taking in her proud stance, Sebastian dipped his chin. "As you wish."

Orford shifted lazily in his seat. "Do get on with it. Tell me, what it is that I am supposed to have done that's got you all roiled up."

Bella's face twisted in anger. "What you have done to Susan is beyond despicable."

Genuine confusion clouded his eyes. "Susan?"

"Is it possible you are such a blackguard that you could ruin a girl and not even remember her name?"

Understanding flashed in Orford's eyes. "Oh, is that all? Darling, surely you are aware that it is not unusual for a gentleman to take his ease with a certain kind of woman."

Her cheeks were awash with color; her eyes shone brilliant in her outrage. She looked magnificent. "With a lightskirt, perhaps, but not an innocent like Susan. Using her like that is abominable."

"I don't know what lies Stanhope here has told you, but the girl's a wanton. She begged me for it. And since Stanhope here had already sampled her—"

"Why you—" Bella grabbed the teacup by Orford's side and flung its contents into his face.

Orford leaped to his feet. "Bella! What the devil?" Liquid dripped from his curls, dribbling down his face, splattering against the white of his shirt. "You could have scalded me. What if you had marked my face?"

"I wish I had. It would serve you right. Now, get out of my sight. You are not welcome in this house, and we are no longer friends."

"Clearly you are distraught, my dear. Once you have calmed—"

"You have one hour to pack up your things and depart. The poor girl thought you had a care for her."

His features stiffened. "That is absurd. As though I would condescend to using her as anything other than...a passing amusement."

"You, too, should know your place." Her words vibrated with fury. "And it's no longer here."

"You are the only woman for whom I have ever genuinely cared," Orford said urgently. "She means nothing to me."

"Is that supposed to make me feel better? If you do not remove yourself immediately, I'll have Davison toss you out and send your possessions to the foundling home. Is that clear?"

"Perfectly." His gaze found Sebastian's and hardened into something much colder, like a snake biding its time before it strikes. "If you will excuse me."

He ambled toward the house as though his altered circumstances were of no concern. Sebastian followed, relieved to be rid of Orford at last. But first he had his own lesson to teach the guttersnipe. His hands curled into fists. The type of lesson he had in mind was best accomplished outside the presence of ladies.

...

Bella turned to Tabby, who had gone pale. "Are you well, dear?" she asked gently. "I'm sorry you had to see that."

"I sometimes forget the true nature of men."

Bella wrapped an arm around the girl's narrow shoulders, knowing she thought of the man who had violated her. "Not all men, dearest. Sebastian and Monty would never behave thus."

Tabby shivered. "But one never knows, does one, until it is far too late."

She guided the girl back to her seat. "There is something I must tell you."

Tabby's large hazel eyes fastened on her. "Is it so very bad? You appear most serious."

Bella patted her friend's arm. "It could upset you."

Worry deepened the subtle lines in Tabby's face. "Has something happened to Monty?"

"Monty? No, Josette says he's away in the country tending to estate business."

"Then do tell me what is the matter before I have an apoplectic fit."

"It is about that scapegrace Dominick Howard."

Tabby flinched. "He hasn't found me?"

"No, of course not. He is dead. He will never harm you again."

"Dead?" The girl paled. "But how?"

"It was a duel. Edgemont challenged him."

"The baron?" Tabby whispered. "Why would he do that?"

"To avenge you most likely. You were his betrothed."

"Oh." Tabby's eyes filled with tears. "You don't think this means he still wants me, do you? I couldn't bear for any man to touch me like that."

Bella hugged her with fierce protectiveness. "He probably just wanted to satisfy his own honor."

"I hope that is the case."

Bella tightened her arms around the girl. "It doesn't matter what he wants. You are safe here with us."

"But if he comes for me—"

"Sebastian will not let him take you. Neither will Monty, for that matter."

"But they have no standing to act as my protectors."

"Nonetheless, both are the best of men who would shield you with their lives." She kissed the girl's cheek. "As would I."

...

Monty escorted Bella through the front doors of Barclay's Bank. "How do you plan to convince them to give you access to the account?"

"I have no idea," she answered, fighting her nerves. "My only plan is to act as if it is my right to retrieve the information."

"Ah, you're going to play the duchess card and intimidate it out of them." Monty chuckled. "That explains the finery."

She was dressed to awe in a silk, metallic-colored pelisse adorned with smart military-style braiding across the high neck and bodice. Full, generous sleeves tapered to a snug fit from the elbow down to velvet-trimmed wrists. Her matching bonnet, flamboyantly adorned with braiding and feathers, perched at a jaunty angle atop her head. "I've no choice but to brazen it out. Orford couldn't find a clerk willing to assist us, even though we promised a generous show of gratitude."

Monty's brows lifted. "A staff that is too honest to be bribed? Perhaps I should move my monies here."

"Another clue into the mysterious Monty," she mused, momentarily distracted. "Have an abundance of funds, do you?"

"A bit," he said easily. "Why do you not dispense with this cloak-and-sword business, and ask Sebastian directly about the funds? The two of you seem to have reached an understanding."

"We have, but that is the problem."

"Getting on well with your husband is a problem? How so?"

"I fear I've fallen too far under his spell." Guilt roiled in her chest to be going behind Sebastian's back in this way. "I'd want to believe anything he tells me. By coming here on my own, if he is innocent, I'll find proof of it independently and put the matter forever to rest."

Monty turned an eye to a man who rushed over to them as soon as they entered the lobby. "The performance begins," he said under his breath.

Bella lifted her chin and looked down her nose at the pale-faced man of middle years who approached them. "I wish to speak with the manager."

It had the desired effect. The man's chest inflated as if to match Bella's display of self-importance. "I am Mr. Roper, the manager, at your service, my lady."

He ushered them into his office, a tidy, nondescript chamber with just enough space to contain the plain wooden desk and a couple of chairs. An elaborate French-style clock hung on the wall behind the desk, the only adornment in the otherwise colorless chamber. Seating herself on a spindle-backed wooden chair opposite the desk, Bella explained her interest in the particular numbered account.

"Very good, my lady," Mr. Roper said. "I presume your name is on the account."

"Not exactly, but it is a Traherne account and I am the Traherne heiress. Consequently, the minor matter of whose name is on the account is hardly pertinent."

She held her breath as Mr. Roper shifted with obvious discomfort. "My lady, that is most unusual."

Her heart skipped a couple of beats, but outwardly she firmed her tone. "I am certain you will find a way to accommodate my request."

Darting a glance at Monty, and seeing no hope of assistance in his coolly courteous expression, the manager said, "Perhaps I'll go and see what can be done."

Bella gave what she hoped looked like a gracious nod. "Yes, please do."

"Poor bugger," Monty said, after the man left. "You've put him in a deuced difficult situation."

"It can't be helped. I have to know the truth." However much it might hurt. Too nervous to remain seated, she stood and paced the small office.

Mr. Roper returned, his smiling face now clear of any previous unease. "Well, now, this is a happy development."

"What is?" Bella swallowed the end of her question when Sebastian's commanding frame filled the doorway.

"Bella." Surprised delight filled his face and he flashed a heart-stopping smile. "What brings you here?" She froze, her heart flailing. Sebastian's glance moved to her companion. "And Monty as well. Have you business with Barclay?"

"As a matter of fact, I do," Monty answered easily, showing no sign of the discomposure gripping Bella. She sent up a silent prayer of gratitude for her friend's quick thinking.

"Lady Mirabella asked to see the numbered account, sir," Mr. Roper said eagerly, obviously thinking he was being helpful.

"Oh?" Sebastian turned to her with a slightly puzzled expression, but what he saw in Bella's face made his smile fade away. "Did she?"

"Yes, indeed," Mr. Roper sounded quite cheery, now that Sebastian's appearance appeared to have neatly solved his own dilemma. "It is a most happy coincidence that you are here."

"What is your interest in the account, Bella?"

"Traherne funds are regularly placed in the account, are they not?"

"They are."

"One thousand pounds per month, I believe it is."

"You are very well informed."

Disappointment cramped her belly. He hadn't bothered to deny any of it. "Would you tell us, Mr. Roper," she said, hoping he wouldn't discern the wobble in her voice, "precisely how much money is in Sebastian's account?"

The bank manager, now sensing something was amiss, darted a troubled look between the two. "About forty-eight thousand pounds, my lady."

"A secret bank account," she said softly to her husband, the pressure of unshed tears building behind her eyes. "I presume His Grace knows nothing of it."

"No, your father has no idea the account exists." He regarded her with a hooded gaze. "Do you have any further questions?"

There was no turning back now. Expelling a rickety

breath, she said, "I understand you've acquired three profitable Traherne properties at well below what they're worth."

The dark slash of his brows inched upward in surprise. "That is true."

Monty shifted on his feet. "Perhaps we should allow some privacy," he said pointedly to the bank manager. Roper seemed happy to oblige, anything to escape the suffocating tension in the chamber.

"Mr. Roper," Sebastian said with quiet gravity. "Whose name is on the bank account?"

The bank manager halted at the door. "I just examined the paperwork at the lady's request. It seems she is the owner. You see," he said to Bella, "your name is on the account after all."

"That's not possible—"

"And who is authorized to remove funds from my wife's account?"

"Just the lady, sir."

Sebastian held Bella's gaze. "Please tell us if any funds have been removed from the account since it was opened five years ago."

"Not a pence, sir. The guineas come in, but they don't go out."

Tension banded around her chest. "I don't understand." But she feared she was beginning to.

"Thank you, Mr. Roper. I am much obliged," Sebastian said, dismissing the bank manager. Monty followed, closing the door behind him. Sebastian turned to Bella. "You gave me your word you would come to me with any questions or concerns."

She bit her lower lip. "I was gathering information before presenting it you."

"I've gravely underestimated you, haven't I?" He picked up a paperweight from the desk and examined it. "This pretense of vapid gaiety with your friends was meant to put me off the trail while you conducted your investigations."

"Don't expect me to apologize for my interest in the duchy's concerns." She swallowed down the lump in her throat. "I am the Traherne heiress. It's my duty to protect the estate from unscrupulous business practices."

"I'm curious. How do you know so much about duchy concerns?"

"I've studied the estate ledgers."

"I do recall Perkins mentioning you'd visited my study once as he was leaving for the day." He wore an expression of avid curiosity, like a scientist trying to classify a fascinating new specimen. "You are able to make sense of the numbers?"

"Yes. I spent my time abroad visiting estates in Spain and France learning about farming practices and how to read ledgers."

Something like admiration glinted his eyes. "To what end?"

"Traherne is my birthright." She firmed her chin, yet her insides were feeling flimsy at the moment. "I won't let it fall to ruin under my watch."

"I see. Do you now have all of the information you seek?"

"No." She forced the words out. "Why is the bank account in my name?"

"His Grace spends a great deal of time at the gaming tables. I don't have the power to limit his access to the

Traherne accounts. The private numbered account was to protect you in case he drained the estate of everything."

She gasped. "My father plays that heavily?"

"He does."

Her scalp tingled as the immensity of her mistaken assumptions set in. "And the unentailed properties that now belong to you?"

"He was going to sell them off to settle a debt."

The pieces began to snap into place in a way that made awful, perfect sense. "So you acquired them to keep them with the estate."

"Yes."

"And whose name are they in?"

"Yours."

Hot confusion swirled within her. All of this time, he'd looked out for her interests, while she'd assumed the very worst of him. "I had no idea."

"It was my duty as your husband to protect your legacy."

"Oh, Sebastian. I have judged you most unfairly." She moved to him, but the icy wall of reserve around him stopped her.

His face drawn tight, he turned a disquieting gaze on her. "You promised to bring your concerns to my attention."

"I am sorry. I thought I could uncover the truth on my own. I didn't want you to know I still had doubts."

He fell silent. Only the ticking of the wood-carved wall clock filled the punishing silence, but even it seemed to condemn her with every harsh click. "I had your word." The soft words rang through the room.

"I know," she said miserably, feeling completely unworthy of this strong, honest man.

"You disappoint me," he said before turning and leaving the room.

Chapter Fifteen

"Where is Sebastian?" Josette asked. "He has been absent of late, *non*?"

"Business matters." Guilt nibbled at the edges of Bella's stomach again, as it had almost continuously since the bank debacle a few days past. "Today he meets with His Grace, a matter involving the lords."

Which gave him the perfect excuse to avoid her. Since learning of her lack of faith in him, Sebastian had retreated back into a polite shell, at times joining Bella and her friends for supper, but otherwise keeping his distance, especially at night. She missed him terribly. He hadn't visited her bed since that awful encounter at the bank.

They were ensconced in the morning room, where Tabby preferred to paint because it offered good light. The cheery chamber had walls the color of sunshine and a wide bank of windows that opened onto the small garden.

"I should like to take a walk," Josette said. "Will you

come with us, Tabby?"

Tabby added a dab of midnight blue to her watercolor's already sweeping swirls of blues, greens, and silvers. Her portrait of Monty was taking shape. "Perhaps later. Just now the light is perfect and I should like to finish this in time for Monty's birthday."

Over Tabby's head, Bella and Josette exchanged raised eyebrows and knowing curves of their mouths.

...

Sebastian spent the same morning in his study tending to business matters. Just before lunch, he received a visit from the Bow Street runner he'd hired to investigate Bella's friends.

"Nash, this is unexpected," he said as the man entered. He gestured for him to sit. "You have news?"

"It's about the gent who calls himself Monty."

Sebastian stilled. "Calls himself Monty? Is that not his real name?"

"I don't know about that," Nash said, wiping his upper lip clean with a kerchief. "I do know that he did not go to his estate a few weeks ago as he claimed."

"If you don't know his name, how do you know whether the estate he went to is his?"

Nash's mouth quirked. "Because I do know who does own the estate he visited."

"And?"

"It belongs to none other than one Baron Edgemont."

"Lady Tabitha's former betrothed."

"It appears your friend met with the baron at the estate.

He spent just one night there before returning to London."

He pushed up from his desk and walked to the window. "So Monty met with the baron, a development which suggests he's working for the man.

"I don't know to what end."

Sebastian strode to the door, anger stirring in his chest. "I intend to find out. Thank you, Nash," he said, walking through the doorway. "Please see yourself out."

He passed the morning room, where Bella and the ladies were apparently discussing something quite amusing, if their giggling was in indication. Taking the stairs two at a time, he rounded the corner leading to Monty's room and tapped on the door to the guest chamber.

"Enter." Monty—or whatever his name was—stood up from an escritoire as Sebastian entered. A hint of surprise registered in the otherwise polite expression on his face. "Sebastian. This is unexpected."

"I'm sure." Sebastian watched the man slip a note into the escritoire drawer as he spoke. Despite the gentlemanly facade, the cove was definitely hiding something and he was damn well going to find out what it was. "I was wondering if you are you up to a bout at Gentleman Jack's later this afternoon?"

"Why ever not? I could use a good workout."

A slow smile widened across Sebastian's face. "Excellent."

He arrived at the boxing saloon a couple of hours later to find Monty already waiting for him on the floor. Sebastian observed the man as they both muffled their fists. Monty stood tall and rawboned, with dark, close-cropped hair and a receding hairline. A cold fury niggled his gut at the thought of this man insinuating himself into Bella's life for nefarious purposes.

They stepped into the ring. He started with a harmless jab to the left. Monty saw it coming and blocked it with little effort. What he didn't see was the blind jab that Sebastian shot out to his right side. Sebastian withheld a grunt of satisfaction when his gloved fist connected with hard jaw. Monty appeared surprised, but quickly recovered, bouncing lightly on his feet.

He had to give it to the man. The traitorous rogue moved well on his feet. "So tell me, Monty, where did you go on your most recent jaunt to the country?"

Monty aimed for his gut. Sebastian allowed the barest connection before easily avoiding the complete impact of the blow. "My estate."

Another jab to Monty's right side. This time a little harder. "And where is that?"

"Oxford."

"A neighbor to Edgemont then?" Taken by surprise, Monty stopped, leaving himself defenseless when Sebastian went for the soft spot of his belly.

With a loud "Omph!" he buckled over from the impact and backed away. Sebastian watched with grim satisfaction. Fueled by anger, he bounced around on the balls of his feet, ready to expend his anxious energy on the lying lout.

Monty straightened and resumed the boxer's stance, both fists up, his eyes watchful. "What do you know of Edgemont?"

Bastard. "Not as much as you apparently." Sebastian swung hard but this time Monty was ready for him and deftly danced out of the way. "Does he hope to steal Tabby away against her wishes? Or does he wish Bella harm because she helped Lady Tabitha escape from him? That's taking hurt pride a little too far, wouldn't you say?"

Monty's left flicked out and managed to catch Sebastian under the chin. "Edgemont wishes Bella no harm. In fact, he is grateful for the service she rendered to Tabby in her time of need."

Monty's hit smarted, but Sebastian hardly felt it. "I won't argue with you there. Edgemont should have protected her honor when her own family didn't." He slammed his fist into Monty's nose—just hard enough to sting badly—but not so bad as to break it, at least not yet. Monty was a competent fighter, but they both knew he was no match for Sebastian.

Monty stumbled back from the force of Sebastian's blow, his eyes cold. "He has done so. However belatedly. Howard is dead." Sebastian faltered for a moment. What was that look in his opponent's eyes?

"Why has your employer sent you into my house? To spy on Lady Tabitha?"

"My employer?"

"Edgemont. The man you report to. I know you visited his estate."

The slight smile that curved Monty's mouth infuriated him. What the hell did the bastard have to smile about? "Edgemont has an interest in what happens to the lady," Monty said. "She is his betrothed."

"Was. I will not allow any harm to come to Lady Tabitha. You of all people know how fragile she is."

"I...we will protect her."

We? Perhaps Monty was the baron's brother or a poor relation. That would explain the gentlemanly bearing. "Just how close are you to Edgemont?"

Monty smiled wearily. "Very close. You could say we are inseparable."

Sebastian delivered another precise chop to Monty's tender side. He was just about ready to finish the whoreson off. "Explain yourself."

Monty grunted at the impact and swung back. "Perhaps the most expedient way to do that is by introducing myself." He paused. "Griffin Snowley, otherwise known as Baron Edgemont, at your service."

Sebastian froze. "Edgemont?"

"Quite."

"*You* are Tabby's betrothed?"

"Monty is a diminutive of Edgemont. It doesn't require a particular genius to parse that out."

Stunned, Sebastian finally saw the truth. What he didn't see was Monty's fist coming from the left, until it struck him hard in the temple, rattling his brain. His teeth chattered in his head and flicks of light danced in his vision before everything clouded and faded to black.

...

"Do you plan to ignore me forever?"

His head still aching from Monty's knockout blow, Sebastian glanced up from his desk to find his wife standing in the doorway with one shoulder propped against the frame, arms crossed under her chest. Her countenance suggested she wouldn't allow him to put her off any longer. Resigned, he dismissed his secretary with a nod.

Closing the door after Perkins, she turned to him. "Well?"

For a moment, he just took her in, the features he knew so well by both sight and touch. "I defy any man to ignore you."

A particular radiance shone off her today and her golden-brown eyes held an impish quality quite at odds with the quiet elegance of her beauty. "You've done a remarkable imitation of it."

"I've had many matters to attend to."

"Apparently. Considering you haven't come to my bed in nearly a week." A delicate brow arched up. "Perhaps you've already tired of me."

"No." Never that. "But I am weary. I've spent my entire life trying to prove myself worthy, first to my father and now to you. I find I no longer have the stomach for it."

"We both know you are far more worthy than I." The fervent tone in her voice surprised him. "Can we cry peace?"

"We are not at war."

"I have a proposition for you."

"What would that be?"

"I agree to absolve you of all guilt—for marrying me as a child and deserting me as a wife." Mischief glittered in her sun-shot almond eyes. "But mostly for denying me the extraordinary pleasures of the marriage bed for far too long."

He bit back a smile. "That last characterization is a bit extreme, but very well, what do you receive in return?"

She sobered. "Your forgiveness, a willingness to truly

make a go of it." She approached him and took his hand in both of hers and brought it to her cheek. "I want it all with you Sebastian—a loving marriage, a family."

He couldn't resist stroking the petal-like skin of her cheek. "Ten children."

She smiled that luminous smile of hers. "For a start."

"That kind of marriage requires full trust."

"I promise to show complete faith in you," she said urgently. "Please tell me I'm forgiven, that it isn't too late. I couldn't bear to make a complete hash of things."

Joyous relief pounded through him. As if he could deny her anything. "There is nothing I want more than to make a life with you."

She launched herself into his arms with a cry of delight. He gathered up the soft, feminine warmth of her body and held it close. "Thank you, thank you, thank you," she said, punctuating each word with quick kisses all over his face. On the last one, he caught her exquisite face with one hand and brought his lips down on hers. She opened beneath him and his tongue delved inside, delighting in her spicy sweet taste.

His body throbbing, he was just about to lay her across his desk when she broke the kiss. "I realize now you are the sole reason Traherne is flush in the pockets." Framed in the window, the sunlight bathed the curly wisps of her hair in an ethereal light. "Why did you never tell me His Grace's gambling almost forced the duchy into ruin?"

"I didn't see the point. It would only serve to lessen your opinion of your father. The truth was that you were an heiress with a fortune."

"A paltry fortune that you made great. And all of this time, you allowed me to mistake you for a fortune hunter."

She glanced around the room, her gaze halted when she finally took notice of the large rosewood desk before the window. "Why do you have another desk?"

"It is for you." He smiled with great satisfaction. "A duchess in her own right should have a proper place to conduct business."

She turned a questioning gaze on him. "I don't need to check up on you."

"It is past time you took a role in estate affairs," he said. "You've already demonstrated a keen understanding of Traherne concerns."

"No, this isn't necessary." She shook her head emphatically. "I trust you to make those decisions."

"This isn't about that. You'll soon be a peeress in your own right and this is your duchy. I do have my own business concerns to look after."

Incredulity tinged her hopeful gaze. "You expect me to attend to estate matters?"

"I assumed we could make decisions jointly."

"You and I. Working together." She cast a longing look at her desk and he could see her turning the concept over in her mind. "It is most unusual."

"As is a duchess in her own right."

"Are you certain?"

"I am. It will be a relief to discuss decisions with someone with a vested interest in the outcome."

Wonder filled her expression. "I never thought any man would willingly give a female power over estate matters."

"It is your birthright. You should take an active role in it."

"I've always wanted to be of real value to Traherne."

The radiance of her smile made his heart flip over. "How can I thank you?"

"There is no need." He took a seat behind his desk, needing to put a barrier between them. Otherwise, nothing would keep him from easing his dazzling wife down on the carpet and having his way with her. "Shall we get down to business? There are several matters you might wish to hear about."

Instead of coming over, she turned and strode to the door to turn the lock. Spinning to face him, she fell back against the door with a smile so laden with wicked intent that even the devil would squirm. "I *insist* on showing my gratitude."

The blood rushed from his head to the place between his legs. He swallowed. Hard. "What do you have in mind?"

She sashayed toward him with a naughty glint in her eye. "Something that will leave no doubt as to how grateful I am to be forgiven."

Already completely and painfully aroused, he shifted in his chair. "You're going to kill me."

She came around and scooted to stand between his legs, trapping herself between him and the desk. Resting her luscious bottom against the desk, she braced her hands on either side of her hips. Her eyes widened when they flicked down to his groin. "It seems you have a very large problem."

He glanced toward his aching lap, where his masculinity strained under his breeches. "Which I have you to thank for, Duchess."

"Duchess, is it? Very well. I command you to show me the problem in its entirety."

His breath quickened. "If you insist."

"I do."

He was already close to losing all control. How had he ever contained himself all of those years without her? He reached for the placket of his breeches and unfastened them, keeping his eyes on her while he did so. She bit her lush lower lip as her eyes followed the movements of his fingers.

"Well?" he asked, once he'd freed his anxious flesh, his voice rough. "What now?"

"Very impressive."

He reached for her but she stopped him.

"No, don't touch me."

He ached to run his fingers along the smooth slide of her silken skin. "I cannot bear not to." With her so close, he swam in her scent, becoming momentarily distracted. "A new fragrance?"

She leaned toward him, her luscious mounds near his face. "Yes, I've finally settled on one I like. What do you think?" The scent of lilies of the valley, laced with subtle notes of cloves, encased her womanly curves in a perfect balance of sensual and spicy. He inhaled, falling deeper in thrall, and pressed his lips against her deep cleavage. "It suits you."

She eased back. "No touching. I'm the duchess here. Do as I command."

God, she was magnificent. He gripped the arms of his chair to restrain himself. "I am all obedience."

She slipped off her slipper, bringing her stocking-clad foot to his anxious flesh. The sight of her slender, pale foot—so small and delicate—against his rampant erection almost made him lose all control right there. She taunted him with her foot, achingly deft and light. Her toes explored him, sliding up one exquisitely sensitive side and down the other, the whisper of her silk stocking heightening the sensation. "Perhaps we should move your desk," he said.

"Why?" she murmured, her foot caressing him.

He gritted his teeth against the building pleasure. "I begin to think we won't get much work done if we're together in this chamber."

Her breathing quickened, the rasping sounds filling the silence of the room. "All work and no play makes Sebastian a dull boy."

Catching her slender foot, he lightly massaged her instep. "We wouldn't want that."

Her eyes sparked in response, but she relaxed her foot into his hold, allowing his hands to do a slow slide up the smooth silk of her stockings until they touched her bared pale thigh. He knelt forward, forcing her thighs to part, and kissed that tempting expanse of flesh. She gave a sharp inhale when his lips touched her bare skin so close to the core of her most feminine place. He licked and suckled that tender little spot of thigh. The musky scent of her arousal swirled in his head, dazzling his senses until he could think of nothing else but spreading her thighs wide right there upon his desk and tasting her fully.

A soft sound at the door knocked him out of his insanity.

Bella startled at the sound, clasping her legs together. She covered her mouth and giggled, her shoulders hunched like a child who'd been caught being very naughty. "Oh, no."

Sebastian groaned and threw his head back against his chair. "Yes, what is it?" he called, not bothering to mask his impatience.

"Sir," Davison's muffled voice sounded through the door. "There is someone to see you. A Spanish solicitor. He says it is a matter of extreme urgency."

Sebastian frowned and looked at Bella. "You were in Spain, were you not?"

Her cheeks glowed with the radiant flush of sensual agitation. "Yes, but I cannot imagine what business he could have with me."

He pushed to his feet, stuffing his aching privates back into his breeches, making himself presentable again. Leaning over, he planted a hard kiss on Bella's mouth. "You undo me."

She gave a shuddering exhale. "What unfortunate timing the Spaniards have. I had such plans for you."

His body pulsed for her, the raging blood in his veins still clamoring to be satiated. "Keep talking like that and I will take you right here with Davison outside that door."

"Proper Sebastian?" She darted away from him toward the door to release the lock.

A bespectacled older man with a high forehead and more gray than black in his hair, entered carrying a satchel. "*Gracias*, my lord," he said, his thin slight form curving into a bow. "Thank you for seeing me without an appointment."

"Please state your business, sir." Sebastian gestured for him to come forward. "And I am not titled, just Mr. Stanhope, if you please."

He pushed his spectacles up the bridge of his nose. "That is why I have come, my lord. To inform you that you do indeed have *sangre azul*."

Sebastian cast a questioning look at Bella.

"Blue blood," she translated for him.

Impatient, he turned his attention to the solicitor. "Yes, I'm the nephew and brother of a marquess. How does that signify, Mr.—"

"Of course, allow me to explain. I am Juan Trevino. For thirty years, I served at the pleasure of Francisco Valdez Marcos, Conde de Vallado, a most noble and fair gentleman. Unfortunately, his lordship passed to the heavens a fortnight ago."

Sebastian sat and gestured for the solicitor to do the same in one of two chairs opposite his desk. Bella slipped into the other seat and turned toward the solicitor, her eyes alight with interest.

"I am sorry for your loss, *Señor* Trevino," Sebastian said, "but I don't understand what any of this has to do with me."

Señor Trevino sat. "It has everything to do with you. You are his lordship's heir."

His first reaction was to snort at the absurdity of it. Trevino clearly had the wrong man. Then his heart lost its beat, shrinking into a sharp-edged icicle in his chest. What if this Conde de Vallado was his natural father, the man with whom his faithless mother had shared her favors?

Francisco Valdez Marcos.

Now the reason Cyrus Stanhope had detested him had a name. "I see." He stood, his cool outward composure at odds with the choking sensation bearing down on his insides. "I am not interested in the man's money. Please distribute it to people in need in your country. Good day, sir."

Señor Trevino pushed to his feet with effort, the pull of age apparent. "I'm afraid you do not understand, my lord. You have inherited your sire's title."

Bella bolted out of her chair. "Is this someone's idea of a

joke? We may be English, sir, but we are aware that even the Spanish nobility does not allow bastards to inherit titles."

Sebastian's heart jolted at how she jumped to his defense. "Please do leave, *Señor*," he said, fighting to keep his voice even, "before I have you forcibly removed."

Beads of perspiration sprouted on *Señor* Trevino's upper lip. "The lady is correct." The words tumbled out. "Bastards cannot inherit. You are the legitimate son born to Francisco Valdez Marcos, Conde de Vallado and his late wife, Maria Teresa Alvarez, Condesa de Vallado."

None of this made any sense. "You think I was born to Count Vallado's lady wife?"

"Your mother died in childbirth. The count took another wife. It was a long and happy union, but unfortunately, he was not blessed with any more children."

Tension contracted every line of his body. "You are mistaken, *Señor* Trevino. I am the natural-born son of Mrs. Matilda Stanhope of Yorkshire in her marriage to the Honorable Cyrus Stanhope. I was born in Yorkshire, not in a foreign country, and most assuredly, not to a Spanish noblewoman."

"I think, my lord"— *Señor* Trevino licked his lips, his nervousness apparent— "if you consult *Señora* Stanhope, she will confirm the truth of what I say."

Sebastian's composure stretched to the breaking point. "You think my mother will know of this?"

"I was present when you were handed into the care of *Señora* Stanhope." The solicitor swallowed hard. "She will confirm she is not the mother of your birth. You, sir, are a count."

Bella frowned, a thoughtful look on her face. "A count?

That's the Spanish equivalent of an English earl, is it not?"

The solicitor looked hopeful he'd won at least one of them over. "*Si, Señora.*"

Sebastian fought an impulse to throw the man against the wall, to demolish his desk, to lay waste to everything in the room. "Please take yourself out of my presence, *Señor*," he said through clenched teeth. "I don't know what folly this is, but I intend to find out."

The solicitor straightened up. "Very well. I shall go. However, you remain the Count of Vallado. I will see myself out."

Sebastian continued to gaze at the closed door long after the solicitor had quit the chamber. Releasing a long, shuddered breath, he said, "It's pure folly, of course."

"Maybe not."

He scowled, redirecting his icy fury at her. "Are you so anxious to be married to a title that you'd believe a Banbury tale like that?"

"I understand you are angry," she said carefully, "but you should at least investigate this business for yourself."

"You want me to inform my mother that her lover is dead?"

"Isn't it well past time the two of you had this conversation?"

Closing his eyes, he struggled to settle his churning insides. "Very well. I shall go and speak to my mother."

・・・

"Sebastian, what a lovely surprise!" His mother hurried toward him, her face radiant at the sight of him. He never called on Matilda unexpectedly. He mostly visited when courtesy dictated it.

He bent over and automatically kissed her cheek. As usual, just a scant skim of his lips against her cool skin. "Madam."

She moved toward the sofa in the family sitting room. "Come, do sit. I'll ring for mineral water with lemon, just as you like it."

"No, don't bother, I won't be staying long." The joy of seeing him melted away, replaced instead with a wary watchfulness. Perhaps she'd already heard of her lover's death. "The Count of Vallado is dead."

All color left her face. "I see." She released a breath. "How did you learn this?"

"His solicitor came to see me. My sympathies, madam, for your loss."

"My loss?" She frowned. "I'm afraid I never had the pleasure of meeting the count."

Impatience brimmed. "Please, madam, let us dispense with untruths."

"It is the truth. I never laid eyes on the man."

"How can that be, madam?"

"I think you know, dearest." Her soft voice was full of sorrow. "He was your mother's husband."

The air in the room flattened against him. "Are you saying, madam, that I was adopted?" Pressure pounded in his head at the possibility he belonged to no one, not even this woman.

"Oh, no." Love infused her voice. "Stanhope blood most assuredly runs through your veins."

Something in his head snapped. "How is that possible?"

"You are Cyrus's natural son."

"No. *No*." He turned away from her, shaking, eyes closed, his hands covering his ears, trying to stop the roar of the truth in them. "That's not possible."

She materialized at his side, her arm on his elbow. "Dearest, please don't be so distressed. Come and sit."

He let her lead him to a seat. He went unseeing, unaware of anything but the fact that this woman's blood didn't run through his veins. A tide of grief and disbelief surged, threatening to drown him. How was it that only now—after he had lost her—that he realized the depth of his feelings for this woman who was no longer his mother? A part of him had never stopped adoring the woman who had embraced a confused boy and cloaked him in maternal love and protection. Only it was all a lie. "You are not my mother."

"From the moment I laid eyes on you, I have loved you as my own."

He closed his eyes against the stunning physical pain ravaging his body. "You did not give birth to me."

Her answer came in a soft voice, infused with tenderness. "You are not of my body, but you have always been the son of my heart."

He searched her face, unable to put a name to the agony rippling through him. "Cyrus was my father in truth?"

She dipped her chin in answer. "You have his blood."

"How can it be?"

She stood and went across the room, and then she was back pressing a glass of water into his hands. "Drink, and I will explain everything."

He obeyed, the boy in him responding to the brisk, no-nonsense mother in her. He brought the glass to his lips, almost choking on the cool water. When he finished, she took the glass, the swishing whisper of her skirts telling him she'd moved away again. Elbows braced on his thighs, Sebastian looked blindly down at the carpet and fought for breath, mindlessly eyeing the swirling designs between his boots.

Matilda told her story in deliberate, even tones. Of how Cyrus Stanhope had married her, a young girl of good standing, not for love, but because of the generous dowry she brought to the alliance. Cyrus, it seemed, had not always been pious and had taken mistresses in the early years of their marriage. But Maria Teresa Alvarez was different. Cyrus met the young daughter of a Spanish nobleman during his grand tour and had instantly fallen in love. They parted because she was already promised to her first cousin, the Count of Vallado. They renewed their acquaintance years later, when the Count and his wife visited London on a diplomatic mission. Sebastian appeared nine months after that trip, once the couple had returned to Spain.

Sebastian finally raised his head to look at the woman who was no longer his mother, who had never been. "What happened to the woman who gave birth to me?"

"She died in childbirth. The count knew you were not his. He told his acquaintances you had perished along with your mother."

"How did I come to be in England?"

"Although he was your legal father, Vallado intended to foster you out to a family in the Spanish countryside. I could not allow that."

His throat closed. How she must have suffered because of him. "How did you bear it when Cyrus asked you to raise his bastard?"

"He did not ask. I insisted. You were just a babe, alone in the world without a mother to protect and care for you. It was our duty to do right by you."

Shame burned in his chest. "How you must have detested me, day after day, having to face the evidence of a faithless husband."

Her eyes went shiny with emotion. "You took hold of my heart the moment your nursemaid put you in my arms." She smiled at the memory. "You had a head full of dark hair, and you looked at me with those green eyes that are so like your brothers'. From that moment, you were mine, and you still are."

He pushed heavily to his feet, feeling as though he dragged a parcel of rocks with him. "Why did my father hate me?"

She did not pretend to misunderstand his question. "Cyrus did not hate you, but it was"— she paused as if searching for the right words— "difficult for him to be reminded of his moral failure."

"Difficult?" He choked out an acid laugh. "For him?"

"You were such a gift to us, for our family. Your sterling character and constancy helped steady all of your brothers, then as now." She placed a hand on his arm. "After you came to be with us, your father changed his ways. I never heard of him taking another mistress. We came to have a genuine care for one another." Which is how Sebastian remembered his mother and father, with a true affection between them.

His understanding of the world shifted, battering his senses. He looked at Matilda and really *saw* her for the first time in as long as he could remember. Certainly since that long-ago day when he'd concluded his mother was a whore. She stood erect and proud, her form still slim and dainty, hands clasped in front of her. To him, she had always been a jezebel masquerading as an angel. Only now, he knew it had never been so. Matilda Stanhope was the embodiment of goodness.

He walked to the woman who had been his true mother and knelt before her. He took each of her hands, soft with the comfortable wrinkles of age, and brought them to his lips, first one and then the other.

"Forgive me, madam, for I have aggrieved you most terribly. Of all of the actors in this sordid drama, only you have acted with true honor and moral rectitude."

She urged him to his feet and brought his hand to her softly weathered cheek. "It was no trial. You have always been so easy to love."

"You deserve a more dutiful and attentive son than I."

"I have him," she said in a certain tone. "No mother could wish for a finer son. You have always made me most proud."

Feeling swelled painfully in his chest. For the first time since he was a boy, he allowed his mother to take him into her arms and comfort him while he cried.

Chapter Sixteen

Bella sat at her new desk unsuccessfully attempting to concentrate on estate business. Sebastian had been gone all night. A note she'd sent around to Matilda the previous evening confirmed he'd left his mother in the late afternoon. So many hours ago. Where could he be?

Davison appeared on the threshold. "My lady, you asked to be informed when the master returned."

"Yes." Relief loosened her tense muscles. "Where is he?"

Worry lines creased his forehead. "He has gone to the mews, my lady."

"The mews? He means to ride?"

Davison cleared his throat. "If I may speak frankly, my lady."

She rose to her feet, pressure bearing down on her chest. Something was wrong. "Yes, what is it?"

"The master does not seem himself."

"He has had a trying time of it. I will go to him."

"My lady, he appears to have imbibed."

"Imbibed?" Sebastian drinking spirits? "He is in his cups?"

"I'm afraid so."

Alarm replaced disbelief. She hurried past the butler. "Thank you, Davison. I will see to him at once."

Rushing to the mews, she wondered what exactly had transpired with Matilda that would drive Sebastian to drink. The sounds of pounding and grunting emanated from the mews as she approached. Entering, she found the grooms standing silently together, their attention fixed on a far corner where Sebastian, stripped to the waist, slammed his fists into a heavy puncher's bag affixed to the rafters with a heavy rope.

His back to them, he pounded relentlessly, grunting at the effort each swing cost him. Sweat glistened off his bronze torso, rivulets of perspiration streaming over the firm contours of his arms and down his powerful back.

"Please leave us," she said to the grooms. "Go to the kitchen. Ask Cook to give you tea." She wanted them far away, outside of the range of hearing.

"Yes, my lady," they murmured in acquiescence, shuffling out of the mews.

"Make certain we are not disturbed," she said, closing the mews doors behind them. Turning, she leaned back against wooden frame, her gaze on her husband. He had bullish stamina; the power of his strokes did not appear to diminish at all. She pushed off the door and approached him, walking to the opposite side of the puncher's bag. The heavy swinging bag almost threw her off balance.

He grabbed the heavy bag with both hands, stilling it

before it could topple her. "You should not be here," he said through harsh breaths. "I prefer you not see me in this state."

"That's just as well since I prefer not to see you in this state."

His tousled hair was wet with exertion; perspiration shimmered over his stark face and strong neck, glinting over well-formed pectoral muscles and the sinews of his hard stomach. "Then we are in agreement. Please return to the house. I'll join you when I am done here."

"When will that be? When your hands are bloodied and you collapse from exhaustion?"

His hard stare met hers, the green in his eyes so dark it was almost black. "I implore you to return to the house."

She laid a light hand on his bare arm. "What happened with your mother?"

He pulled away from her. "It seems the old Spaniard knows of what he speaks." He gave a harsh laugh. "Turns out I'm as much of a Stanhope as Cam—or Edward, Will, or Basil for that matter."

"So," she said slowly, processing his words. "Cyrus was your true father."

"I've got the old bastard's blood in my veins." His stormy gaze met hers. "All these years I thought he detested the sight of me because I wasn't his son. But it seems the fact that I *am* of his blood is what made me contemptible to him."

"But why?" The ache in her chest deepened for him. "That makes no sense."

He swooped down to grab a bottle of open brandy from the floor. "It seems I reminded Mr. Perfectly Pious of his human failings. I am the product of his adultery." He tipped the bottle into his mouth, the cords of his throat worked as he guzzled from it.

She cocked a brow. "I doubt drinking will be of any more help than pummeling that bag."

He wiped his mouth with the back of his hand. "I don't believe I asked for your opinion."

"When have I ever waited to be asked for my thoughts on anything?"

He looked at her with red-rimmed eyes. "Get out."

Her heart clamored in her chest. She'd never seen him like this before—unkempt, foxed, and raging—so unlike the controlled gentleman she'd become accustomed to.

His eyes narrowed. "I said get out, madam."

"No."

His face darkened in a way that frightened her. He leaned toward her, his posture threatening. "Leave me, or I will not be responsible for what I do to you."

Fear uncoiled in the pit of Bella's belly, but she straightened her spine. "You could not harm me. I know the man you are."

He erupted, leaping at her and forcing her up against a wooden support beam. She smelled the spirits on his breath and forced herself not to recoil from it. He brought his face close to hers, his breath whipping lightly against her cheeks. "You know me, madam? How is that possible when I don't know myself? A stranger's blood courses through my veins. Neither of us knows what I am capable of."

"I know you don't have it in you to harm me. You will not frighten me away."

A dangerous glint entered his eye. "You think not?"

Without thinking, she curved a hand around his neck

and pulled him to her lips. He came willingly, bringing his lips roughly to hers, forcing her mouth open, driving his tongue mercilessly inside, obviously expecting her to protest. She did not. Instead, she opened her mouth wider and softened into him, inviting him to take whatever he wanted. Whatever he needed. He kissed her with a fierce recklessness, a passion so different from the considerate, controlled way he usually loved her. She sensed that beneath the anger and roiled feelings that she, finally, was getting a glimpse of the real Sebastian.

The scents of exertion and perspiration, heat and emotion, laced his masculine essence. The raw force of it fired Bella's blood and she kissed him back with equal vigor.

He pulled back abruptly, torment etched in his face. "Why do you accept me? I am not worthy."

"You will never convince me of that," she said breathlessly. Putting her hands behind his head, she pulled his mouth back to hers and kissed him with everything she had. Her tongue delved into the damp heat of his mouth, taking in the swirling taste of brandy.

His mouth softened against hers and he took voracious control of the kiss. Plundering deep, he stroked inside her mouth with greedy, feral movements, provoking a maelstrom of sensation that threatened to knock her off her feet.

He stopped abruptly, backing away from her, leaving her cold and empty.

She ran her hands over the wide expanse of his bare chest, both soft and hard under her fingers. She touched her lips to his damp, salty skin, peppering light kisses all along it. Her fingers ran down into the waist of his breeches.

He groaned and tried to pull away, but she would not

let him. She pushed him up against the wall, pulling open his breeches, reaching in to stroke the hardened male flesh.

"I will not allow this to continue," he uttered, struggling to control himself. "Stop." His hands flattened against the rough wooden slab of wall behind him, as if he did not trust himself not to grab for her.

He gasped when she dropped down to her knees. He reached to pull her back up, the gentleman in him trying to prevent her from doing what she intended. She shook off Sebastian's hand and took him into her mouth, sucking hard, determined not to let him leave her now. Falling back against the wall, he closed his eyes and let out an anguished sound, pain and desire etched on his face. His release came quickly and he tried to pull away before it did, but she would not let him. She suckled harder, greedily pulling on him until she sampled the sweet, salty taste of him.

She let him know she wanted him, all of him—even now. Especially now. She didn't care who gave birth to him or who had fathered him. She wanted him as he was. And she knew in that moment, as clearly as she breathed, that she loved him completely, with a fullness she'd never known possible. And always would.

...

Losing himself in her mouth shattered what little remained of Sebastian's self-control. Leaning against the wall, the rough wood digging into his back, his senses scattered as he let himself go for the first time since he could remember.

The way her luscious lips sealed around his male flesh—drawing out all she could— completely unmanned him.

He saw black when he exploded into her hot wet mouth, blasts of light pierced his vision when his body convulsed powerfully around her. Drained of strength, he slid to the floor as the last tremors of release shook him, the wood scraping his bare back.

Shifting her body, she settled beside him and leaned back against the wall. She tipped her head back and closed her eyes, allowing him to take in the fine lines of profile, the firm chin and elegant turn of her delicate throat. She released a sigh. "That was unlike anything—"

"You could obtain a divorce, you know."

Her eyes opened. "On what grounds? A surfeit of pleasure?"

He shook his head, shame and mortification heating his insides. "I don't know what possessed me to allow that."

Her mouth curved as she gave a lazy stretch, her lush breasts straining against her bodice. "It was an impulse. One can't always be in control, Sebastian."

"I'll not have your pity."

Her throaty laugh contained genuine mirth. "I assure you I am not *that* philanthropic."

His chest squeezed at the thought of releasing such an enchanting creature. "You could divorce me for fraud. I am not what you thought when we married."

"I was thirteen. I barely knew your name much less who you were."

"Please be serious. This is hardly a laughing matter."

"What is the fraud? Should I protest that instead of a mere mister I find myself wed to a Spanish earl? I would be laughed out of the Lords."

Pain pulsated in his head. "You're to be a duchess in

your own right. Your children should not bear my muddled bloodlines."

"Muddled? You've seen His Grace. The Traherne line could use an infusion of fresh blood."

"Please be serious."

"I am," she said in that firm way of hers. "I married Cyrus Stanhope's son and you are that."

A fresh wave of pain swelled in him at the thought of the father who all but disavowed him. Trying to swallow it away, he tipped the bottle back, welcoming the bitter burn that set his throat and chest ablaze like the fires of hell. He lobbed the emptied bottle into a bale of hay, where it landed with a useless *thud*. "Whoever said drinking dulls the pain was an arse."

She scooted up off her bottom and knelt before him, folding her legs underneath her. "If anyone's been swindled, it's you. You've been cheated out of your birthright."

Did she think he cared about the title? "I have no real right to Vallado. We all know it. For God's sake, even the solicitor knows it."

She shook her head. "I'm not talking about the title. You are a true Stanhope. You are Cyrus Stanhope's son. You deserved better than what you got from him."

A fresh swell of emotion roiled over him. "I won't challenge you on that."

Pushing to her feet, she held out her hand to him. "Come along. You need a hot bath and an even hotter cup of coffee."

He obliged, wrapping his hand in hers, hoping she could pull him to safety. Once they returned to the house, she ordered the bath and dismissed his valet before disappearing into her adjoining chamber. Sebastian sank into the steaming water, savoring its enveloping heat, although nothing could wash away the truth.

Returning in a dressing gown, Bella took the soap and began to wash his back. He leaned forward to give her better access. "My valet could do that."

Her hands glided over his back. "I don't mind."

"I've put you through enough."

"Lean back and close your eyes." She poured water over his head. Its warmth splashed over his closed eyes, running down his face and shoulders.

She began to wash his hair. "You are always taking care of me or the duchy or the foundlings." She pressed a kiss against his neck. "Let me take care of you for once."

Closing his eyes, he sighed and leaned back against the tub. She massaged his head as she washed his hair. Her fingertips moved to his temples in soothing, circular movements. A warmth stole over him.

"What are you thinking?" she asked after a while.

"That I have no idea who I am anymore."

"You are still you. This changes nothing."

"It changes everything. Everything I am, everything I've done up until now is a result of who I thought I was."

"Matilda Stanhope's bastard."

"Yes. Because of that, I wanted to be worthy of my father." A fresh onslaught of grief twisted hard in his chest. "I tried to emulate his moral rectitude. If I had the best character, if I excelled in my studies and sport, I thought perhaps he could tolerate me better."

"Those were his failings," she said quietly, her hands still moving in comforting patterns in his hair. "Lean forward and close your eyes."

She splashed water down on his head again to rinse the soap out of his hair. When she was done, he wiped the water from his face. He felt emptied of everything, left with a gaping hole where the man used to be. "I based my entire being, everything that I am, on a fraud, a lie. He was an adulterer."

She moved around to the side of the tub. Her hands soaped his chest in round motions. "You are not. You are honorable and decent."

The heat of anger poured into the gap within him, filling it to bursting. He slammed his hand down in the water with a loud slap, splashing water everywhere, splattering her face and the front of her dressing gown. "Do you not hear me? None of it is real."

She wiped the water rivulets from her face. "What you have done for the foundlings is very real," she said with equal force. "Without you they'd be dead, diseased, whored out to perverts, or worse. Your business sense is not an illusion. You've saved Traherne from ruin, rescued the estates, ensured a good life for the tenants and their families." She gripped his face, forcing his tormented gaze to meet hers. "And you've rescued me from a lonely wandering existence, from a life devoid of purpose. Am I not real? Am I nothing?"

"You are everything."

She kissed his forehead, each of his closed eyes, his nose with urgency. "I love you, Sebastian. Please don't withdraw from me."

Her admission stunned him. She loved him? Even now? "How can you love me?"

She stood and removed her dressing gown. She wore nothing underneath, baring pale, glistening skin to his anguished gaze. Full breasts quivering, their rosy centers pert, the soft slope of her belly, the exotic tangle of curls that guarded her femininity. His ache moved from his heart to much lower.

She climbed into the tub with him. "How can I not love you? You make the world a better place to be in. You fill a hole in my soul in a way no one else ever has."

Opening his arms, he pulled her to him, flattening her warm, soft breasts against his chest, kissing her long and hard—hot, wet, and openmouthed. Slipping inside of her with a smooth, easy stroke, they moved together in a sensuous rhythm. Making love to his wife, with no secrets left between them, was almost agonizing in its intensity.

In the presence of her life force, the hole inside of him began to fill, revealing his true self: the blood son of Cyrus Stanhope and the woman called Maria Theresa Alvarez; son of Matilda Stanhope's heart; rightful brother to Cam, Edward, Will, and Basil. Even—as improbable as it was—the Count of Vallado. But most of all, he was the beloved of this woman who infused his ordinary existence with exuberance and light.

Shed of the constraints and assumptions of the past, he felt curiously light, as if a lifelong burden had lifted. And the realization came to him that for the first time in his life, he was free to carve out a destiny of his making.

His own man at last.

Chapter Seventeen

"Count Vallado had no other heirs. You may be quite certain he intended for you to inherit."

Sebastian eyed the Spanish solicitor, who'd taken it upon himself to travel all the way out to Traherne Abbey to speak with him. "How can you be certain of that, *Señor* Trevino?"

"He recorded proof of your birth and retained the papers of your identity."

Examining the documents Trevino had brought with him, Bella listened to their exchange from behind her father's enormous mahogany desk and resisted the urge to sneeze. The air in the study was musty from lack of use. Although Traherne Abbey was the duke's countryseat, His Grace was rarely in residence. Bella hadn't wanted to visit either. Being in the empty old mausoleum dredged up unwelcome feelings of loneliness and abandonment she'd felt as a child growing up here. But Sebastian had insisted, saying it was their duty to visit the vast property. What he hadn't explained was why he'd also insisted she wear her finest day dress this afternoon.

He looked splendid as well, dressing for whatever occasion he had in mind. His silver, tailored tailcoat stretched snug across his expansive shoulders and his blue waistcoat had subtle silver designs threaded through it.

"If Vallado had wanted me to inherit, why did he send me away while telling people I had perished along with my mother in childbirth?"

"He hoped to sire a son of his own," Trevino said. "When his second wife failed to provide an heir, it became obvious the blame lay with him."

"I have no interest in claiming what is not rightfully mine. Surely, there is a worthy distant relation who can take the title and do justice to it."

"There is no one but you. The count knew this. He watched from afar and was impressed with your progress."

"Watched me?"

"Yes, when it became clear he would have no more children, he attempted to reclaim you as his legal son, but *Señor* Stanhope refused."

Pausing from her examination of the paperwork, Bella looked up with interest at this latest revelation. "The count wanted him back?

"When was this?" Sebastian asked.

"You were perhaps eleven and a fine child who excelled in all he attempted," the solicitor said. "The count saw this and felt you would do credit to his title."

"And Cyrus refused to send me? Why?"

"He insisted you were his son and no one else's. He was quite firm that your place was with your true family."

"I'd have thought Cyrus would jump at the chance to be rid of me. The more I learn about the man, the less I understand him." He shook his head. "None of this makes any sense. How could Vallado desire for me to inherit his title when his blood does not run through my veins?"

"Ah, but it does. The count and your mother were first cousins. So, you see, the blood of the late Count Vallado—and of all the counts before him—does indeed run through your veins."

"I thought I wedded a mere mister," Bella said, "yet it seems you are even more noble that I."

"Nonsense." Sebastian shook his head and exhaled loudly. "Very well. If there is no one to whom this title should truly belong, I suppose I should become acquainted with my new responsibilities."

Relief glimmered in *Señor* Trevino's eyes. "If it suits you, I shall arrange for the count's…er…your man of business to come meet with you when you are back in Town, my lord. Unless, of course, you plan an extended visit here in the country?"

"Not at all. We have one very important matter to attend to and then we shall travel back to Town. I shall see your man of business there."

After the man was gone, Bella said, "One very important matter to attend to?"

A mischievous glint lit his eyes. "Indeed."

"Which is?"

"I will tell you shortly." He gestured toward the documents in front of her on the desk. "What have you learned?"

"There don't appear to be any problems with the estate."

"I am assured it is quite profitable," he said morosely.

She laughed. "Most men would be grateful to have an entire earldom dropped into their lap."

"It is not something I've earned, and I am not the rightful heir."

"Legally, you are." She rose from her seat and walked over to him. "And Vallado wanted you to inherit, likely because you were as close to a blood son as he was ever going to have."

"I already have my hands full with Traherne and my own holdings."

"Then it is just as well that you've given me a desk in Town and forced me to attend to Traherne matters."

"Forced you, did I?" he asked with amusement, taking her hand in his large, warm grasp and guiding her out the door.

"Where are we going?"

"To attend to that very important matter."

Which apparently required she be blindfolded during the carriage ride to wherever they were going. "At least tell me our destination."

"That would negate the purpose of the blindfold, now wouldn't it," Sebastian's voice answered from where he sat beside her in the forward-facing seat. "I told you it's a surprise. Stop being so impatient."

"The last time someone surprised me I ended up married."

His chuckle sounded close to her ear. "And look how well that turned out."

"Yes." She smiled. "I doubt this surprise could surpass that."

"We shall see."

Impatient, she fidgeted with her blindfold. "Why must I wear my finest day dress if I'm not even to be allowed to know where we are going?"

His voice—low and full of intent—brushed against her ear. "You will know when you are meant to."

Suppressing a shiver at the warm puff of his breath, she maintained a purposely petulant tone. "What if I don't like it?"

"You will like it. I do know what appeals to you." The carriage lurched to a stop. "We are here."

She fingered the sides of the coach. "Am I supposed to step out of this carriage blindfolded?"

"Not at all." She felt his fingers removing her blindfold and then he helped her alight. Squinting against the sudden infusion of light, she focused on the strong lines of Sebastian's face.

Looking beyond him, she realized they stood in front of Traherne's white stone chapel. A chill stole across her heart. This was the place where they had been married all of those years ago, before he had abandoned her. She had avoided it ever since.

She shot him a wary look. "What are we doing here?"

He grinned, a flash of white against his warm skin tones, that lone dimple creasing high on his right cheek. Swooping her off her feet, he carried Bella into the small structure with long, purposeful strides, not setting her down until they were inside the tiny vestibule.

Stepping forward into the chapel, Bella saw it was not at all as she remembered it. It had seemed so forbidding all those years ago, full of cold wood and hard edges. Now she saw the quaintness of its whitewashed stone walls and the solid wooden benches, which held so much of Traherne's history within their sturdy confines.

She'd never seen so many flowers. Primroses, daffodils, cowslip, and cuckoo flowers—in every color—adorned the aisle, while an enormous arrangement graced the altar. Their scent, the lightly fragrant layered with darker spicier varieties, filled the air.

Tabby and Monty—Edgemont as they all knew now—had recently reached an understanding of their own, and stood at the altar with expectant smiles on their faces. "What are they doing here?" She turned to Sebastian. "What are *we* doing here?"

Her last words melted in her throat as Sebastian knelt on one knee and took her hand. "Miss Wentworth, would you do me the great honor of becoming my wife?"

A surge of tears tightened her chest. "Has it escaped your memory that we are already married?"

"I would like to do it properly this time, with Lady Tabitha and Edgemont as our witnesses. You would make me the most fortunate man alive if you'd consent to be my wife. Of your own accord."

"Oh, do get up you silly man," she cried, her heart exultant. Pulling him to his feet, she threw her arms around him and smattered kisses all over his face. "Yes, yes, of course I will marry you."

Cupping her face with large strong hands, he gently brought his lips to hers. He kissed her long and slow, infusing it with all of his love and tenderness. She savored his sweet, masculine taste with its ever-present tanginess. She would never again partake of lemon without thinking of him.

Breaking the kiss, he spoke in a roughened voice that belied his emotion. "Come then, my love."

Placing her hand on the solid curve of his forearm, he led her down the aisle to their friends, the waiting vicar, and the ceremony that would seal their fate together once and forever.

"I do," she whispered as they neared the altar. "And I always will."

Acknowledgments

I have to give special thanks to my friend, Megann Yaqub, for reading every possible version of this book through numerous edits and revisions. Although it is invisible to the reader, her influence is on many of these pages.

I'm grateful for the support and camaraderie I enjoy in the writing community, especially among my talented author friends at The Dashing Duchesses and Violet Femmes romance blogs.

An abundance of gratitude goes to the best editor in the business, Alethea Spiridon-Hopson, for her guidance and expertise, and also to the premier agent in publishing, Kevan Lyon, for her patience, business savvy and sound professional advice.

I'm fortunate to have a husband who picks up the slack (without being asked) when I'm facing a writing deadline and that my sons, Laith and Zach, don't complain too much about Mom's lack of attentiveness when she's obsessively tapping away at her keyboard. I love you guys.

About the Author

Diana Quincy is an award-winning former television journalist who decided she'd rather make up stories where a happy ending is always guaranteed.

Her books revolve around the Regency world of dashing dukes, irresistible rogues and the headstrong women who capture their hearts. New York Times bestselling author Grace Burrowes called Diana's debut novel, *Seducing Charlotte*, "Sweet, steamy, and thoroughly enjoyable."

Growing up as a foreign-service brat, Diana lived in many countries and is now settled in Virginia with her husband and two sons. When not bent over her laptop or trying to keep up with laundry, she enjoys reading, spending time with her family and dreams of traveling much more than her current schedule (and budget) allows.

Diana loves to hear from readers. You can keep up with her on Twitter, Facebook, and by visiting her website. www.dianaquincy..com

Are you feeling...

SCANDALOUS?

Our readers know that historical doesn't mean antiquated, that's why they choose Scandalous-an Entangled Publishing imprint-for love stories from eras gone by.

Our romances are bold and sexy and passionate. After all, torrid love affairs are even more illicit when forbidden by social mores. Take a little time for yourself, escape to another era, and discover a timeless romance. There's never been a better time to fall in love.

Never miss a release by subscribing to our newsletter, and join us on our social media pages to keep up with our specials, giveaways, prizes, and what is new with scandalous authors.

www.entangledpublishing.com/category/scandalous

Other books by Diana Quincy
COMPROMISING WILLA
Book Three of the Accidental Peers Series

England 1805

Lady Wilhelmina Stanhope is ruined and everyone knows it. Back in Town for the first season since her downfall, Willa plans to remain firmly on the shelf, assuming only fortune hunters will want her now. Instead she focuses on her unique tea blends, secretly supporting a coffee house which employs poor women and children. If her clandestine involvement in trade is discovered, she'll be ruined. Again.

No one is more shocked by Willa's lack of quality suitors than the newly minted Duke of Hartwell. Having just returned from India, the dark duke is instantly attracted to the mysterious wallflower. His pursuit is hampered by the ruthless Earl of Bellingham, who once jilted Willa and is now determined to reclaim her.

Caught between the clash of two powerful men, a furious Willa refuses to concede her independence to save her reputation. But will she compromise her heart?

Printed in Great Britain
by Amazon